Coveted

Coveted

A DEMON WATCHER NOVEL: BOOK 3

by

GINNA MORAN

SUNNY PALMS PRESS

To my readers,
Forgive me for being wicked—just kidding. Brace
yourselves.

Prologue

A BETTER PURPOSE

MY DEAREST DAUGHTER,

I never in my wildest dreams imagined I'd ever be so lucky to bring such a beautiful, precious gift as you into the world. Within your good soul lies the power to tame even the most evil, vile demon. I know this because I see it already in your father as he presses his hand to my stomach, his eyes lighting every time you kick him. He says you're already quite the fighter, and I know he's right. I see it in my dreams, feel it imprinted on the soul that ties us three together.

You're going to not only survive in this trying world, you're going to thrive and make the most of it. We'll see to it. I refuse to believe anything short of amazing could come from the love your fa-

ther and I share.

Even if loving a demon isn't easy. It definitely isn't ideal. And sometimes, it's downright terrifying, but I'm strong. If there's one thing in the world I can pass down to you, it's my strength, which you're going to need in this world as Raphael Blackwell's daughter.

It might feel tough at times, but I want you to listen to the advice your grandma gave me when I thought my world was falling apart. Evil isn't something to fear and evil is subjective. And your grandma was right. Because despite the demon blood inside you, you'll never be evil no matter what anyone says.

You were not born from evil. You were born from the best parts of me and your dad—his all-encompassing, devoted, powerful heart and my good soul, a soul that can withstand the dark. These two things are all you'll ever need to create a life as beautiful and as powerful as you are. Which you will. I know it. The thought is what keeps me fighting, though all the world seems against me. Against you. Against my beautiful Raphael.

With your life, the world will see how incredible things can come from the dark. They will see how even a fall from grace won't destroy the universe because a fall from Heaven doesn't steal away the best parts of someone. A fall only means you have to figure out how to travel through life differently.

You can still rise to defeat true evil. Because a fall doesn't steal love or hope. It doesn't steal faith. And you, my daughter, will make them see. You've showed me how you can change someone who the world thought would remain the same. You will change the world in the best way.

Though your father no longer has his wings, he still has light in his blood. He has a new, better purpose. He has you. Never let him forget that. Never let the darkness win.

Forever yours,
Mom

1

COVETED

A WATERFALL OF black blood cascades through the air in my direction. Covering my face with my hands, I shield myself from the spray of putrid demon guts even Ezekiel can't save me from.

The mist of the Veiled Realm clouds my vision, and I take a step back at the bright light falling from the sky. My heart races at the sight of the avenging angel who has been stalking me through the veil for weeks, but it's easy to ignore him when all I have to do is drop my hand. He can't touch me with the protective shield Kristin, my self-appointed witch caretaker, put in place to block me from Heaven. But Heaven—especially this annoying angel who keeps asking me for forgiveness for ruining my eternity—persists, trying to get to my soul that lies in my charming fallen angel's hands.

The angel unfurls his white wings, staring at me without a word, and I jerk my hands away from my face.

Ezekiel stands a foot away, tilting his head to the side. "You need to work on your reflexes."

Groaning, I swipe the remnants of the demon Dad just ripped the heart out of from my face and flick it at Ezekiel. "Maybe I needed an excuse to get out of here."

The last few weeks have been nothing short of miserable, all because I've lost my freedom. I'm supposed to live the rest of my human life protected by the two demons I love, but it doesn't feel like living. I feel like I'm trapped in my own hidden veiled world with an eternity in the hands of the demon who possesses my soul. If Ezekiel doesn't hold it tightly, I'll fall to Hell alone forever. The thought never leaves me, consuming me.

And then there's Dad. He's taken demonic affairs to a new extreme. But they're still as boring as Hell. Dad has been immersing himself in a lot of them lately to try to assure the angelic army that he's still a good, powerful demon who knows his purpose in the universe. Even if Heaven wants to avenge whatever they think needs avenging, they can't touch him through Kristin's spell unless they visit him in the one place they hate to go, the place my stalker angel doesn't seem to leave as he taunts me through the veil. In the daylight prison world, Dad is invincible.

"All you had to do was ask," he says, smirking.

"Well, what's the fun in that? I also needed an excuse to steal your shirt unless you see any towels around here." I clench my jaw to stop myself from smiling.

I'd much prefer to tease Ezekiel than admit he's right about my slow reaction. It's been a while since I've worked out. I used to practice combat with Cadence, but now I'm alone most of the time. I spend nearly all my daylight hours trying to break and melt off the locks on my bedroom door, but they're spelled by Kristin to contain me. When I'm not trying to prove to Dad he can't control me, I watch Ezekiel in the daylight prison realm.

I knew I was capable of loving a demon, because I love my dad, but I didn't think I could accept Ezekiel's fall like I have or how easily I've forgiven him for not returning my soul to me, though I never stop asking. Because with my soul, he can feel my humanity if he wants to. He still carries the memory of his love for me despite not feeling it in the same way.

But maintaining a life with Ezekiel doesn't change the fact that I'm Hell-bound because of him and disgraced by all of Heaven for not letting them take him from me.

I shouldn't complain, but this isn't the life I imagined. I feel like Dad's preparing me for my eternal torture in Hell unless Ezekiel somehow manages to keep my soul with him for eternity. Even then, I'll never have the peace I expected or wanted—the peace I still want if Heaven could forgive me.

I lift my hand to my eye again to glare at my heavenly stalker.

He waves.

I drop my hand. *Stupid angel.*

Ezekiel holds out his shirt to me, pulling me from my inner thoughts. I hadn't expected him to actually take it off, but now that he has...

Trailing my eyes from his broad chest and down to his bone-hard abs and the curves of his hips, I drink in the sight of him. We rarely get any time alone at night because Dad thinks Ezekiel's had enough alone time with me while we were on the run, but I'm kind of glad for it. I think Dad's worried Ezekiel will take our relationship places he wouldn't have as an angel, and I wouldn't be able to resist. Which he might be right about. It's as easy to lose myself in Ezekiel's darkness as it was to get lost in his light. But it's more than next-level stuff. I think Dad's more worried about the state of my heart. He knows what being a demon did to my mom. He'll never stop trying to protect me.

Ezekiel closes the distance between us when I don't move to take the shirt. Rubbing the soft fabric across my cheek, he cleans the dead demon from my skin. Fire dances in his mocha eyes, locking me in their intensity. His eyes turn from fire to emptiness in a matter of seconds—an emptiness I can't seem to fill as much as I want to.

His heartbeat resonates through me, beating in a low thrum I always focus on to push the rest of the world away. I force to break our stare, finding myself watching his mouth, his bottom lip puffing with the breath he releases.

"If we leave now, we can lose Raphael until morning," Ezekiel whispers softly so Dad can't hear him if he's eavesdropping.

A smile crosses my lips, and I nod my head, standing on my tiptoes to peek at Dad too busy cornering another demon against the wall. The man snarls at Dad, revealing his true body—a creepy blood-red mass of muscle and bone with what looks like organs on display through a spiked cage of ribs. The demon's horns twist into spiral points sharp enough to impale anyone with a butt of his head.

Ezekiel links his hot fingers through mine, tugging me toward the front door of the dingy apartment in a complex overrun with Hell's minions. Cool night air engulfs me, and I shiver. Sliding his hot arm around me, Ezekiel pulls me close, letting me steal his body heat.

Dad's Mercedes idles in the front spot, the purr of the engine quieter than his Ferrari he complains about never getting to drive anymore with the "excess baggage" he calls Ezekiel since he never leaves my side.

I cut Ezekiel off before he can slide behind the wheel and hop in first. He raises an eyebrow but doesn't argue because Dad could obliterate the demon and finish up whatever he's dealing with in the demonic world and be on his way to find us.

I don't really know how Dad handles things these days. I've heard him talk on the phone with Cami Anders, the reigning demon queen who watches over the night on behalf of Heaven, but he manages to stay away from angels. He also manages to keep me by his side through everything, but on the sidelines, using Ezekiel's obsession with me to protect me while sending any demonic threats to Hell before my name burns across their tongues.

The last thing he wants is for all of Hell on Earth to hunt me down. If anyone apart from the angelic army knew I had magically resurrected—which Heaven has done me a favor by keeping my life a secret—I'd be the most coveted demi-demon in the universe. Loved by Heaven's two traitors and able to break the veil between worlds. Capable of ruining the world.

I hate my life. If it's not witches and hellhounds—it's something else.

"You should let me drive," Ezekiel says, leaning in the seat.

I take a moment to put on my seatbelt while Ezekiel watches me. No need to accidentally assist Heaven by risking my safety, as Dad would say. "You drive worse than you used to fly."

He chuckles. As much as it pains me to remind myself that he no longer has his beautiful black wings, I continue to do it for him. Because I'm afraid if I don't, he'll forget who he was to me even if his body's no longer the same. I know deep inside him lies the angel I fell in love with and the angel who truly loves me instead of just remembering that he did—obsessing over me like I'm a possession he takes pleasure in stealing away from Dad every chance he gets.

"Because there's no time to waste with you, Faith," Ezekiel

says, touching my leg and squeezing his fingers into my bare thigh peeking from my hiked up dress.

"Don't remind me," I say, backing out of the spot and stomping the gas pedal the second we enter the quiet street.

Channeling my inner demon, I speed down the road well over the speed limit in the direction of our new fortress nestled in a valley surrounded by tall trees to protect us from the sky. Ezekiel shifts in his seat, peering out the back window. He's always on guard now that he no longer has his angelic light to shield us from the world.

But most demons won't mess with Ezekiel. His power was gifted to him by Hell for fighting for his place on Earth. He's as powerful as Dad, if not more, because he holds my soul and neither Dad nor I would ever allow him to end up in Hell. It's bad enough that's where my eternity leads.

"Come on, Faith, you can drive faster than this," Ezekiel says, grinning at me in the side of my vision.

He's purposely challenging me, trying to poke at the demon within me. Ezekiel used to beg me to keep it at bay, but he now tries to unleash it every chance he can. He claims to love my darker side, love the power he feels radiating in him from my soul, and maybe he does, but I still can't find it in me to shut off my humanity. It's the only thing I have left that still feels like me.

"You just can't wait to get me home, can you?" I ask.

"Well, I'm pretty sure you're going to want to shower."

I laugh and bat his leg. "You wicked demon. You were

counting on my slow reflexes, weren't you? Always trying to corrupt me."

"It's fun," he says. "I love seeing you blush."

"And I miss seeing you bl—" I snap my mouth closed.

Reaching over, Ezekiel runs the back of his knuckles across my cheek. "I'm sure you could still make me if you tried."

"I don't think my nerves could handle such a challenge," I quip.

Ezekiel leans his head back on the headrest and laughs. In moments like these, where it's all banter, life doesn't feel so dooming. Ezekiel still feels like my Ezekiel and not the demon I turned him into. Moments like these give me a reason not to fall into the empty part of me left in the wake of my soul. I can even excuse Ezekiel for not bargaining with me over my soul. Without it, I'd lose him. He'd be a soulless demon, and I'm not sure I could live with that. But I have to. I need to. It's the only way.

Jerking the wheel, I make a hard right at the end of the street, sending the back of the car fishtailing on the road damp from an evening rain shower. Ezekiel laughs as I release a scream and get the car back under control, though I hit someone's plastic trash can left out on the street. Garbage flies through the air, hitting the windshield and blocking my view. If I were a demon, I'd keep driving with no concern for what was in my path. But I'm not a demon.

I hit the brakes, skidding to a stop, and Ezekiel jerks in his seat, bracing himself on the dashboard. Releasing a tiny breath,

I shove the gear into park without moving out of the road. Ezekiel flings his door open, swiping a trash bag from the windshield to the street. I unbuckle my seatbelt to help.

"Time to switch, Demon Spawn," Ezekiel says, striding around the hood to open my door. "I might drive like a maniac, but I'd never risk your safety like you did."

"It was a trash can," I argue, gripping the wheel without moving.

He doesn't give me a choice by leaning in and scooping me into his arms to set me on my feet. "Could've been worse. You're not invincible."

I place my hands on my hips. "You sound like my dad."

"Well, he makes a point. You've gotten soft and can barely take care of yourself, Faith. You mope around when you should be practicing your skills."

I tighten my jaw. "You said you'd always keep me safe."

He releases a groan and spins, lacing his fingers on the back of his head. "If you'd cross the veil with me, I would."

"Ezekiel," I whisper. "You know I can't go back there."

"Then you could—"

His hands light up in blue liquid fire the same time a guttural growl sounds from behind me. I summon my own Hell power and swivel to face the flaming hellhound slinking through the night in our direction. Ever since I killed Mary, the hellhounds have been causing even more havoc in the night. They might not have their witch, but they still have Hell in their veins and won't submit to demons or the angelic army.

And until now, I've managed to evade them and their interest in me like I'm their earthly salvation because Mary chose me.

"Stay away!" I yell. "I'm not in the mood to deal with you."

The hellhound doesn't stop. Its heavy paws thump on the asphalt as it moves closer. From here, I can smell the burning flesh of its skin ignited by Hell's fire, and I cover my nose. Kristin said the hellhounds might turn toward me, seeking me for something I don't want to offer, because I killed their witch and pack leader, but they should know I'm not the answer to their eternity. I can't save them or help them maintain an existence on Earth. Not after they ruined mine.

If Heaven can't forgive me, then why should I forgive the beasts responsible?

I shoot a blast of power in front of it. "I said stay away."

My hands tremble with more power, the beast's human eyes meeting mine. Fury clenches my chest, speeding my heart with painful beats. The way the hellhound watches me pokes at my demon within, reminding it of how incredible it felt to make a wolf bow, though my humanity fights back, reminding me it was the most horrible experience in all my life.

Ezekiel tugs my elbow. "Faith, wait in the car. I'll take care of this."

Panic erupts in my chest, washing ice through the fire burning in my veins at the sound of his words. Against my better judgment, I turn my back on the hellhound and press my palms into Ezekiel's bare chest, feeling his heartbeat and muscles tense and relax under my touch. He looks past me instead of meeting my gaze. If I wasn't already pushing him toward the car, he might tug me in its direction without giving me the choice of bringing him with me so he doesn't do something I might not want to see.

"You're not taking care of anything," I say.

"You can't show them you're weak," he says. "They'll take advantage of you."

I cringe that he calls me weak. He's never done that before. I was always the powerful daughter of Heaven's Traitor to him. A mortal with Hell in my veins and a darkness in my heart that I could unleash at any second.

"Ezekiel..." I don't have it in me to defend myself.

Because he's right. I stopped fighting back. I've thrown everything I've been taught about the demon world into the silent air no longer blessed by my watcher's breathtaking wings. I no longer see reason to prove I'm worthy to be the daughter of Raphael Blackwell, because now I see things differently. I can feel my most horrible parts deep inside me, threatening to consume who I am.

Facing my inner demon, watching how it yearns to destroy the world, forced me to chain that part of myself away in an unbreakable prison not unlike the one Dad turned our house into. And locking away my demon does leave me weak and vulnerable. But I'm also not trying to be powerful. I'm trying to prove I'm not a threat.

The fire in Ezekiel's eyes dims, snuffing out as he takes a hard look at me. Tears blur my eyes, and I pull away and stroll to the driver's side door of the car. He'll do whatever he thinks he must regardless of how I feel just like Dad always has. It's the demon life, one I'm struggling to reacquaint myself with after so many weeks graced with Ezekiel's light. But that light's gone. All that remains are his shadows.

He touches my shoulder, turning me to face him again. Sucking in a deep breath, he stares at the tears splashing onto my cheeks. An indecipherable look crosses his face, furrowing his brows, and he runs his fingers over my tears.

"Please, don't do that," he whispers. "I don't like how it feels."

I huff a gasp, a cross between a laugh and sob. "You don't like how it feels? You can't even feel!"

"That's not—" Ezekiel shoves me toward the car, pushing me into the cold metal. Fire warms the air behind him, the hellhound landing in the spot I was standing. It releases another growl, snarling, sending fear through me.

Igniting his power, Ezekiel prepares to launch it at the hellhound, but it jumps again, landing on the hood of the car only to dart off and a few feet forward. A strange noise claws at my ears over the sound of the hellhound's growls and my own heart ramming against my ribcage, trying to pound through to Ezekiel.

"Faith, get in the car and drive," Ezekiel whispers.

But I can't move.

All I can do is swivel in the direction of the monstrous demon twice the size of Ezekiel as it glares our way.

THE VEIL BREAKER

THE GROUND SHAKES beneath my feet as the demon stomps closer despite the snarling hellhound. Ezekiel nudges me again with his elbow, refusing to take his eyes off the demon. Running goes against what Dad taught me, because I should always put a threatening demon in its place, but Dad's not here to protect me if things go wrong. Physically this demon could do some serious damage. Ezekiel will fight, but he doesn't know the demon world as much as I do and Dad would always approach demons like the business man he is—Ezekiel? He's ready to send him to Hell.

I link my fingers through his hand, stopping him from

shooting power at the demon. Ezekiel jerks his attention to me for a second, and the ground shakes again, causing me to grip the roof of the car.

Summoning power into my hands, power unmistakable as my dad's, I step into the open to face the demon. "What do you want?" I'm not even sure what to say to a demon. This one is clearly a mid-level demon who's more likely to fight for a soul to gain power. The only one here with a soul is Ezekiel and the hellhound, so he might not even be after me. But Ezekiel does possess my soul in a way no one else can since he fell with it in his hands. It's why angels don't keep souls. It's dangerous.

The towering demon smiles, splitting his oval head across the middle where his nose should be if he could create a human façade properly. Sharp black teeth reflect the light of the moon, reminding me of the onyx path in the Veiled Realm.

He turns his gaze to Ezekiel. "What is the cost to take her off your hands? Just the body, not the soul."

Nausea rolls through me. "Are you kidding me?"

"I can deliver twenty hell-bound to you before dawn," he adds.

"Twenty people? That's it?" I ask, offended he thinks he could take me from Ezekiel for twenty people.

"She's right," Ezekiel says. "She's worth at least a thousand."

My mouth drops open, and I smack his arm.

He laughs. "Well, maybe five hundred when she's causing trouble."

The demon rubs his chin with long, boney fingers. "I do like trouble."

Chucking my power, I hit the demon in his tree-trunk thick legs, making him hop into the air. The asphalt smashes under him, the action creating an earthquake strong enough to knock both me and Ezekiel off our feet.

And the ground doesn't stop shaking.

The demon rushes us while we're down, taking advantage of Ezekiel already physically possessing my soul without a contract. Kidnapping me in my soulless state doesn't have much consequence apart from facing my dad. Who knows what he could do in the time it'd take Dad to find me. But Ezekiel won't let that happen.

Ezekiel launches to his feet, summoning power to throw. He grips the roof of the car to keep himself standing, and I struggle to even get to my hands and knees.

A low growl erupts in my ear, and a flash of firelight draws my attention to the hellhound. It evades the demon only to return to my side. Pressing its burning nose into my waist, it rolls me with enough force that I end up under the car at the same time Ezekiel charges away to face the approaching demon straight on. While his power can hit the demon from afar, it's better to close the space, hit it with enough force to blast its chest wide open if that's even where its heart is. If only it were a lower level demon. Even an untrained human could take out one of those.

I'm just thankful the demon isn't the same caliber as Dad

or Ezekiel.

"You should've accepted my first offer!" The demon roars, swinging out his fist at Ezekiel.

He dodges the demon and blasts him with his liquid blue power, burning the front of the demon's chest. The skin melts away, revealing a holey, honeycomb-like texture that seeps black liquid.

Ezekiel jabs the demon, knocking him back a few feet. I've always known Ezekiel was strong, but seeing him in action now, using his demonic power and strength instead of the heavenly light and wings I'm used to does something to me. I can't take my eyes off him. He's not my beautiful fallen angel. He's my fiercely protective demon.

The hellhound drags me out from under the car. It barks and snaps its teeth until I use the door frame to get to my feet.

"Faith, get out of here!" Ezekiel yells.

But I can't. I can't leave him.

Igniting more power into my hands, I thrust it toward the demon Hell-bent on trying to make Ezekiel agree to his poor excuse of a bargain. It's why he wants me to leave. If I'm not here, he has nothing to take.

The fear in Ezekiel's voice pokes at my inner demon. It's not until this moment that I realize it's my panic rushing from me to him, threatening his ability to fight like a demon as my humanity opens him up and leaves him weak. Why he suddenly allowed me in, I have no idea. He's been all fire and steel for weeks, only playing with my human desire.

Something must have gotten to him.

Ezekiel shoots power at the demon. "Faith, I mean it. Drive!"

The demon roars, swinging his arm at Ezekiel and knocks him into the front yard of a nearby house.

Pushing myself into action, I scramble into the car and slam my door. The demon punches the side window, sending glass spraying over me. A flash of fire lights the dark night, and the hellhound launches at the demon, using its giant, flaming body to knock the demon away.

The demon hits the ground, the force of his fall keeping Ezekiel off his feet, though he throws another burst of power.

Giant fingers grip the doorframe, bleeding black onto the leather upholstery. Metal screeches as the demon tries to pry the door open without sticking his hand in to unlock it. Black ooze secretes from his grossly holey chest, sending the car smoldering with burning leather. I stomp the gas pedal, but the tires only spin in place. The demon won't let me leave so easily.

The demon leans down and peers at me. "Knock it off before I throw this whole car at your keeper and really give him that soul of yours."

I ease off the throttle, because he might really kill me if he can't have me. "Do you even know who I am?"

The demon smiles again, sending my heart sliding into my stomach. He doesn't have to say anything for me to know he does. He sniffs the air. "You're the veil breaker. I can smell it all over you. Now, get out."

It's the first time a demon has called me something other than Dad's spawn, and I'm not sure being known as the veil breaker is better, especially because he can smell it on me. Ugh.

Blue liquid power explodes on the side of the demon, making him roar again.

Stomping the throttle, I try to break his hold on the car. The demon hollers, spraying me with the fluid leaking from his honeycomb-like chest. I cover my face and turn away, the world morphing from Earth to the Veiled Realm. Pain splatters across the bare skin of my back because Dad insisted I wear a dress tonight, and now I wish I had argued.

Ezekiel blasts more power from his spot on the sidewalk as he slowly makes his way to me as the demon stomps like a raging two-year-old. I bet the whole neighborhood thinks the world is coming to an end.

Burning rubber clouds the air, stinging my eyes with tears, but I don't let off the throttle. The demon continues to rip at the door like an idiot, probably because he's never driven or owned a car in his existence.

He sprays me again, pelting my back with his hot fluid, and I cover my eyes once again. Bright light shines in front of me, and the avenging angel stands so close he could touch me if he wanted. But he doesn't. He continues to silently watch me.

A scream escapes my mouth, more pain erupting on my skin, and the avenging angel jerks his hand out like he can pull me away from the demon and into the Veiled Realm. Fear forces me to drop my hands, blocking the angel, and I fling power at the demon.

The hellhound bites his arm, hanging onto it, slowing the demon down. The demon punches the hellhound away and in doing so, loses his grip on the door. The car thrusts forward, screeching while finding traction, and I lean back in the seat.

My back burns against the cool leather seat, and I drive to the end of the block and hit my brakes. Peering in the rearview mirror, I watch the demon rush in my direction instead of to Ezekiel. The demon, while not smart like an upper-level demon, still has a need to survive. Attempting to kill Ezekiel will only get him sent to Hell. He knows he can't win in a power match, so he's willing to risk stealing me like someone who does a smash and grab at a jewelry store when the security guard is too far away.

But Ezekiel's armed.

And so am I.

As much as I want to drive away, I can't let this demon think he even has a chance to take me. I'm not some possession. Ezekiel was right. I can't show my weakness.

Shifting gears, I stomp the gas pedal and drive in reverse toward the demon. Ezekiel shoots power, knocking the demon off his feet and out of the way of the car. I slam my brakes, sending more burning rubber into the air, and shove the gear into drive and accelerate. The demon doesn't have the chance to move out of the way, and I run into him. His monstrous body hits the hood and smashes into the windshield before denting the roof.

The whole world shakes around me, and I bounce, unable to brace myself. The car smashes into a short, decorative block wall. Cool air whips around me as the force of the crash throws me through the windshield.

I squeeze my eyes shut, bracing for a world of pain, but I never hit the asphalt. A burning hot body knocks into me mid-air, sending me rolling over and over through the soft grass of the front yard of a house. If it weren't for my demon blood, for my resilience, I would've been far worse off.

I finally stop when my body thuds against a planter. My chest heaves from the quick motion, and I struggle to catch my breath. Hot hands grip my wrists, yanking me to my feet, and I scream out.

"You should've run," Ezekiel says, pressing my face into his bare chest to smother my scream.

I groan and open my mouth to say something, but the world shakes again. The demon gets back to his feet, rolling his shoulders. Instead of rushing for us, he turns to run away, knowing well enough he lost his chance to attempt to capture me.

I wiggle in Ezekiel's arms until he has no choice but to set me on my feet. Without thinking, I hobble forward, pain radiating through my whole body. There's no way I'll ever catch up with the demon, but I can't let him get away.

"Faith, let him go," Ezekiel says. "We'll let Raphael handle him."

"He knows who I am. Word will spread," I say, pushing

my legs to work through the pain. "I can't let that happen. I have enough fear as it is. I don't need—"

Ezekiel hooks his hand around my waist, picking me off my feet. I expect him to drag me away. I expect him to swear he'll protect me, always make sure I'm safe. I expect him to lie to make me feel better.

But all he does is charge forward after the demon.

"This guy's a beast," Ezekiel says. "Summon as much power as you can."

"Me?" I ask.

"Perfect time to work on your skills again. I'll back you up," he says. "We might only have one chance."

Hooking my legs tighter around Ezekiel, I gather so much power into my hands that I barely manage to hang onto it through the quivering world. The demon picks up speed, but his monstrous body is no match against Ezekiel's fit and powerful form, even with me in his arms. A gust of wind pushes against me, and I swear I feel the breeze of Ezekiel's missing wings.

I turn to look at his back, but there's nothing there.

It's in my head.

"Faith, now!" Ezekiel yells, drawing my attention back to the demon before us.

The edges of my vision shadow, and I glimpse a shift in my power turning from ruby red to vibrant orange. My inner demon threatens to rip through my skin to take over if I hold onto such power much longer.

Jerking my hands out, I thrust my power away sending it at the fleeing demon. It smacks into the demon's back, knocking him forward. He collides into the ground, skidding across the asphalt, and Ezekiel closes the distance between us.

The demon rolls over and holds his hands up. "Let me make a deal. Whatever you want. I'll get it."

"I want you dead." My voice comes out deeper, smokier like I have a sore throat. It's the voice of my inner demon. "You'll tell the demonic world my secret."

He cringes. "I'll serve you. Bow to you. You'll have hundreds of souls waiting for you when you descend."

I suck in a quick breath at the thought. "No."

"Wait!"

I don't. Jumping from Ezekiel's arms, igniting more orange power into my hands, I land hard on the demon's broad chest. Black ooze squirts from him, smoldering the hem of my dress, but I don't let it stop me.

I ram my power right into him, breaking through his muscles and burning slime. His heartbeat pulses in my fingers and instead of ripping it out, I force it toward the asphalt, pulverizing it through his back.

He explodes beneath me, spraying guts and innards all over the place. Ezekiel, yanks me back, wiping the burning blood from my skin as fast as he can.

"Now that's one way to rip someone's heart out, pretty little demon," a masculine voice says from nearby.

Before I can look, ice water sprays into my face, rinsing

away the burning residue of the demon. Footsteps sound over the running water and the familiar sound of bones cracking and shifting cuts through the air. Ezekiel tugs me from the spray of water, and through my blurry eyes, I watch the hellhound dart away into the night.

I thought the hellhounds left me alone, but now I'm starting to think they've been around me all along.

Ezekiel pulls me against him, hugging me until I stop trembling, and then strides to turn off the hose, set to automatically spray from its holder. Ezekiel's wet chest steams in the night. I shudder a breath at the sight of him, so hot and sexy with the Hell in his veins calling to my darkness. My whole body relaxes with the motion, and I nearly make it to my knees before Ezekiel hooks his arm around my waist to keep me on my feet.

"Raphael would be proud of you," Ezekiel says, inspecting every inch of me. "But he's sure going to give me Hell."

I release a cross between a laugh and a sob. "Think the car still runs?"

Sweeping his eyes around the area, he turns his gaze to Dad's crushed Mercedes. "It's totaled." He points at an old black sedan with peeling paint and bubbling window tint. "But that one will work."

"Ezekiel, we can't steal someone's car," I say.

He raises an eyebrow.

I sigh. "Okay, but I'm going to have Kristin return it in the morning."

"If it survives your dad."

I wobble toward it, shaking my head. "It might be the only thing that does."

3

STALKER ANGEL

I'D SAY TONIGHT was the worst night ever, but it still could never compare to the night Ezekiel's wings were severed. But I still hurt like Hell. At least it's all physical, and I'll heal by sunset.

"I think you should let me call Kristin," Ezekiel says, handing me the burn cream I keep with the first aid kit in my bathroom.

"She's visiting with her wolf pack." And by wolf pack, I mean her familiars. She's been hanging out with the rogue pack at night more and more lately while I'm in the care of Dad and Ezekiel. She's had a bleeding heart for misfit werewolves since the first day I met her, and I can't help but wonder if she's afraid to leave Greg, Lola, and Calvin alone since hellhounds can cross holy barriers in their human forms. Though, if they try hard enough, the hellhounds can do it in their Hell forms as well as long as they haven't been leashed by a demon. It was something I didn't know possible until Aria broke through one to try to scare Kristin and the Traitor Pack when I was still in Heaven's good grace. I wish I saw it sooner. If I had, Ezekiel and I wouldn't be in this position. Maybe. I can't dwell on the what-ifs.

"She always visits them," Ezekiel says. "She'll understand. You're in pain."

"How am I to toughen up if you always try to baby me? You said it yourself. I'm weak and out of practice. I'll take the human approach with medicine," I argue.

"Faith."

I roll my eyes. "Why don't you just kiss them?"

"Kiss them?"

"And make them feel better," I answer, smirking. "Like…"

Ezekiel doesn't reciprocate my smile, turning from annoyed to full on pouty. For being a demon, he still sometimes manages to hold the same gentleness he did as an angel. Even if he lacks wings, I can't help wondering if maybe it's still in his blood.

"I've lost my healing touch, Faith," he finally says, his voice deepening, tickling the bare skin of my shoulder. He brushes his lips across a purpling bruise anyway.

"I doubt it. There's only one way to find out, though. Unless you're afraid I might let you corrupt me."

Ezekiel brings his gaze to mine, searching my face for answers I don't give him with my voice. Instead, I kiss him. His hot lips tease mine with a whisper of a touch, not all-consuming like I expect from him. I shift onto his lap, grazing my fingers around his neck to slide across his muscular shoulders.

He moans a breath into my mouth, standing up to shift me to my bed, so carefully I can forget the blisters and bruises splattered across my back as long as he keeps kissing me like it's all he wants to do until the sun rises to steal him away. Even then, he might convince me to cross through the veil. Because I hate feeling like my soul is missing when he's not on the same plane. If only it didn't wreak havoc on my mortal body and pull the inner demon out of me in visions too realistic to ignore.

The front door to the house slams shut, drawing Ezekiel's attention away from me. I cup his face in my hands, trying to steal his focus back. But he doesn't give it to me. The fire in his eyes, lit by the adrenaline of the night, of letting my humanity get to him, disappears with the hard thuds of Dad's dress shoes on the sleek wood floor leading to my wing of our fortress.

"Let me handle him," I whisper.

Ezekiel rolls off me and helps me to my feet. Swiping the robe off the edge of my bed, I hide the damage caused by our fight with the demon. I allow strands of hair to fall into my face to obscure my sun-burned looking skin, and pad across my soft rug to meet Dad before he can thrust open the door without knocking.

"Ezekiel!" Dad yells as I crack open my door. His gaze darts over mine, fury pinching his brows, and then he tries to shove my door open.

I block it from opening with my body, knowing Dad won't actually push hard enough to knock me back. "Whatever it is, it wasn't his fault."

Dad huffs and stands back, crossing his arms over his pristine suit. "You were in his care."

"He's my boyfriend, not my babysitter."

"He's the destroyer of your eternity is what he—"

"Dad!"

Ezekiel comes up behind me, his body heat warming me through my robe. Dad tries to push my door open again, but now with Ezekiel behind me, he'd really have to slam against it. He doesn't. Fire ignites in his eyes and he flashes his true body for a split second. But Dad, even in all his hellish glory, doesn't scare me.

"Before you try to take the house down, you must know we have a problem, Raphael," Ezekiel says.

Dad punches the wall, leaving a crater behind. "You think? You wrecked my car and abandoned it for the Hunter's Alliance to discover. There were remnants of a demon splattered across the street. Property damage. We're trying to lie low, not have the angelic army circling. Faith might be protected against their good grace, but it's a bandage to our problem and bandages aren't permanent fixes."

"Don't blame Ezekiel, Dad. I wrecked the car and killed the demon. I just—I couldn't let him go. He knew who I was."

"The whole demonic world knows who you are, Faith," Dad argues.

"As the veil breaker?"

His eyes dart to Ezekiel, who remains firmly behind me, nearly sandwiching me into the door I refuse to open completely in case Dad's still in the mood to punish demons. Dad and Ezekiel share an incredibly annoying silent conversation, and it takes me slipping away from Ezekiel and into the hallway, shutting the door to block my brooding boyfriend off, to get Dad to turn his attention back to me.

I glance over my shoulder to make sure Ezekiel doesn't open the door. "I can't live like this, Dad. The constant fear is getting to me. I don't want to have to defend myself every second of the night."

He twists his lips. "Then you can stay here with Ezekiel. As much as it annoys me, I've accepted this as my eternal punishment. But remember, Faith, he's not your watcher anymore. He won't be gentle with your—"

"I'm tough, Dad," I say, cutting him off. Shrugging my robe down my arm, I show him my blistered and bruised shoulder.

I really, and I mean really, don't want to go in the direction this conversation is heading. Dad's a demon. Nothing about humans fazes him, and he never holds back in telling me what's on his mind, no matter how uncomfortable it makes me. I actually think he does it on purpose to punish me in his own twisted way. Having any sort of mortal desire sex talk with Dad is basically Hell.

Dad's eyes widen, and he reaches out to touch my skin, but I pull my robe back up. "Oh, unholy Hell. I meant he wouldn't be gentle with your heart, Faith. How—"

"Relax, Dad. This wasn't—"

Dad snarls, hooking his arms to my waist to physically lift me off my feet to set me off to the side. He lunges at my bedroom door, his true body breaking free from his human façade. I jump forward and grab the back of his jacket and yank him hard enough to send him to the wall behind us.

"How could you let him do that to you?" he asks, his wild eyes burning at my door like he could somehow blast it open with his glare. "He knows how fragile you are. And—"

"Dad," I say, laughing. I can't help it.

He points at me. "You think this is funny?"

"I—"

"Ezekiel!" Dad yells without letting me explain how he's got the wrong impression. "Just because I can't send you to Hell doesn't mean you're not going to experience an eternity of torment on this plane."

My bedroom door swings open, and Ezekiel stands in the doorway with his arms crossed over his bare chest. Dad launches from the ground at Ezekiel, who doesn't even fight back as Dad knocks him off his feet. They slide across the floor together, crashing into my small kitchen table since I don't even have free range of the house come dawn. My room is like an apart-ment, which doesn't bother me much. I don't have a need to mess with Dad's personal belongings.

Dad summons power into his hand and aims it right at Ezekiel's face.

"Dad, stop! This wasn't Ezekiel. It was the demon I killed. I swear to God if you hurt him I'll—"

Dad snuffs his power out. "He didn't do that to you? I swear, Faith, if you're lying—"

"Some of it was a hellhound, too," I add.

"Those damned beasts. I'm going to break them all." He jabs Ezekiel in the chest. "And you will help me."

I tug the back of Dad's suit, and he lets me pull him off Ezekiel. "No one is breaking anyone. That's what got me in this mess."

Dad sighs. "I'd much prefer to blame Ezekiel."

"Whatever you want, Raphael." Ezekiel pushes to his feet, closing the distance to me. Instead of wrapping his arms around me from behind, he only holds my hand. I'm sure he's ultra aware that I'm doing everything I can to ignore the pain radiat-ing through me.

Dad raises his eyebrow. "My daughter's soul."

"She's safe with me."

"Obviously since you don't even have a damn scratch on you."

"You two, please. I—" I wobble on my feet, the adrenaline of confronting Dad now wearing off. The edges of my vision shadow, making my head spin.

Dad jets his arm out, pulling me away from Ezekiel before I end up in his arms. My stomach rolls, and I blink a few times to clear my vision. I was fine a second ago, but something strange sneaks through me, threatening to knock me unconscious.

"Faith? What's wrong?" Dad asks.

"I—" I can't get the words out.

Chills grab hold of me, shaking my whole body. Without having to ask, the moment I peer into Ezekiel's eyes, I know something is incredibly wrong with me. I cover my eyes with my hands, the world fogging with the silver mist drenched in the light of the hovering moon.

Hot fingers pry my hands from my face. "Faith? Stay with us, okay? I think you're having a reaction to the demon's secretion. Your burn blisters are changing."

I open and close my mouth. Nothing comes out.

Dad's voice sounds through the air. "You better hope she survives until you get here or you won't be leaving my estate ever again, Kristin. The sun is rising, and we can't stay with her."

Ezekiel brushes my hair from my face, his forehead wrinkling with concern. "Don't listen to him. You're going to be fine."

My teeth chatter from the sudden cold of the room, and I reach out to Ezekiel to pull me closer. He doesn't.

"You're already burning up. I'll make it worse," he says,

pressing his lips into a line.

But I'm not sure it can get any worse.

Darkness swallows me.

"I should've never let your feelings get to me like I did," Ezekiel says. "I just—I know how much you yearn for me to embrace your humanity."

He stands behind me on the dream beach of his making, the one reminiscent of my home in Moonlight Shores. It's so familiar it hurts. Or maybe it's Ezekiel's words. Either way, if my soul could weep, I'm sure I'd drown us both in my grief.

"What are you saying?" I ask, hating that I know the answer.

"I have to suppress what your soul does to me," he says.

"Ezekiel, please. I'd suffer all over again to make you feel something. I don't care. I don't want to lose that part of you," I say.

"This is why I must. For you."

Tears blur my eyes. "Please."

His shadow cuts across the sand next to me, but I refuse to look at him as he breaks my heart. Dad was right. Ezekiel can't be gentle with it. Not like before. "Don't think I'll give up. I'll drag every damn feeling out of you if I have to."

He sighs. "I want you to shut your humanity off, too. It's damaging you. All it does is cause you pain. You need to accept the Hell in your blood and now in your soul."

"I don't."

"Just think about it, Faith. You're suffering for no good reason."

"I'm—"

"Demon born and demon bound. Hear my spell, hear the sound. Use the veil to pull you in. Summon your demon and let it win." Kristin's voice prods at my essence, threatening to rip me from my own mind. "Blood to blood, red to black, let the veil take your body back. Your demon within, will get to you. Use its body to see you through."

The world blinks in and out of my vision, but Ezekiel's presence never wavers. He doesn't leave my side. Fear clenches my heart as my dream beach turns into the light prison realm, and the sand beneath me transforms into dirt next to the eerie onyx road.

I cover my face with my hands, startling at the sight of Kristin in my bedroom, her pack of three staring right through me. I'm in bed but not, as I peer through the veil from the other side at them.

"Oh, no," I whisper. "Did I? Am I?"

"Faith, take a breath. It's going to be okay," Ezekiel says, squatting next to me in the dirt. He rubs his hand over my shoulder, and I tense. Because his hand isn't hot for once since he descended. We feel the same.

I suck in a deep breath. "Oh, God. I died."

"Faith."

Digging my fingers into the dirt, I squeeze my eyes shut. I'm going to be sick. "Mary was right all along."

"You need to calm down, Faith." Dad's voice sounds from behind me.

I shake my head, hitting my face with my sweat-drenched hair. "I can't be here. This can't be it."

Ezekiel shifts and takes my face in his hands. "This was the only way to combat the poison in your skin."

Tears burn my eyes. "To make me descend?"

"No," Ezekiel says. "You crossed the veil."

"I—" Before I can get the words out, my stomach heaves, and I jerk away to throw up into the sand next to me. I suck in another breath, but the air doesn't want to enter my lungs. This is worse than the last time I came through the veil. It's like the world is trying to drag my inner demon from the prison I've locked it in.

"I need to leave," I murmur. "I don't feel so good."

"You'll have to manage another few hours," Dad says.

Not happening. The world is rejecting my humanity, and I refuse to let my inner demon loose again.

"You're strong," Ezekiel whispers. "You'll get through."

I groan, covering my eye again. "You called me weak last night."

Ezekiel combs my hair from my face. "Your humanity. Not you. Just turn it off. You'll feel better here if you do. This place isn't meant for humans."

This can't be happening. "Which I am."

"Not completely." Leaning in, he brushes his lips to my forehead. "Not forever. You don't have to be scared of who you are."

Dad clears his throat. "Listen to Ezekiel, Faith."

But I can't.

Fighting through another bout of nausea, I get to my feet and take a few wobbling steps. I need to get out of here. I don't care if I have to break the veil again. If I don't leave, I'll lose myself. I might relent to Ezekiel's suggestion. Desperation pushes people into making crazy decisions, and if I can't suppress the horrible feeling that I'm about to descend, I might unleash my demon.

"Faith, stop," Dad says. "You don't know the realm."

I stumble away faster and into the trees. Summoning power in my hands, I blast one of the twisted trunks of a silently screaming tree in an attempt to break the veil so I can cross back over because I don't know how to portal the other way back without Dad or Ezekiel. They connect to my blood and soul. I have nothing connecting me to Earth.

"Faith!" Dad yells.

But neither he nor Ezekiel comes after me.

A flash of light blinds me, and I scramble to stop before I crash into my stalker angel here in the flesh. My heart pounds in my ears, and the soft sound of ruffling feathers smashes my heart to pieces, reminding me of all the angelic army ruined because of me.

"Stay back," I say, summoning more power into my hands. My usual ruby power burns orange, and the angel's eyes widen at the blackening skin of my hands glowing with Hell fire in my veins.

He doesn't. Flapping his wings, he launches forward at me with his arms outstretched. His brilliant white wings encase me in the purest of light against the hazy air. I squeeze my eyes shut, bracing myself to be sent to Hell at any second.

The world spins, my stomach twisting again. My vision flashes from pure white to red, and I release a loud scream.

But I don't feel the fires of Hell.

All I feel is cool air, and I can breathe again.

Snapping my eyes open, I peer around the front lawn of my fortress. My skin steams against the moisture of the wet grass, and I bend forward to puke black blood everywhere. When my stomach stops heaving, I lean back and stare at the azure sky peeking though the lush branches of a tree.

I prop myself up on my elbow and peer around, still shaking. Slowly covering my eye with my hand, I glance through the veil at my angel stalker. He holds his finger to his lips, shushing me, and then bends his knees and takes flight. Dad and Ezekiel stroll through the gnarled trees on the other side of the veil and catch sight of me.

I drop my hand. I can't face them right now.

"Faith, what happened?" Kristin's voice draws my attention from my racing heart and to her and her wolf pack standing in the doorway to my mansion. "How did you cross? I didn't summon you back, and I know you didn't break the veil because Ezekiel would be with you."

Instead of answering, I say, "How could you do that to me?

I don't belong there."

She motions for Greg, Calvin, and Lola to stay inside and strolls closer to plop down next to me in the grass. "Whatever demon you encountered last night poisoned you. Your blisters weren't caused from burns. They were filled with some sort of substance that was killing you. I don't even know if you should be here yet." Reaching for my shoulder, she shifts me so she can look at my back. "A lot of them popped and seem okay, but there are still quite a few."

"I'll be fine. I'm not going back." Something sharp stabs my shoulder blade, and I yelp, jerking away from Kristin. "Ouch. What the Hell!"

"I wanted to save you the pain of doing this," she says, reaching to poke my back again. "But since you're acting stubborn like your dad, it must be done. You're lucky you don't have nearly as many blisters as before. You're probably down to fifty compared to who knows. I couldn't count."

I groan. "Make it quick."

"Then lets go inside. The other's can help."

Warmth crawls up my chest into my neck. "You need better spells."

"And you need to stop getting into trouble." She takes my hand and pulls me to my feet. "Now, hurry up. We're running out of sunlight and you're going to need to get a little sunburn when I'm through."

"Did I mention your spells suck?"

She laughs. "At least I haven't asked for your blood."

"Yet."

"You're right. The day's not over."

4

LEGION OF DEMONS

"WHY DO YOU insist on doing things the hard way?" Ezekiel asks, hovering next to me in the veil.

Kristin sets her lancer onto a towel and then dips a washcloth into a bowl that suspiciously hums with the sacredness of holy water. I jerk as Kristin rubs it over my skin, burning away the last of the demon poison from my skin.

I grind my teeth. "This was easy compared to a day in the daylight prison realm."

Ezekiel's fingers graze the veil between us, shocking my cheek. "You mean a day with me."

"That too." Because being with Ezekiel in the daylight prison realm is more painful than looking at him there through the veil. Especially after what he asked of me. Turning off my humanity would change me like descending changed him. I'm afraid if I do I'll forget what's important to me, which is reminding Ezekiel who he is despite what he is.

"It doesn't have to be hard." Ezekiel kneels down to peer into my eyes. In the Earth world, I'm lying on my bed. In the veiled realm, I seem to be on a rock of some sort. It always freaks me out how things mirror the Earth world but in a creepy way.

Kristin taps my arm, drawing my attention away from Ezekiel. "Time to go outside."

"Dad will be furious."

She rolls her eyes. "I'm coming with you. The others are already on watch in the forest. I think we'll be okay. Maybe Raphael will invest in a block wall or moat or something so you can have more freedom."

I drop my hand from my eye, cutting Ezekiel off without commenting on his statement. I'm not in the mood to argue. He might be charming. He might ignite my heart with his beautiful flames. But turning off my humanity for me? It goes against everything ingrained in me. I know what happens to those who do such a thing, and Ezekiel taints my soul with Hell enough as it is. I want to be able to beg Heaven for mercy and to be redeemed once I figure out how to get my soul back from Ezekiel. If he's so insistent on turning off his access to it, then what's the point? He'll act soulless regardless.

Kristin holds onto my waist, carrying some of my weight from my trembling knees. My aches and bruises are ten times worse since last night. I have to remind myself that it always gets worse before it gets better. If only I didn't have to deal with this at all.

"So, your dad mentioned a hellhound," Kristin says, opening a side door that leads to a garden now dead from the lack of care. Dad's cut back our entire staff since my return, and it really shows.

"He helped me." I'm not sure how I feel about it. Hellhounds ruined everything. They still threaten the balance of the universe. But I understand where they're coming from. I always have. It doesn't make me want to suddenly befriend them, though.

"I know you feel the bad blood still, and Mary left you scarred because of it, but I think this is progress. If the hellhounds wanted you dead, they'd have made it known. We could use this to our advantage."

"Our advantage?"

"Against the unrest. The world is changing, Faith."

Spreading out the blanket, I plop down in the grass outside of the tree line. "I wouldn't know."

Kristin heaves a sigh. "I'm doing my best to make Raphael see reason. He's just overwhelmed by everything that has happened. Just be patient."

"It's not like I have a choice."

She lies down next to me on her stomach, taking my hand in hers. "Heaven's Traitor's daughter is more than a vessel. You were meant for great things, Faith."

"Knock it off with the prophecies," I say.

She laughs. "But they're so good."

"Doubt it. I'm going to end up in Hell, remember?"

She frowns. "Even so, you will rise."

That's what I'm afraid of. There's only one way to rise from Hell, and it's the last thing I want to be.

"You're acting like quite the angel, Demon Spawn," Ezekiel says from next to me.

The muffled voices of the restaurant sound through the open archway to our section which Dad managed to get closed off from the rest of the patrons.

He sits across from me, sipping red wine while messing with his phone. Turning his gaze to me, he raises an eyebrow. "It's quite annoying."

I stab at my pasta like it'll come to life and strangle me if I don't. Going out to dinner to a nice restaurant and forced into another gown was the last thing I wanted from my night. Kristin left with her wolves the moment the sun set, and it took everything in me not to chase after her to beg her to stay. But the rogue wolves don't trust Dad or Ezekiel, which I can't fault them for—even if they knew Ezekiel as an angel and saw him fall, they treat him like the demon he is.

"I don't see what the big deal is," Dad adds. "You were

sick, and I wanted you to heal. Can you fault me for loving you?"

"This isn't about that," Ezekiel says, sliding his hand over the tablecloth to try to hold my free hand.

I jab my fork between his fingers without saying anything.

He laughs, steals my fork, and takes a bite from my plate. "Forget being angelic. You're still worth five-hundred Hell-bound, troublemaker."

I glare. He laughs about his own teasing from last night when the demon tried to barter twenty Hell-bound people for me. I bite my bottom lip between my teeth, refusing to let Ezekiel summon even one smile onto my lips. I'll give him the angelic silent treatment until dawn for the whole humanity suggestion.

Too bad demons love these types of games, and I'm losing.

Dad misses Ezekiel's inside joke and ignites power in his hand. "You better not be equating my beautiful daughter's worth to a bunch of humans."

"Five hundred when she's being a pain," Ezekiel quips, smiling at me. Without tapping into my humanity, he clearly doesn't care what Dad thinks and isn't afraid to provoke him.

Snatching Dad's hand, I snuff out his power, linking my fingers with his. "It's a joke, Dad. Ezekiel obviously thinks I'm worth more. If he didn't—"

Dad burns his fiery eyes at Ezekiel. "Don't remind me."

Ezekiel points my fork at Dad. "You should appreciate I think Faith is priceless."

Before Dad starts power blasting Ezekiel, I shove back from the table and stand. I throw my cloth napkin down and glower at them. "Try not to burn the place down while I'm gone."

Both Dad and Ezekiel get up.

I shake my head. "No way. I'm only going to the bathroom. You two stay here. I mean it. If you think I'm acting angelic now, you just wait."

Ezekiel laughs while Dad groans into his hands, mumbling about how he should've known the universe would repay him for all his sins. I peek over my shoulder once, pointing my finger at them to stay behind and make my way to the back of the restaurant where the restrooms are located.

Dozens of eyes fall on me, watching my every move. Being a demon's daughter always draws attention, even from those who have no idea of the Hell lurking in my veins. Mortals, especially the Hell-bound, will find me alluring. It used to be easy to ignore, but with the whole world seemingly out to get me, I'm more aware of everyone.

"Well, aren't you a pretty little demon," a man says from his seat at a table near the bathroom.

I meet his gaze, his voice sounding too familiar. Fire dances in his eyes, making me tense, but I force myself to straighten my shoulders instead of turning to run back to Dad and Ezekiel. We're in a public restaurant. The man won't come after me here, especially not with two full-blooded demons waiting for me.

I enter the bathroom and smile at the bathroom attendant

perched on her chair. I hold my hands under the faucet and splash water on my still sensitive face, lightly pink from both the demon and the sun. If the hellhound last night hadn't squirted me with the hose, I'm sure my face would've been a blistered mess as well. The woman hands me a towel from her basket, and I pat my face dry and stare at my reflection.

"On a terrible date?" the woman asks, offering me lavender lotion. "I can have a server deliver an urgent message so you have an excuse to leave."

I turn my gaze to her, smirking. "There is no emergency imaginable that will end a dinner date with my dad, unfortunately."

She hums under her breath. "How about a quick escape? I think I can come up with a distraction."

The door to the restroom swings open again, and the man from the table pokes his head in. I automatically summon power in my fingers against my better judgment. But my inner demon automatically reacts.

"Thirty seconds if you want to leave," he says to me.

I frown. "You heard?"

He taps his ear. "Now or never. You know you don't want to be a daddy's girl forever. We can offer you the same protection."

My breath catches as I realize the two people cornering me in the bathroom are hellhounds, and I'm pretty sure the man was the one following me last night. Fear trickles through me. They are insane if they think I'll go with them or that Dad would even allow it.

"I—"

The man releases a low growl. "Sorry, kid. Time's up."

He closes the door, disappearing with the sound of his quick footsteps, and the woman strolls toward the back of the bathroom. She enters a linen closet where I spot an open window. A burst of fire lights from outside, and I catch the scent of burning flesh.

Leaning my palms on the counter, I take a heaving breath. The door to the bathroom swings open again, and Ezekiel comes in without even thinking about it. One look at my face tells him something's wrong, and he links my fingers with his and tugs me from the bathroom without even hearing what happened.

Dad stands near the now empty table, looking from the seat to me. Under the restaurant patrons' scrutiny, he maintains his steely façade despite how much he wants to unleash Hell upon the place.

"One left out the window," Ezekiel says to Dad.

"They're brazen. Unafraid," Dad quips.

Ezekiel peers around the room. "I don't like this."

"We'll fix it. I'll unleash Hell to protect Faith."

His comment reminds me of what the man said, his words swimming through my head. He offered me his protection. But from Dad? Why? Is this some ploy to lure me away from Dad? Are the hellhounds messing with my humanity? Is there another witch now helping them? The man called me the same thing

Mary did—a pretty little demon—and now all I want to do is run home and hide. I'm through hunting hellhounds and witches.

But it seems they aren't through with me.

I twist my hands together. "I'd rather you just took me home instead."

Dad sighs. "And let the hellhounds think they got to us."

"Yes, exactly that. I'm tired and still hungry. I just want to grab my dinner to go and spend the rest of the night in my bed. Maybe soak in the tub some more."

Ezekiel's eyes light up though his mouth remains hard. He's torn, because I'm sure my plans sound as good as Dad's to him. "I can take Faith home."

Dad narrows his eyes. "Do you think I'm going to trust her safety in your hands after last night? Not to mention if it's an entire pack of hellhounds taunting us. They're wild beasts. I need you to watch my back, and Faith needs to send them a message that they will not be allowed to bother us."

I groan. "You're the worst, you know."

Dad smiles. "I try."

Hooking his fingers around my arm, Dad pulls me to the entrance of the restaurant with Ezekiel flanking my other side. I'm basically the safest girl on the planet, yet I can't stop the panic from turning my hot blood icy. But it's not fear for myself. It's for the hellhounds. *They made their choice. They ruined your life.* The dark thought sneaks up on me, and I shove the smoky voice of my inner demon to the back of my mind.

If I expect Heaven to forgive me, I might as well follow that thinking as well. Life isn't exactly easy for anyone with the world in constant battle for who controls what and who.

"At any sign of danger, don't back down," Dad says to me, summoning power into his hand as we exit. "Send them to Hell if you have to, but I prefer you only weaken them enough to break."

"Dad."

"Faith, this is our world. I know you struggle with yourself, and I love your beautiful humanity and how it reminds me of your mother, but you must adapt if you want to survive. Things are changing. Not even the sunlight is safe for you." Dad narrows his eyes, searching the dark parking lot for signs of the Hell beasts. "Not with the beasts around."

"They don't want to hurt me," I say, basically being dragged between Dad and Ezekiel.

"You talked to them." Ezekiel isn't asking. He knows already without having to. I guess I need to work on my own steely façade. "What did they want?"

"Nothing."

"Everyone wants something," Dad snaps.

I yank my arms away and stand to face my personal legion of demons. "Just stop. I don't want to do this tonight. I want to go home."

Firelight bursts in Dad's eyes. "After."

"No, now."

Summoning power, I hold it up and glare at Dad. All he

does is twist his lips in annoyance, knowing the ruby red orb matching his won't do him harm. He knows I'm full of empty threats.

An eerie howl sounds through the air, making me shiver.

I might be full of empty threats, but the approaching hellhounds aren't.

Dad and Ezekiel throw power at the same time. Growls rip through the air, but I don't even have time to react. Two hellhounds launch at Dad and Ezekiel while another one bites onto my gown, yanking me back. I stumble, and the beast drags me across the parking lot and away from the restaurant.

I thrash, trying to break the hellhound's hold. "Let me go!"

The beast doesn't, even when I ignite power in my hands. It might sense that I don't want to hurt it. Because this isn't an attack. The hellhounds aren't attempting to rip Dad and Ezekiel apart. They're only messing with them.

But Dad will show them what happens to those who do try to best him.

So I do the only thing I can. I scream. "Dad, help me!"

Both Dad and Ezekiel stop chasing the hellhounds, turning their attention to me. Dad reveals his true body, his jutting horns spiking toward the sky. He snarls, gathering more power in his hands. He'll throw it at me, knowing while it'll wind me and smolder my dress, the power won't hurt me.

The hellhound releases me as Dad runs toward me with Ezekiel by his side. Power sparkles through the air, hitting the car next to me, and the flaming beast jumps on the hood to disappear on the other side. Ezekiel scoops me from the ground while Dad launches past us, landing on the hood of the car right after the hellhound. He chucks more power, sending a few swear words toward the sky, and then turns to peer at me in Ezekiel's arms.

"He should've never touched you," Dad says. "This could've ended badly."

"But he didn't want to hurt me," I argue.

Dad launches another orb of power in the fleeing hellhound's direction. "That's not what I meant. Ezekiel was right. You've grown weak, Faith. I saw more fight in you as a little girl."

I straighten my shoulders, clenching my jaw. "Well that little girl grew up and knows that the world expands farther than her dad's shadow and realizes the damage her devotion could do."

Dad doesn't respond. He silently stares at me with a strange look crossing his face.

"You let that angel get into your head, Faith," Ezekiel says, cutting into my conversation with my dad. He knows what the avenging stalker angel told me when he severed Ezekiel's wings. I'm sure it's the one thing he'll remember if he forgets everything else—how an angel made me cry and forsook me. Because Ezekiel never would. "You know as well as I do that you could never destroy the world. You're meant to change it. Make it better."

But for whom? Ezekiel doesn't see or feel what I feel any

longer.

I don't respond because I can't see how I could possibly make the world better the way I want to. Not with my soul in his hands.

Dad closes the distance to me, touching my chin so I have to look at him. "You must have faith, my beautiful daughter. It's why I gave you such a name. Your mother would've agreed it was perfect for you. And I'll help you. You can always count on me. But first, I must be certain you rely on yourself. You've been sulking around long enough. It's time you embrace your demon."

Ezekiel touches my shoulder. "You don't have to be afraid of yourself, Faith."

I swallow the burning in my throat, my heart speeding at the idea. It's not me who likes it though. It's my inner demon.

"We'll start training again tonight," Dad says.

I can only nod.

Because as much as I don't want to think about it, Ezekiel is right. I am afraid of myself. Because my inner demon is me. I can't pretend it's not. I am my own personal demon.

AVENGING ANGEL

THE WALL BEHIND me explodes in ruby flames, and black smoke clouds the room. Gathering power into my palms, I summon energy from the depths of Hell, using all my annoyance and disappointment in Dad for forcing me into practicing when all I want to do is lie down.

Another blast of power, this time from my right, whizzes past me and sets the sleeve of my shirt ablaze in hypnotizing blue light. My skin burns, pain rushing over me. I release a small scream and rip my shirt off, tossing it to the ground.

"Damn it, Ezekiel!" I yell.

I don't get the chance to move when another one of Dad's

ruby red orbs of power collides into my stomach, sending me crashing into the sizzling wall. Shadows edge my vision, blurring my eyes, and I fall to my knees.

They were right. I suck.

"Get up, Faith." Dad's footsteps sound over the pounding in my head. "If we were anyone else, you'd be dead."

Groaning, I shake off his hand and push to my feet to stand on my own. "Well, it's a good thing you're not."

"That's my point. Next time it might not be. You've been sought after twice in two days. What happens if the Hell beasts come to tear the place down come dawn?"

"Kristin spelled the place. If I can't get out, there's no way anyone's getting in."

Dad shakes his head. "That's beside the point."

"Is it, though?" I ask, sarcasm lining my words.

Ezekiel slides up next to me without a word, snuffing some of the annoyance away with a pout of his lips. Firelight shines in the depths of his mocha eyes, a stark contrast to Dad's blue ones. The two demons stand before me, gazing at me in completely different ways. Where Dad scowls, crossing his arms, probably thinking about adding an additional ten locks to the house the longer he dwells on my safety, Ezekiel drinks me in, trailing his eyes from my lips to the lacy bra I regret wearing instead of a practical sports bra. But I wasn't expecting to tear my shirt off in front of Dad.

"You're hurt worse than I thought," Ezekiel says, closing the distance to grab my arm. His fingers brush over the new cluster of blisters from where his power grazed me. "I'm sorry. You make it so easy to forget how fragile you are."

"Like a porcelain doll," Dad says, taking my arm from Ezekiel, stopping us from hugging in front of him. But I could sure use a hug instead of getting blasted into a wall with Dad's idea of toughening me up.

Ezekiel glances from Dad to me. "Or a bomb."

Dad chuckles, dropping my arm, the firelight extinguishing from his eyes as he settles down. "The hellhounds will surely find out. Heaven better be careful, too."

Hearing Dad and Ezekiel discuss me like something the world needs to fear erupts a bout of sorrow through me. They claim I'll change the world, but I think they now mean after I destroy it first.

Rolling my eyes, I slide between Dad and Ezekiel, striding from the gym before Dad can stop me. Dad promised to permit me to use his gym during the day if I please, probably trying to persuade me to stop arguing with him, but I just shrugged. Because it doesn't make up for anything, and it doesn't change that he's gone into full on demon dad mode. It's like the hellhounds flipped his humanity switch off and now he's doing things as a demon and not my dad. *He's always done things as a demon. He hasn't changed. You have.*

I push the thought away and break out into a sprint to my room.

Ezekiel's footsteps sound behind me, following me at the same pace, though I refuse to peer over my shoulder to look at him. He deserves my fury as much as my dad. He might think he can shut out my humanity, but I know how to get to him. And ignoring him is one way. It not only drives him crazy, it also elicits burning emotions within me that will get to him and make me easily lose myself and forget about how much he's changed. Like Kristin told me before—I have to fill his demonic emptiness with all that I can.

He jogs in front of me to walk backwards, not giving me any other choice but to pay attention to him. "There's still an hour to sunrise," he says, reaching out for my hands, tugging me along and toward my bedroom. "Let me make tonight up to you."

I smirk, faking a glare I can't maintain. It's incredibly hard to resist his charm. "You don't have demonic things to do?"

Firelight burns in his eyes, his smile widening. "Only with you."

I laugh, letting him pull me the rest of the way to my bedroom. Pouting and unleashing fury won't give him the desire to want to feel my humanity again. It was the fear that made him suppress it in the first place. So maybe I need to remind him of the good things.

Ezekiel shuts the door behind us and locks it as if Dad doesn't have the key. Leaning down, he closes the space between us, brushing his lips to mine. His warm mouth, tasting of the dark chocolate scent that clings to him, makes me kiss him harder. He devours every kiss I offer him like he can't get enough. Like he's starving and wanting to gather my kisses to hold him over through the day when we're apart.

His hands comb through my hair, tossing it from my shoulder so he can graze his lips down my neck and to my bare collarbone. Heat blossoms from every spot he kisses, working its way to my heart beating wildly, trying to escape my ribcage.

"You're incredible," he whispers, his breath tickling my chest under the black feather tattoo marking my skin. It's gone from a reminder of the angel he used to be to his personal claim on me like I'm a possession. It drives Dad crazy and makes me roll my eyes. Silly demons. "I wish you'd try to come with me through the veil again. It's agony leaving you." If he keeps kissing me like this, I might consider it. What am I even thinking? I felt like I was dying last time.

Ezekiel hooks his thumbs to the waistband of my workout pants, tugging my hips to his to feel our bodies completely aligning together. When we're this close, breathing the same breath, my skin against his soft shirt, it almost feels like my soul is mine again. He makes me forget that he'd have never allowed me to get this far without stopping as an angel, and I want nothing more than to lose myself in everything he is in this moment. Because even after last night, he doesn't feel demonic. Not like Dad does. He feels just like the angel I fell in love with and like I'm still his sole purpose in the universe.

I tug his shirt over his head and let him spin me toward the bed. I hop up, wrapping my legs around his hips, pressing our chests together while running my hands over his shoulders. My fingers touch the mostly smooth skin on his back apart from the nearly invisible scars from where an avenging angel severed his wings.

Ezekiel tenses, his muscles bunching for a split second, but he doesn't force me to stop. I can remember the softness of his feathers, a phantom feeling racing through my mind as quickly as my heart.

I pull away, my breath heaving. "Ezekiel," I whisper. Because as much as I used to tease Ezekiel about corrupting him, and he now reversed the role on me, I'm not ready to allow him in completely no matter if it could open him up to me. His desire burns differently. He can't feel exactly what I'm feeling. And until he opens himself up to the effect my soul has on him again and I can truly have him, I'm not putting my heart on the line even more than I have. I hate that Dad's attempt at a sex talk really got to me this time.

A tear splashes onto my cheek, surprising me. I thought I had come to terms with the idea that Ezekiel is now forever a demon by my doing. But something about this moment, about everything that happened and might happen because of the hellhounds, opens up my wounds to pour everything out of me all over again.

Ezekiel's muscles ripple as he shifts me, and he tilts his head to the side. "What's wrong? Did I hurt you?"

I swipe the heel of my hand across my cheek. "I'm fine. My arm is tender is all." My even voice and smile are enough to cover the emotions I try so hard to suppress without doing what Ezekiel has asked and turning off my humanity to embrace the demon who would never shed a tear over something like missing wings.

He rubs his lips in a thin line and turns to carry me toward my bathroom. Setting me on the sink, he moves toward my cabinet to grab the first aid kit from the shelf. The action stirs a small ounce of joy inside me, because emotionless demons don't bandage wounds or kiss boo-boos away, and Ezekiel looks ready to do both just like after the demon attack when I teased him, and he told me he was missing his healing touch.

Opening the kit, he sighs at the empty container of bandages I haven't had the chance to refill.

"I'm fine, really," I say, scooting off the sink to stand on my feet.

He raises an eyebrow. "Don't move. I'll be right back." Kissing me once more, Ezekiel heads from my bathroom. Taking care of me, ultra aware of his ability to accidentally hurt me, treating me just like he's always treated me, but even better, makes my life feel like maybe the destruction I've left in my wake was worth it. That maybe I won't destroy the world after all.

I cover my eyes with my hands, sucking in a deep breath to control my still racing heart. White mist swirls through the Earth realm as the Veiled Realm appears before me as I use my sight to see through the realms.

"You've been busy," a whisper of a voice says, trickling through the veil to me. "The demons treating you kindly now?" It's the first time my stalker angel has said two words to me.

I should drop my hands. I shouldn't let him bait me. But something snaps inside me, especially after encountering him in the sunlight prison world.

"Better than you ever will," I mutter, turning to glance at the terrifyingly beautiful angel with his annoying workaround to the magical spell Kristin cast to block Heaven from finding me.

"Forgive me for that. I was hoping my divine intervention would persuade you."

I frown. "What?"

"I helped you portal away from Heaven's Traitors."

I blink a few times. So that explains how I crossed the veil without Kristin summoning me or me breaking the veil. I thought the angel was trying to grab me to end my life, but he helped me.

I stare at him, words lost to me.

"You're a force I've learned I can't forsake so easily," he adds. "So will you please forgive me?"

Angels and their dumb need for forgiveness.

I huff. "Maybe if you give up on me. I'm not going to destroy the universe despite how you feel. And if my dad finds out you've been sneaking around the Veiled Realm hunting me, he'll see to it you fall by his side."

The angel grimaces, his pouty bottom lip doing nothing but annoying me. It doesn't get to me like Ezekiel's—or maybe the infuriating angel's flaming sword seared any reaction away. "Yet you haven't told him. You know, he'd take great satisfaction in that."

It's my turn to pout. "You say that like you know him." I refuse to acknowledge his other statement about not telling Dad about him yet. Because the truth is, even though I know I should, I can't help but wonder if not telling Dad and proving the angel wrong about me will somehow help me in the end.

He cocks his head. "I do."

I glare. "You don't. You don't know anything."

"I know my purpose."

I should yank my hand from my eye and force him to disappear from my view. I shouldn't argue with a celestial being who was quick to raise his flaming sword to my chest to seal my eternity. But I've never been good about listening to my good senses—senses I doubt I still have. There's just something about knowing my enemy, letting him near through the protection of the veil that makes me feel better. Like my existence isn't lost completely. With him, I see a chance to redeem myself.

"I swear to God if you say it's me you better fly your haloed head out of here before something terrible happens to you," I say.

He hums under his breath, unfurling his brilliant white wings. "I can see why my brother is so enamored with you. Your humanity is quite endearing. I'm thankful you're strong enough to resist the allure of turning it off."

I groan. "I'm offended you sound so surprised. You're a jerk for being in good grace."

"My apologies."

I wish he'd quit this. "And you know what? Ezekiel's not your brother. He's not even your friend."

The angel flaps his wings, sending a gust of rose perfumed air in my direction. The light shining from his golden eyes, the same color as his hair, burns brighter than his glorious wings, but no matter how much it pains me to watch him, I don't turn my gaze away.

"And he's not *your* keeper," he says. "Neither is your father. But you'll never see that. While your humanity is so precious, it does nothing for your judgment. It allows you to make excuses for this deadly situation."

Anger rushes through me, and I ignite power in one hand, blurring the two worlds around me. "Deadly situation? It's my life and now my eternity. I'm not a situation."

His shoulders tense, his gaze darting to my power. "Careful, Faith. I'm not here to threaten you. I'm here to ask you to make it right. You're obviously conflicted about the state of the world. I know you still care."

Make what right? I don't know what it is he wants apart from ending my life and damning me to Hell all because he believes I'll allow Hell to reign again. "I don't understand."

"You can't live as you are. You know this."

I glower. "I'm not damning myself to Hell."

"So, you'll damn everyone else."

Fury turns my vision red. Raising my hand, I chuck my demonic power at the avenging angel, sending him launching into the sky. How dare he do this to me or ask this of me especially after everything? I'm not who he thinks I am. I'm not. The last thing I want is to damn the universe.

The world rocks around me. The veil morphs, distorting my view of the angel and the dead desert landscape. The cool night air warms with a brown haze from the soon-to-be rising sun, and I summon more power in my hand to launch it at the avenging stalker angel.

Despite my sneer, he lands in front of me, holding his hands in front of him. "I'm sorry, Faith. I didn't mean that. It's just I've never dealt with someone like you."

"A demi-demon?"

"Raphael might be a demon, but he wasn't always. And Grace Blackwell somehow managed to remember that despite the new fire burning in his veins. You weren't born like normal mortals, Faith. You're different. Dangerous. Can't you see that? I know you're in love with a demon and you're a devoted daughter, but imagine what'll happen if Hell breaks loose. You're out of control, creating portals between realms by accident, thinning the veil, dragging mortals through with you. Your blood is powerful enough to break free will. You were born from unruly magic and powerful blood. You're an abomination." He can list all the things he thinks is wrong with me, but it still won't make a difference. Because I know how to handle danger.

"I won't cross anymore," I say, ignoring his honesty since angels can't lie. "You don't have to worry about me."

The angel reaches out his hand, linking his fingers around

the wrist of my hand I hold over my eye. He yanks my hand from my face, startling me, and my bedroom disappears completely from my view. Panic seizes my chest, sending me reeling, and I stumble back, igniting Hell power between my palms.

"Stay back!" I scream, scrambling to my feet.

He doesn't. Strutting forward, he closes the distance to me. A flaming sword materializes out of thin air, and he aims it in my direction. "You proved my point."

"Please," I beg. "Show me mercy. Don't you think I deserve it after everything? You said it yourself, Heaven failed me. And you know what? Even though you want me dead, even though you ruined my Demon Watcher with the sword you threaten me with, I still don't want to hurt you. I don't even blame you. But I need you to give me a chance. Please. I'll do anything if you give me time to get my soul back." Because I can't go to Hell. I can't.

He lowers his sword before it disappears. "Okay."

Surprise raises my brows. "Okay?"

The corner of his lips pulls up into a ghost of a smile. "Despite what Raphael has said of me, I don't want you to spend eternity in Hell. You should've never been in this position, Faith."

I release a relieved breath. "So now what?"

"Cross back over, get your soul back, and don't destroy the world in the process," the angel says, making it sound simple enough. If only.

"How much time do I—"

"Blood to blood from dark to light, bring Faith back, control her sight." Kristin's voice hums through the air, pulling at my very essence. "Demon born and Hell-bound, hear my words, hear the sound. A father's smite, and a lover's plea, open the veil, let us see."

The angel expands his wings, taking flight without giving me the answers I need. Blood blossoms through the air, coating an invisible wall in front of me. I stare in shock at Dad, Ezekiel, and Kristin standing before me in my bathroom.

"Faith, what happened?" Dad asks, reaching his hand up to press against the veil dividing us. His black blood coats the spot between us.

I shrug. "This was an accident. I saw—" The words stick to my tongue, and I clear my throat, but nothing comes out.

Ezekiel's eyes widen. "This is Heaven's doing."

Horns erupt from Dad's forehead, his true body unleashing for me to see. Black blood drips down his face. Fire burns through his eyes as he tries to peer around the Veiled Realm behind me.

"Dad, calm down," I say, taking a breath. Raising my hand to my eye, I close the space between us, crossing back through the veil and into his arms. "I'm fine."

"You're not." He turns to Kristin. "Ready another spell. You and Faith must leave at dawn, understand? We will catch up come nightfall."

"Leave? We don't need to leave, I've—" Again, the words remain locked in my throat.

"Don't argue with me, Faith," Dad snaps. "Not after the demon and the hellhounds. Now this damned angel."

Before I have the chance to argue, the sun rises, lowering the veil for a split second to lock Dad and Ezekiel back in their prison world. A white feather drifts through the air, and I catch it before it can land in Dad's blood.

Kristin clears her throat. "What the hell? That belongs to an angel."

I shrug, tucking it away in my pocket. "Have I mentioned—" The words stick in my throat.

"Damn angels. He found a way to contact you in the Veiled Realm."

I nod as she fills in the blanks I can't say. Angels can protect themselves by making it nearly impossible to talk about them with people they don't trust.

"For how long?"

I expect the words to stay locked up but manage to spit out, "He's been watching me for weeks, but today I accidentally crossed over." Maybe the angel wants Dad to realize his plan to keep Heaven away is failing or that I'm failing because I've kept it a secret.

She sucks in a breath. "Weeks? Why haven't you said anything? Faith, Raphael's going to kill—"

I cringe. "You can't tell him."

Narrowing her eyes, she gazes at me, determining whose side she'll pick. "You're so lucky he can't hurt you there."

I frown. "He can't?"

"Why do you think you're still alive?"

I open my mouth to tell her about the angel granting my last request, but something holds me back, her words digging into me. Angels are sneaky and manipulative. I'd have never agreed to give myself over as long as my soul was intact if I had known he couldn't have sent me to Hell right there. He wasn't granting me mercy, he was using a moment of my weakness Dad will definitely point out again to get into my head.

"That damn angel," I say, fisting my hands. "He tricked me."

"What do you mean?"

"I thought he was going to kill me, and I begged for mercy, so he—" Again, the words don't come. I can't tell Kristin about him granting my sort of last request since he couldn't actually kill me.

She sighs. "And they say demons are bad. He was messing with your humanity."

"So what now?"

"We pack our bags like Raphael asked."

"That's it?"

She stares at me for a long moment. "Why are you looking at me like that?"

"Because I was hoping you'd say we would hunt an angel."

She laughs. "There will be plenty of time for that. No one messes with Raphael and Grace Blackwell's daughter."

She's right. The stalker avenging angel will see. And I can't wait.

MERCY

I PEER AT the sunlight prison realm around me. Dad and Ezekiel stand a few feet away, screaming at each other so loudly I can hear their voices through the sound-muting veil. Ezekiel would've never dared to enter a screaming match with Dad, but now that they're on the same level power wise, nothing stops the two from embracing their demonic nature. If only I wasn't always dragged in the middle.

Strolling forward in the empty parking lot, I close the space, getting next to them without stepping between them, and place a hand on my hip. If I wasn't using my sight, neither would see me, and they only can now because they each share a part of me—Dad with blood and Ezekiel with my soul.

Ezekiel notices me first, turning away from Dad to reach out and graze his fingers over my cheek, sending my skin buzzing. "You okay?"

Slowly, I nod. "Yeah, just annoyed."

The veil thins with the last rays of sunlight, releasing them back to Earth.

"You think you're annoyed?" Dad asks, pushing Ezekiel away from me so I'm forced to give him my full attention. "Do you know how difficult it is to arrange things when I'm the one stuck here until sundown?"

I shrug. "Welcome to my life of being imprisoned. At least you get to roam the night on your own."

Dad closes his eyes, composing himself. "Faith, I know it's hard, but it won't last forever. The angelic army backed off from me already. We haven't given them anything to worry about. You're just lucky you didn't damage the veil crossing over."

Because I didn't want to break it. Like with the time I crossed over to Dad, something about the avenging angel allowed me through. "That only happens with my power. I don't even know how it happened. One second I was in my bathroom and the next I was there."

"She used a portal like when she left the daylight realm," Ezekiel says.

"Only angels can do that," Dad snaps.

Both demons turn their attention to me, looking me up

and down like somehow glorious wings and heavenly light will manifest from my back. I want to tell them about the avenging angel and how he grabbed me to take me over, but I can't find the words.

"And she's not even Heaven-bound," Ezekiel says, stirring up a wave of sorrow through me. He says it like it's a good thing, because if I were, our eternities would eventually drift apart. And they still might. I hate to even think it, but it's how it has to be. I love Ezekiel, I loved him as an angel, and I still love him as a demon, but the universe is against us.

"Which is a good thing," Dad adds, making it worse. "She still has a chance to—"

Summoning power into my hands, I ready a ruby orb in my palms to chuck at them for having this conversation about my eternity like I don't get a choice in the matter.

"If you dare say what I think you're going to say, I'll blast you both back and cross the veil," I say.

Dad scrunches his brows, grimacing at my words. Despite the power in my hands, he hugs me against him, breathing his vanilla-scented breath in my ear. "Faith, I don't think you understand the situation. I've thought about it long and hard, and I can't find another option. There is no other choice. I will not see you fall to Hell nor will I allow Ezekiel to hold your soul hostage for eternity. Humanity can be regained with the appropriate spell, and—"

I blink, angry tears clouding my eyes. "Are you serious?"

He hugs me to him. "Very. I know this isn't ideal, but we

will work through it. I'm afraid we're running out of time. It's going to be okay. I will help you through everything. We won't let anyone hurt—"

"I'm not going to let Kristin cast a spell to bring another life into—"

"It'll be for Ezekiel with a hum—"

I can't even believe what I'm hearing. No wonder Dad hasn't threatened eternal punishment for Ezekiel or has freaked out more than he has about me, because he's been coming up with his own plan for my eternity—one that doesn't involve Heaven or Hell. He expects me to accept my fate as a full-blooded demon on Earth—the one thing I've been fighting not to happen to me all along.

I groan. "A human?" This is so demonically twisted, and so something I should've seen coming, but oh, God.

"Well, you're already half demon, and I'm not so sure the two of you can concei—"

"Dad!" I yell, shaking him off. Embarrassment and rage flourish through me as Dad discusses the idea of me and Ezekiel having children as a way to maintain some sort of normalcy, making my own existence seem less important because Dad already uses me as his vessel for humanity—but still. A child? I'm not even eighteen for another month. Not to mention the world wants to see me perish.

Ezekiel reaches for my hand. "Faith, be reasonable. There's no sex involved if that's what you're worried about."

I lose it.

Igniting power into my hands, I launch enough through the air that Dad and Ezekiel back off and take cover behind the nearest car. My vision tints red, and I heave, my insides tensing, threatening to spill out of me. If I didn't know any better, I'd think my inner demon was already ripping through my skin to reveal what my true body would look like.

I cover my face with my hands, sucking in a deep breath before I accidentally tear the world apart. A flash of light blinds me, sending me reeling. My back hits the asphalt, winding me, and the glorious avenging angel stands above me, his brilliant white wings pushing my blond hair from my face.

He holds out his hand to me, a serious look on his face. "You look like you need an escape."

I don't take his hand, keeping my hands covering my face to peer through the veil. "Leave me alone."

"Come on, Faith. I granted you your request. I'm not going to hurt you." The angel locks me in his golden eyes the same way Ezekiel used to as he searched for my soul. But now, whatever the angel sees inside me dims the light shining from him.

"You manipulated me," I snap.

His shoulders droop, and he lowers his arm to his side. "I'm sorry."

I shift away to drop my hands to return my attention to the Earth realm where I've blocked out Ezekiel and Dad's voices, but the angel's presence distracts me, begging me to give him another moment of my time. "Just leave. I don't trust you not to damn me the second I get my soul back."

"I'd never. Your soul will be sav—"

"How are you so sure I can even be Heaven-bound after everything?" I ask.

He doesn't respond, which means he doesn't truly know and angels can't lie.

I sigh and look up at the sky through the veil, the stars blurring as they blend together through both worlds. "This isn't fair. What have I done to deserve this?"

The angel lowers his wings, and they disappear on his back. Bending down, he kneels next to me and reaches out, resting his hand on my knee, causing my skin to hum through the veil. "You've done nothing wrong."

I jerk my leg away. "I wasn't talking to you."

"I know, but I wanted to answer you."

"Just go away," I whisper.

Closing my eyes, I push the world away and focus on my heart beating. Wind gusts around me as the angel launches into the night, leaving me lying on the black onyx path of the Veiled Realm. Lowering my hands from my eyes, the Earth world returns into view.

Ezekiel and Dad stand in front of me, peering down at me with emotions no demons should have masking their faces. Pressing my palms to the ground, I get to my feet and turn my back on them without a word.

"Who were you talking to, Faith?" Dad asks from behind me.

"Who do you think?" I ask, because even if I wanted to tell Dad, I couldn't. I don't even know the angel's name.

"That bastard!" Dad roars, throwing his fists into the sky. His orb hits a power line overhead, sending sparks bursting through the air. The lights flicker out, leaving us with only the glow of the moon. "What did he say, Faith?"

I stare at the ground and don't answer.

Dad hollers again, shooting more power toward the sky. If any angels were flying around, they'd get caught in his crossfire.

Ezekiel clears his throat and knocks Dad in the arm with the back of his hand. "Go check on Kristin and see if she's come up with something. You're not helping the situation, Raphael."

I expect all Hell to break loose, for Dad to unleash his true body to lash out at Ezekiel, but he surprises me by huffing and turning toward where I had left Kristin in the motel room. Ezekiel offers me a smile before opening his arms wide to invite me in for a hug. I'm sure he hadn't planned on starting off the night discussing my eternity so blatantly in front of me, but I can tell he and Dad were probably negotiating something they'd never tell me about.

"Are you okay?" he asks, enveloping me in his arms, trying to obscure me from the rest of the world even without his wings. "I didn't want you to hear any of this until everything was worked out."

I stiffen. He notices and buries his face into the crook of my neck.

"So then we could make a decision together," he adds, his

heart pounding so loudly it's all I can focus on.

"The only decision you can make is whether or not you will give me my soul back, Ezekiel. And it shouldn't even be something you have to negotiate or think about." I don't mean to snap, but I can't help it. "Do you even know what you're doing to me by keeping it?"

"Faith," he says.

I shrug away. "You're ruining my eternity."

"And you ruined mine, but we can fix this." He says it like it's not a huge deal. And the fact that he can no longer see that it is a massive, world-changing deal makes it utterly heartbreaking. "You have no idea how freeing it is not having to constantly worry about serving an unfair purpose. You said it yourself, your human life is a losing battle, but it doesn't mean we can't win in the end. If I return your soul to you now, then what? Who will protect it? It's part of my very being, and honestly, I don't think you really want me to let it go."

I'm stunned silent. How do I respond? How do I tell him I want to stick with the plan I've always had for my eternity. A plan I was afraid I'd never accomplish. But now that the avenging angel granted me a last request, I have the option. I can see if my soul can still be saved.

I swallow the burning in my throat, thinking about how no matter what my future holds, I should come to terms that the cost of anything I want comes with the steep price of a short mortal life.

"I won't need you or Dad or anyone to protect my soul,

Ezekiel," I say, my voice barely coming out a whisper.

The softness in his eyes hardens, and he tenses. I can imagine him unfurling the beautiful black wings no longer on his back as he turns into a warrior, reading my thoughts without me even having to form the words. Ezekiel knows me.

"Do you understand the consequences of what you're considering?" he asks, firelight igniting fury in his very being so hot that my skin warms from even a few feet away. I expect him to reveal his true body, to fling out power into the universe, to show me his true demonic side not unlike what Dad showed minutes ago.

But he doesn't. He never has, either. Not to me.

"If you loved me you wouldn't abandon me for them." His low voice cuts through my chest, slicing me open to spill my aching heart across the dirty ground between us.

I shuffle a step closer. "We're supposed to all be on the same side, remember? It's not them and us. You know I don't want to be a—" The pain sweeping across his face ravages through me, stopping me from finishing my sentence.

"You say it like it's the worst thing in the world. Have you forgotten the blood that flows through your veins?"

I straighten my shoulders. "You should understand."

He hooks his fingers to the hem of his shirt, yanking it over his head while turning around to show off the faint scars of his lost wings. "Look what they did to me, Faith."

My whole body tenses as fire suddenly bursts from his skin, eating away his human façade to reveal his true body. But he doesn't let me see his face. He keeps his back to me, showing me the sizzling scars that were barely visible moments ago, now glowing with the fury that comes when sacred objects touch unholy things.

Tears rim my eyes, and I blink. Ezekiel composes himself, hiding his demonic side, and spins back toward me. "Tell me how I should understand now. What changed, Faith? You were willing to risk your whole eternity before."

I sniffle. "Because I always thought you'd save me, Ezekiel. But now? I don't know. I love you, but do you honestly think I can survive all eternity? Heaven will obliterate me even if we were successful. And if I'm a demon..."

"You'll be too powerful to stop."

"But the world—"

He brings his fingers to my lips, cutting off my words before leaning in to kiss any other argument from my mouth. "Just imagine it, Faith," he whispers. "We will have an amazing eternity together."

I want so badly to do as he says and think about all the possibilities of a future with him without having to worry about anything, but that kind of future is pure fantasy.

Instead of arguing, I nod my head. "How about we get through the night?"

He smiles. "Want to sneak away? We're near the beach. I know how much you miss the ocean."

I close my eyes and concentrate on the noise outside our hearts beating. The sound of the crashing waves stirs up a mixture of emotions within me, reminding me of all the years I've spent staring at the sea, watching both the sun and moon set.

Nodding, I hold out my hand to Ezekiel. "Just no more talking about our eternities tonight."

"I'm sorry for that, you know."

He laces our fingers together and tugs me away from the motel where I can hear the hum of Kristin and Dad talking through the open door. Bringing my hand up to his mouth, Ezekiel kisses my knuckles. Warmth blossoms over my skin, and he grins at me in his peripheral vision.

His apology is enough to remind me that even if Hell now flows through his veins, he can still manage to hold onto who he was as an angel even if it's faint. It makes me realize how he might be right about our eternities. Because how can I abandon him for those who dare forsake us?

As we walk hand-in-hand toward the moon-lit waves of the Pacific Ocean, I know I'd walk through Hell for Ezekiel. If only it didn't mean I'd have to give up my humanity, the part of me he fell in love with. The only part of me that keeps me from destroying the world.

RUIN THE WORLD

"DAMN, THE WATER'S freezing," Ezekiel says, standing on the shore in front of me.

Hearing him swear still makes me giggle every time. I grin and kick seawater at his moonlight-soaked bare chest, sending steam sizzling from his skin. He glares, stepping back into the dry sand and out of my reach.

"It's not so bad," I say, my own hot skin steaming into the clear night. "Come on. I'll keep you warm."

Holding my arms open, I curl and uncurl my fingers, motioning for him to come closer. He doesn't move from his spot, glancing from me to the waves pulling the sand back to sea from under my feet.

"How about *you* come to *me*?" he asks.

Laughing, teasing Ezekiel, sets my heart aglow and not in demonic light. The world doesn't feel like it's ending as long as we both keep smiling.

Instead of closing the distance, I tug my shirt over my head and throw the damp fabric at him, hitting him in the face. He chuckles, yanking it away to look at me, but I dive into the water, letting the cool current wash over me.

I pop back to the surface to meet Ezekiel's dark eyes. A chill rushes over my skin, and I shiver. He raises an eyebrow, making me laugh again, and I dash to him and jump up into his arms. He releases a yelp as my icy skin touches his hot, muscular chest when I press against him.

I quiver again in his hot arms. "Not s-so b-bad."

He laughs and spins us around to set me onto the sand. Leaning on his elbow, he holds his weight over me while I stay utterly still under him, thinking about how our bare stomachs touch together.

"You're beautiful, Faith," he whispers into my ear before kissing the spot beneath it.

I react to his touch, desire rushing over me. I don't know if it's the events of the day or what, but all I want is for Ezekiel to pick me up and carry me somewhere no one can find us. Sitting under the bright moon on the beach reminds me of all the nights we spent together alone in the Veiled Realm.

Ezekiel runs his warm hands down my body, pushing away

the goosebumps prickling my skin. He releases a low moan, making his way to my lips to kiss me. I brush my lips to his, just teasing him for a second before sliding my tongue into his mouth to kiss him deeper. He sinks into me, resting his legs between mine, making me gasp against his mouth. His hands dig into the sand under me and graze over my bra so slowly, just testing me to see if I let him continue.

And I do let him, feeling his warm fingers against my skin, sending my heart thrashing against his. I suck his bottom lip between my teeth, and he moans again, making me smile.

"Faith," he whispers, breathing my name into my collarbone. "Let me take you inside before your dad comes looking for us."

I nod and kiss him again. "I'd like that."

"Yeah?" he asks, a huge smile crossing his face.

"Yea—"

A low growl cuts off my agreement, and Ezekiel vaults to his feet, igniting blue liquid power in his palms. Without saying a word, he thrusts the orb over my head, sending sand spraying across me. I scramble to my feet, summoning my own Hell power and turn to face three werewolves in human form, glowering at us from the pathway.

"This town belongs to the Sunrise Cove pack," the man in the center says, puffing out his chest like his sheer size could actually intimidate us. "The girl's free to go back to her motel, but you have to stay here until morning and then leave, demon."

Ezekiel raises his hand and throws power at the wolves again. The man grunts as the blue liquid smolders the front of his shirt, but he doesn't run away like any normal werewolf would do in the face of a demon, which means he's a hellhound.

I snatch Ezekiel's hand midair, making him drop another orb of power at our feet. "I'm not leaving without him, and you might want to be careful who you speak to like that. My dad is up the beach and he's had it with—"

A huge, flaming beast launches from behind the small building with the public restrooms and over the wolves directly at us. Ezekiel hooks his arm around my waist, dragging me back to the icy waves. The Hell beast lurches forward through the sand, stalking us, forcing us deeper into the water.

But it remains on land.

Though ignited with the fires of Hell, the hellhound's flames are no match for the ocean. Ezekiel blasts more power at the beast, sending it jumping out of the way.

"Like I said, he stays until sunrise, and you're welcome to go," the same man says. "If you don't then it's going to be a long night for you, honey. The water's cold."

The rest of his lurking pack glares for a moment before strolling away with the man.

This was a warning and nothing more. A power play.

I glance at Ezekiel steaming in the waves. "I'll go get Dad."

"No. Those hellhounds aren't leaving," Ezekiel mutters, tossing another orb of power at the Hell beast taunting us.

"They'll go after you the moment we're separated."

"I don't think they'll hurt me," I argue.

"Even so, you'll never make it to Raphael."

Unless Dad shows up now, we'll be stuck here until the sun rises and steals away its hellish façade with the rest of the demons, including Ezekiel. The wolf remaining in the hellhound's place will have to face my wrath alone, and I've had enough with people messing with me just because they think they can get away with it.

"What happened to your faith in me?" I ask, tugging away from Ezekiel's steaming skin.

Ezekiel stays on my back, his body warmth trickling to me through the salty sea spray. "You would more likely let them take you than hurt one of them."

He might be right. "I—"

"Don't worry, though. I think I can break it and send a message."

Hearing Ezekiel suggest such a thing releases a waterfall of fury over me hot enough to combat the freezing ocean around us.

"Break it?" Why couldn't the hellhounds leave me alone? They have to realize they're poking at a demon by doing so. They don't have their witch to bring them an eternity on Earth, so why risk damning themselves to demon servitude?

"Your dad was right, you know. We'd be doing the world a favor," he says.

My whole body tenses at the idea. Ezekiel would've never

suggested something like this before his fall. He knows how awful I feel about stealing someone's freewill. Doing so jeopardizes what's left of the already broken truce in the world, sending the universe back to the time before the uprising where the hunters of the Hunter's Alliance put humans first and a time where demons broke werewolves as power plays.

"Ezekiel, no," I say. "Let me handle it, okay? I won't go to Dad but I can't stand here while you do something unthinkable."

He sighs. "Hellhounds don't deserve your mercy."

I purse my lips. "Everyone deserves mercy."

A wave crashes into us, sending us rising with the tide. The hellhound backs away from the rolling surf toward the dry land. Summoning more power, I stomp toward shore, anger washing over me. While the start of the night wasn't exactly great, it was turning better by the second, and these power hungry unleashed hellhounds ruined it.

"Faith, be careful," Ezekiel says from behind me.

I glance at him over my shoulder. "Just get ready."

"Ready for what?"

Without responding, I stroll another few feet forward and into ankle deep water. The hellhound growls, charging forward, but it stops short of attacking me. I raise my hand to my soulless eye, peering into the misty Veiled Realm.

A shining light erupts before me, standing next to where the hellhound growls. The avenging angel tilts his head and studies me from his side. His eyes don't wander from mine, though I'm standing in only a bra and wet jeans in front of him. It reminds me of how pure he is. How something like my state of dress won't distract him.

"I need your help." My voice drifts on the wind created by his wings.

"My help for what? You ready to leave your demons behind?"

I grimace. "No, not that. Can't you see it?"

The blank stare he gives me speaks volumes. He can't see through the veil just like Ezekiel can't. He has the same limitations. But how can he see me? We have no connection. Ezekiel has my soul. I share Dad's blood.

This angel? The only thing he can possibly control now is my life.

Oh, God.

I can't believe I didn't realize it before. There's a reason he's been following me for weeks through the Veiled Realm. He can't get to me on Earth, yet I'm sure he can't leave my side. This avenging angel isn't just out to kill me. He's my new Demon Watcher.

I should've known when Ezekiel fell that Heaven wouldn't have let me go so easily.

Fire erupts on my chest, stealing me away from my distracting thoughts and the avenging angel. The hellhound rams into me, searing my skin under its flaming paws. It tries to bite onto my leg to yank me from Ezekiel, but I flail back. Screaming, I fall into a wave, and Ezekiel's power sparkles over me.

But I don't get the chance to move.

The hellhound bites my leg again, tearing into my flesh through my jeans, and drags me from the water and onto the beach. It snarls above me, dripping frothy black saliva from its jowls. I shove my hands against its chest, thrusting it back with a bout of power I summon in my palms. It stops it for a second, long enough that I can bring my hands up to protect my face.

It doesn't bite me. It's trying to steal me away.

Cool hands latch onto my wrists, yanking me to my feet. Ezekiel's yells and the hellhounds growls disappear as my newly appointed stalker angel tugs me through an invisible portal in the veil.

"What in Heaven?" he asks, finally turning his attention to the damage to my body.

I jerk my hand back up to my eye, peering at the Earth realm. Ezekiel launches power at the hellhound, knocking it to the ground. He struts from the waves and kicks it in the side. Its body rolls to the water, and it howls as a wave washes over its back.

Something shifts on Ezekiel's face. The spark of hellfire I see in his eyes grows, licking across his skin. I gasp, dropping my hand from my eye, my chest heaving at the sight of my beautiful fallen angel now revealing his true body in front of the hellhound.

"Faith, what happened? Tell me what you need," the angel says.

I wave my hands in front of my face, trying to stop tears

from stinging my eyes. I can't speak the words locked in my throat. The angel can't give me anything I need. He can't give Ezekiel his wings back. He can't stop the hellhounds from trying to rule the night. He can't do anything for me.

Cool arms wrap around me along with the softest feathers whispering over my skin. I startle at the feeling of being hugged by an angel, and without thinking, I slam my hands into his chest and knock him back.

"I need to leave!" I scream, spinning away from him, searching for a way to return to the Earth realm. Every step I take leads me down the onyx path and no closer to Ezekiel.

Through the veil, I stare in horror at the hellhound lying at Ezekiel's feet. Ezekiel's jeans smolder, now ruined from the Hell he manages to combat with the ocean. Blood red horns cut through his once smooth forehead, streaking two shadows across his smoldering face under the moonlight. He positions his palms apart, growing an orb of blue power between them into the size of a basketball. All it would take to kill the hellhound would be to drop it over his chest.

"Ezekiel, no!" I scream, my voice cutting over the humming ocean as I cross back through the veil, much easier in the night world I've grown used to. It's the daylight prison world that gives me Hell.

Ezekiel jerks his head up, his usually dark eyes now glowing orange, his chest heaving under blood red skin. Steam pours from him, clouding the crystal night above. A sneer crosses his face, and he raises his hands higher, turning his attention back to the hellhound.

My fingers tremble, my heart aching at Ezekiel in his true body. He no longer looks like my beautiful angel but the true demon Heaven broke him into when they sliced his brilliant black wings from his back.

"Ezekiel, please," I whisper. "Please. It gave up. Just come with me."

Ezekiel releases a low growl from his throat. "I can't, Faith. We must prove our power. These beasts will doubt our control if we let them roam free."

I shudder at the deep sound of his raspy voice, no longer soft and musical. I wish he wouldn't say anything at all. I wish he'd listen to me.

"You're only proving their fears right. Don't you get it? They're like this because of demons. They think it's the only way to survive now after what demons have done. What Mary did. Please, I'm begging you to let it go and come with me. We can go back to my room and—"

Ezekiel roars into the night, his voice loud enough to make me wince and cower back. I stumble, hitting my backside on the ground. Ezekiel jerks his arms to thrust his power, and I cover my eyes with my hands to obscure the world from my view.

My new Demon Watcher sits on the ground next to me through the veil, his lips turned downward in a frown that hurts my heart. Even now, even with this avenging angel who nearly destroyed my world, watching an angel cry stirs horrible grief through me, my own pain reflected in his golden eyes.

I drop my hands in time to see Ezekiel's power explode in the sand next to the hellhound. He kicks the beast once more into the water and turns his back on it, neither killing nor breaking it into his personal guard dog.

Our gazes lock, and he shakes his head, the firelight dying in his eyes the longer I capture him in my blurry stare. His heartbeat trickles to my ears over the sound of the crashing waves, and I expect him to close the distance between us, but instead, he shifts away and strides down the beach alone, taking a moment to tilt his head to peer up at the glittering stars suspended in the midnight sky above us.

I scramble to my feet to chase after him, my own heart still trying to calm down. "Ezekiel, stop."

He doesn't listen. "Go back to the room, Faith. I don't want you to see me like this anymore."

I grimace and push my legs faster to catch up. "Ezekiel, please wait. I—"

He spins around to face me, his true body still overtaking his human façade. "You're looking at me like I'm some sort of monster."

I swallow, stifling the sob trying to escape my throat. "No, I—"

"I smell your fear, Faith. You're afraid of me." He summons power and tosses it at the waves, sending spray into the night. "And why wouldn't you be? Look at me. I just—I can't control it. Seeing that beast drag you forward..." Turning away, he hides his face from me.

I don't even know how to respond. Revealing his true body during a fiery moment of attack is part of his nature. He was bound to reveal himself to me eventually, and I thought I'd be better prepared to see him in all his demonic glory, but I wasn't ready. I didn't prepare myself enough. And now I feel horrible for letting his revelation get to me.

Striding forward, I reach out and gently grab his smoldering shoulder to turn him around. My fingers burn against his skin, but I don't pull away. I meet his fiery gaze and draw my other hand up to touch his cheek, cupping his face in my hand.

"Ezekiel, I'm sorry. You are not a monster to me. I don't care if you have—" I press my lips together and run my finger to his forehead to touch one of his bone-hard, blood red horns. "Seriously impressive demon horns."

His face smooths as he composes himself.

"I bet my dad is wickedly jealous," I add, now smiling.

Leaning forward, I kiss him, hugging him against me, letting him encase me in his muscular, still burning arms. He shifts away, burying his face into the crook of my bare shoulder, just breathing in the scent of my now icy skin.

His true body disappears completely when he pulls away to meet my gaze again. We're both a mess, covered in sand and singed clothing, but at least I managed to yank Ezekiel back from the grips of Hell.

I link our fingers together. "Thank you," I whisper.

He furrows his brows, looking at me in his peripheral vision. "For what?"

"For not killing or breaking the beast."

"You have no idea how badly I wanted to—but seeing your face, the way you looked at me—Faith, I always want to do right by you. Having you look at me like I was ending your world was far worse than losing my wings, you know. For a moment, no matter how hard I tried, I couldn't suppress your humanity."

I suck in a breath. This wasn't how I wanted to pull it from him, but it makes no difference now. I know I have it in me. I know I can help him see past his demon blood.

"I still wish you wouldn't try to suppress it," I say, stopping in place.

"And I wish you did," he says. A tear splashes onto my cheek, and Ezekiel smears it away with the pad of his thumb. "You wouldn't always feel so bad, you know."

I frown, rubbing my hand over my cheek to dry another uncontrollable tear. "You're wrong."

"How so?"

"Because I need to feel everything to help me remember who I am and who you fell in love with," I say.

"Is that what this is about? You're afraid I won't love you?"

"Partly." I don't have it in me to tell him I'm afraid of losing the part of me that loves him, too. That I'm terrified there would be no coming back from such an act, that all of my pain and suffering would have been for nothing. Losing his wings? It would've been for nothing. Even if he can't see it. "I want you to keep it on to remember who we are together, Ezekiel."

"I could never forget."

I run my fingers across his face. "Why risk it? You were never afraid to feel before."

He shakes his head, his kissable mouth turning pouty, making him almost look human instead of the hardened demon he's become. "It's torture. Feeling nothing is the only way I'm going to survive this eternity and protect you. I told you this."

"So as long as we're alive nothing matters? Even if you can't feel your love for me?"

He steps forward, tugging me to walk again. "My love for you is the worst of all. Deadly."

I freeze and tug away from him. "What?"

He shrugs, like what he didn't say isn't breaking my heart. "Faith, don't you get it? My love for you makes me want to ruin the world. The universe, even."

DEMON WATCHER

"I NEED YOUR blood, Faith," Kristin says, slapping her ivory dagger against her palm.

I scrunch my face. "What for?"

"Just give her your palm," Dad snaps from near the window. "If you plan on using your humanity against Ezekiel to save every damn hellhound we come across, then we need to double your protection. Dawn is coming, and I can't relocate again. I have business to take care of tomorrow night. I won't hear the end of it from Cami if I don't show. She's already annoyed I moved without warning."

"She'd understand, Dad," I say, a blip of sadness overtaking me. I haven't seen Cami since the night Kristin faked my death.

"Understand? She'd blast my ass to Hell if she knew you were still alive and I didn't tell her," he says.

"What?" I had assumed she knew and Dad was keeping me away because he didn't trust her Demon Watcher. I knew he was meeting up with her in the daylight prison realm to discuss business. Now I wonder if Kristin's spell included Cami. Of course it would. Her soul belongs to Heaven.

He sighs. "The fewer people who know about you, the better. The angelic army hasn't been quick to announce your sudden resurrection for a reason, and as much as it infuriates me, I agree. There's enough tension as it is, and I will not allow anyone to break your heart when you see where their loyalty lies—and Cami's? It's with Heaven."

I never thought I'd ever be jealous of Cami until this moment. If anyone understood me, it would be her. She knows what it's like to be cast out of good grace while trying to do the right thing, but she still managed to get it back. It's all I can hope for. Maybe if I can convince Dad to let me see her...

"Dad, I—"

He shakes his head. "Faith, I promise when the time is right, she will be the first we go to considering she can pull you back from Hell if Kristin can't get her spells straight."

Kristin aims her ivory dagger at Dad. "I'll have everything in order. Faith is different now that she touched Hell and shares her soul with Ezekiel without a contract. The only demons we need are you and him."

"And I'm in," Ezekiel says from behind me.

Dad glares from his place near the window, watching the ocean. "You better be."

I open my mouth to argue when Kristin jerks my hand up and slices my palm without warning. A strange sensation crawls over me, shadowing my vision, and I freeze at the sight of black blood pouring from my wound. *Oh, no.*

"Blood to blood, red to black, thin the veil and keep him back." A shudder runs up my back at the darkness awakened in me by her spell—one that feels different than usual. This one twists my insides with panic.

And him? Who is she referring to? I thought she was casting a spell to protect us from all the hellhounds. "Kristin."

"A demon's mark and angel's smite, take Faith's blood, and give us sight." Reaching into her pocket, Kristin tugs something out and hides it in her hands, rubbing my blood over whatever object she cups.

Gasping, I tense, another wave of fear seizing my muscles. Her spell beckons to my demon blood, poking at the evil creature inside me who would love to break free. It reminds me of the time she used my blood to break a wolf or when Mary tried to make me bow. "What are you doing? This isn't about the hellhounds," I say. "It doesn't feel right. This isn't a protection spell."

Ezekiel grabs me from behind, wrapping his arms around me. Pressing his lips to my ear, he whispers, "The hellhounds come next. This is for the watcher, Faith. We knew you'd argue if we told you otherwise, but don't worry. This spell will help us protect you."

"My watcher? How did you know he was your replacement?" I regret the way the words come out.

Ezekiel tenses. "No one can replace me."

I cringe at the demonic possessiveness in his voice. He's locked my humanity out completely. I can feel him slip away even though he embraces me tighter—if only he were trying to hold me together as I fall apart instead of keeping me back to let Dad and Kristin do something insane. Something that very well might ruin how I feel about them.

I elbow Ezekiel a few times, but he doesn't waver. "Please, stop."

The room hazes around me with the mist of the Veiled Realm, and my Demon Watcher materializes into view before me. He expands his brilliant white wings, raising his flaming sword to the sky, sending both fear and awe through me. But he's not directing his attention to me, he's bracing for what happens next. He must sense the darkness slicing through the air like I do.

Ezekiel growls in my ear. "Jesaiah," he whispers. "Of course Heaven would assign him. They must be shaking at your existence."

"You see him?" Something's wrong. An angel never lowers his shield.

I flick my gaze to Kristin as she splatters the wall in front of us with my blood from a… I swear under my breath, realizing she must've stolen the feather that drifted from the Veiled Realm I pocketed last night. I had no idea she could possibly break a shield since Mary couldn't, but Mary didn't have my blood or an angel feather either.

"With the rise of dawn on the coming day, sear his vision, make him stay." A bright streak of lightning cracks through the Veiled Realm at my Demon Watcher's feet. He flies back from the force, yelling out while covering his face.

"Help me." The angel's words drift through the thundering world, his voice a soft plea to no one I can see, staking me directly in my humanity.

"Kristin, stop!" I scream, the sudden realization of what her spell will allow my dad to do.

All Dad needs is a moment. If he can see him for a second, he can break the shield. He can make him stay. And there's only one way to truly stop an angel from seeing me and watching me in the way a Demon Watcher does. My stomach rolls, the worlds blending in and out with the rising of the sun. The spell is holding my watcher long enough for Dad and Ezekiel to cross.

"Don't watch, Faith," Ezekiel whispers. "I'll see you come nightfall."

Oh, God. "Ezekiel, what are you doing?"

"Just don't watch." His voice hitches, and I know if I could get one more minute, I could break through the Hell fire of his desperation. I could bring back the part of him who would never agree with Dad. I could—

I don't get the chance.

Dad and Ezekiel disappear with the rise of the sun and into the sunlight prison world. I hold my hand over my eye and stare in horror as Dad blasts his power at my new Demon Watcher, too stunned to take flight and disappear.

In that world, they're numb to humanity. They can live with all the horrors that come with the Hell in their veins.

But this? Something is different. Dad threatens to break an angel's wings all the time. He threatens to inflict eternal punishment on them when they annoy him. He never goes through with it. His threats have been empty until now. And his actions are seeping into Ezekiel and Kristin. Dad says the world is changing, but I can't help to think that he's the one changing.

I barely recognize him.

"No!" I scream, summoning power into my hands at the sight of Dad's true body breaking through his skin. I can't let him hurt the avenging angel as Ezekiel stands by without intervening. But why would he? This is the angel who severed his wings. This is Ezekiel's justice—a justice Hell seems to favor, because demons believe everyone gets what they deserve and they're happy to assist. Heaven's more forgiving.

Dad circles my new watcher, thrusting power at him, not giving him a chance to fly. He'll not only steal his sight, but I'm certain he'll try to force him to fall because angels can't die, and Dad drowns in the bad blood he shares with Heaven's army.

"Faith, please stop watching," Kristin says, tugging at my

hand.

I thrust my power at the wall. "How could you do this? I trusted you."

"How could I not? He manipulated you. He's been stalking you. He wants to kill you like you're some kind of monster because he can't grasp that evil is subjective. You know this."

I step forward, hitting the wall of the motel room. "He wants to save me." If something happens to the angel—Jesaiah—any chance of me ever returning into Heaven's good grace will disappear like demons do in the sunlight.

And Dad's right. There's no way I'm spending eternity in Hell, which means... Why does my life keep turning full circles, always spinning back to transforming into a demon? I hate the idea with my very being. The creature that haunts my sleep, full of untamable power, will surely destroy who I am. Dad thinks he can handle it, that he can somehow manage to immortalize me as I am now, but something deep down tells me he can't. The person I am will be gone and no one or nothing will ever get me back. I've felt this way since discovering an eternity on Earth was possible. My body might be alive, but I'll be dead. Just gone from existence.

Kristin locks her fingers to my shoulder and yanks me back. "Faith, I'm sorry. He can't save you the way you want to be saved."

"But I'll ruin the world if he doesn't get the chance to try." I rip myself from her to focus on what Dad's doing. "You and I have both seen what my inner demon is capable of. It's what I'll turn into because there is no way I'm allowing you to create a vessel and without one, Ezekiel will never return my soul to me." I can't even put the thought of what it really means to create a vessel of humanity out loud.

"You say that like you're—"

"A possession? Right now, that's how I feel, Kristin. You guys have locked me in a box. You plan my eternity without consideration for what I want. You keep using me over and over. I'm tired." I slam my hands against the wall. The world buzzes and sparks. "I'm tired of everyone not letting me live or die or just breathe even."

"Faith, stop."

"No!"

She pinches my shoulder. "You're damaging the veil."

"Good! Maybe it'll finally open. I'm not letting them hurt him. I've paid enough for Dad's sins." Two burning hands appear in front of me and bang against the veil, sending sparks of light through the air. The world morphs around me and distorts the motel room. Sucking in a deep breath, I gather more power, and the demon within me begs for control, now dancing in front of me with its soulless eyes.

Wind blows my hair back over my shoulder, the scent of roses wafting through the room. I draw my gaze away from my demon contorting its body in front of me. Behind it, both Dad and Ezekiel gape in my direction, no longer focused on the avenging angel.

My new Demon Watcher locks his gaze with mine for a second, glances at the sky, and disappears into the brown haze. Dad blasts power in his wake and then toward me, but all it does is disappear through me. He can't access the veil like I can, and I didn't break it.

I drop my hands from my face, cutting off my view of him striding closer. He'll undoubtedly unleash the fire of Hell upon his return, but he's not the reason I cut off my connection. I refuse to risk accidentally looking at Ezekiel after what I've done. I'm afraid to see his reaction to me interfering in the spell and saving the angel who severed his wings and tried to damn me to Hell. He won't understand—he's incapable of understanding me anymore, not like he used to.

"Faith, your dad's going to—"

A booming knock on the motel room door cuts off her words. My speeding heart steals my breath, and all I want to do is crawl into bed and hide until nightfall and not deal with what I'm assuming might be the disgruntled wolves from last night. Ezekiel did leave the Hell beast roughed up, and Kristin was too busy complying with Dad's desires that she hasn't started the real hellhound protection spell. I suppose this will teach Dad a lesson for concerning himself with a watcher who can only do that—watch me through the veil.

Neither Kristin nor I move to answer it. Whoever it is will have to break down the door. Kristin shuffles to peer through the peephole, and then sighs and turns to face me. "Raphael told me I had another day."

"Another day?"

"Kristin, open the door," a familiar voice says. "Come on, I've been driving half the night since Raphael called. I want to sleep for a bit before I surprise him. It's been weeks since I've seen him."

A smile crosses my face, and I hop to my feet to race to the door. Dad hasn't mentioned Cadence at all. I thought maybe they broke things off after my fake death. But here she is, standing outside the door because Dad invited her. I shouldn't be so involved with Dad's personal relationships, but out of everyone in the world, Cadence has never been one to snub my decision to fight to remain Heaven-bound. It helps that her soul is Heaven-bound. She's been the only other mortal in my life for years before Kristin came along, but then, Kristin doesn't count. She barely looks older than me since witches live long lives if they can manage to survive.

"Faith, no," Kristin whispers. "Not yet. Not before Raphael talks to her."

I scowl at her. "He'll get over it."

Kristin steps in front of me. "I mean it. Don't. You'll put her in unnecessary danger."

Groaning, I spin around and flop on the bed. "Fine." Because she's right. The last thing I want is to put Cadence in the line of any fire, demonic or otherwise. She might be the only person who can help Dad see reason. She might stop him from adding another angel to my list of those who fell because of me. She might—I shake my head, pushing the thoughts away. How will I ever tell her what I've done? She knew Ezekiel. She'll never look at me the same.

Kristin holds her index finger to her lips and waits a moment to make sure I remain quiet and frozen in my spot on the bed. Slowly, she cracks the door an inch, blocking Cadence from entering the motel room.

Kristin fake yawns. "Raphael arranged the honeymoon suite for the both of you at the Sunset Cliffs Plaza. Did he forget to tell you?"

I close my eyes and focus on listening to Cadence, soaking up the familiarity of her heartbeat, how she sucks in a breath at Dad's undeniable ability to romance her.

"The bastard did forget," she says, humming under her breath. "But he's been distant lately. I thought maybe because of..." Her voice trails off.

"Raphael is fine, Cadence."

Cadence clicks her heels on the ground as she shifts. "You sure he isn't losing his humanity? Because if he does, I need to prepare myself to—"

"Shove a dagger in his heart?" Kristin asks.

Cadence huffs. "God, no. I was going to say if I have to go through a damn demonic breakup."

Both women laugh, and I lean back and stare at the ceiling, finding solace in how abnormally normal their conversation is about Dad. I never thought much about the consequences Dad faces if I somehow manage to be saved. He knew it was coming. A mortal vessel can only live a human life once—though if I turn into a demon with my soul intact... *Stop seeing reason in his desire. He can't protect you for all eternity.*

"You don't need to worry about the aftermath if it ever came to that," Kristin says. "The Storyteller already assured your safety, and Raphael doesn't break his word."

I wish I could see Cadence's face that comes with the silence from Kristin's revelation that Dad and Vivian, Cadence's grandma, worked things out because the old seer helped me.

"When the heck did he—"

A howl sounds through the air, cutting off Cadence's voice. She swears, and I hear her swipe her dagger from her hip holster, a sound I've heard so many times before I can envision her doing it in my mind, how her red-tinted black hair sways with the motion, the fierce shine in her honey eyes.

"Back off, wolf," Cadence says. "You have five seconds to get out of here before the Hunter Alliance comes to take over your town for threatening me."

Digging my nails into my palms, I listen to Cadence's heels tap away from the door. If I were her, I'd threaten the wrath of my dad, but Cadence would never admit to aligning herself with demons. It's her evil little secret that hangs in her closet behind a door made of opaque glass. People whisper about the possibility, but her good soul always gives reason for people to doubt it.

Kristin motions me from the front door. "I need more of your blood. Hurry."

Jumping up, I jog across the room and allow her to cut my palm without protest. I'd normally argue, but Cadence is outside. I want Kristin to help her subdue the wolves or get them to leave without my involvement. I'm afraid if I do try to help, I'll have a bunch of dead wolves on my hands. I don't want to hurt them, but if they try to hurt Cadence to get to me? God, I hate my life.

Kristin holds her hand open, catching my blood in her palm. "Stay here and lock the door."

She rushes outside before I even respond. I flick the lock and move to the curtained window to peer at the parking lot through a small crack. The same wolves from last night stand near a car with various weapons—a bat, a tire iron, what looks like a pathetic kitchen knife—and they create a barrier around Cadence as she yells at them.

"Hell-bound and leashed to night, tame these beasts, destroy their fight. With demon blood, black and true, create a chain, binding you."

Another guttural howl rips through the air at the sound of Kristin's spell. The werewolves charge Kristin, trying to stop her from casting magic on them, and Cadence punches the tallest man in the face, jerking his head to the side. Glass shatters, making me startle. But it wasn't the window in front of me.

Summoning power, I swivel and face a wolf growling from under the window that leads to the beach. Dad was right when he complained about the corner room I begged Kristin to take since it was the last one with a beach view. He warned that it would leave us vulnerable.

"I will melt your face off if you take a step near me. I don't want to hurt you," I say.

The wolf slinks closer, cautiously yet determined like it wants to see how far it can push me into a corner before I fight back. It growls, baring its sharp canines at me, and I reach behind me to unlock the door.

The door slams into my back, knocking the wind from me. I hit the floor with a thud and accidentally set the bed smoldering with my unleashed power. The wolf snaps at my face without attempting to bite me, trying to put me in my place. Scrambling away, I ram into a pair of legs that don't even wobble from my force.

"If you try anything with that Hell power of yours, consider your friends outside dead," a feminine voice says, drawing my attention up to a woman. She narrows her green eyes at me, pursing her lips, but doesn't attempt to harm me. "We've been patient long enough, and it's time you come home with us. Now get up. Slowly."

Obeying her order, I push from the floor and to my feet. She reaches out, digging her nails into my shoulder and spins me around so I can't face her. Something pinches my wrists, and she submerges my hands into cool liquid. Without having to test my power, I know she's dipped my hands in holy water to try to stop me from using my power.

"Sorry about the holy water, hon. It's a safety precaution."

"What do you want from me?" I ask. "I have nothing to offer you."

She pushes me forward. "Your demonic ties are ruining

you. We want to help. You deserve everything Mary had to of-fer—an eternity where we help each other."

"Help you? Are you kidding me? I want to be left alone."

"Your demon will never allow it."

I scowl, though she stands behind me. "I don't own him."

She releases a deep, breathless laugh. "You do. Just like you own your demon daddy, sweetheart."

I sigh. "Obviously you don't understand my situation."

She shoves me hard only to rip my bound arms back to stop me from falling to the floor. Pain swells through my shoulders at the force, and I cry out. Werewolves have always been tough, and they use these sort of tactics to keep their packs in line, but I'm not a part of their pack. Pushing me around won't do anything but piss me off.

If I didn't see the twelve werewolves outside, blocking Cadence, distracting Kristin with other wolves lying in wait in the shadows, I'd blast this bag of holy water off my hands and accept the burns that come with letting it touch my power. But the pack is too big for even me to handle.

This is more about power than revenge, so I shuffle where the wolf leads me along the pathway in front of the rooms without Kristin even realizing I'm being kidnapped.

"I'll send you to Hell if you don't keep your word about not hurting them," I snap, trying to peer over my shoulder.

The woman flicks my cheek, nearly hitting my soulless eye. "You sure you want to threaten an ally, daddy's girl? Last I heard, you were on your way there yourself. You're lucky it's in my best interest you stay alive for the time being."

I groan. I can't help it.

Pinching my shoulder again, she says, "The feeling's mutual."

"At least you had a choice."

"Which you stole away by killing Mary."

I close my eyes for a second, realization sinking into my bones. Werewolves are cunning and smart. They've had to face demons forever, always worrying about the possibility of being broken. It's what helped Mary rise. I should've known better to think they were turning to me because I killed their witch and angels and demons are against them. Like me, they won't accept an eternity in Hell. They still have a lot of fight left with the power Mary gave them.

"I really can't help you. You need a witch," I say.

"You have one of those, too," she snaps. "Word has it that your dad found a way to activate your birthright without divine intervention. We know he won't be quick to help us, but if we can get a moment with him—"

"You're wasting your time. Dad will never agree."

"We'll see. We know how important your eternity is to him. But if you accidentally fell into the wrong hands..."

A van idles in the street at the end of the building with a familiar hulking man holding the back door open for me. The female wolf shoves me forward, and I trip and spill across the pavement, scraping the skin off my elbow.

Black blood drips to the ground, sizzling in the sun. Something changed inside me since the last time Kristin drew blood from me. I thought my blood would turn back to red after Mary's death, but something prevented it. *Ezekiel's fall. Another step closer to Hell.*

"Get your ass up and quit acting like we're monsters," the man says, nudging me in the stomach to roll me over. "You should thank me for helping you the other night with that damn demon."

I don't move or answer the man I recognize as the hellhound from the restaurant who offered me protection, the same hellhound who helped me fight the poisonous demon. But something shifted in his demeanor. Maybe he's offended and pissed he couldn't so easily charm me away from Dad only to use me against him.

I stare at the cerulean sky overhead and the bright sun sending starbursts through my vision. He kicks me again, much harder, but I still don't move. Bending down, he grabs my hair and yanks me to my feet, the action reminding me of Joshua and his bad attitude when he didn't get his way.

I bite my tongue to stop from yelling out. I refuse to give him any sort of satisfaction of seeing me weak and malleable to shape into something he can use to his advantage.

"Drake, I think we might be wasting our time with her," the woman says.

The man's name sounds familiar, pulling at my subconscious. "Maybe we're doing things wrong. She was raised by a demon after all. Her humanity rejects us but maybe her demon blood won't."

"I don't think it's worth it."

"Pleas—" I don't get a chance to reason. The man—Drake—swings his arm around my neck, cutting off my airway.

"This could've been so easy," he whispers into my hair.

I thrash, fighting in his death grip, panic sweeping over me as my vision darkens. This can't be happening. I was supposed to die by a flaming sword in the hands of my new Demon Watcher with a chance to be saved. The hellhound can't kill me like this because I won't comply. Right? But I can't breathe. He's suffocating me.

I summon power in my hands, shocking and burning myself because of the holy water. Drake grips me tighter, my eyes bulging from the lack of oxygen, my mind spinning out of control.

"Shhh," he whispers in my ear. "That's a good demon."

I open and close my mouth, and the world blurs.

I expect to see the gates of Hell before me. I expect to hear the screams of the damned call my name. But all I see are the shadows. Because I won't go to Hell unless Ezekiel releases my soul. At least that's something.

Darkness claims me.

THE SUNRISE COVE PACK

"EZEKIEL," I WHISPER, my voice disappearing in the misty world reminiscent of the dream beach Ezekiel creates for me. "Please, Ezekiel, show yourself."

I never thought I'd ever be so thankful for Ezekiel possessing my soul. I didn't know what to expect from death with my soul in his hands, but if it's going to be an eternity like this, alone on a beach, maybe I'll manage. Maybe it won't be so bad. Anything's better than the pits of Hell with Uncle Lucifer, who'd probably punish me for refusing to willingly join his ranks.

Ezekiel materializes in front of me, his arms crossed over his chest and fire burning in his eyes as he faces me. It takes everything in me not to throw myself at his feet and apologize for protecting my new Demon Watcher just to make him stop glaring at me. Having him look at me this way is a whole new form of punishment, but I won't apologize to him because I'm not sorry for intervening.

He should've never let Dad try. He should've never held me back. If Ezekiel would have at least tried to get Dad to stop, I could've handled it. I know Dad and how he behaves when he doesn't get his way or feels threatened. All I have ever known Dad as is a demon. But Ezekiel? I still cling onto who he was before. I'm afraid if I don't, I'll lose myself now in this strange eternity scorned by my beautiful fallen angel.

"I thought you'd want to be alone after this morning," Ezekiel finally says, trapping me in his dark eyes for what feels like forever.

"Never," I whisper, my voice choking. "I don't ever want you to leave me. Please."

A smile lights his brooding face as he misses the pain in my voice, and he steps closer to kneel in the sand next to me. "I wasn't sure you'd forgive me."

I'm not sure if I have. I don't tell him that, though. "You really want to talk about that now? It doesn't matter anymore. Nothing matters. I've lost."

He frowns, tipping his head forward, confusion marring his handsome features. "What is that supposed to mean?"

"Can you not feel it?" My heart crashes into my ribcage. I don't know exactly what the sunlight prison realm does to him, but I do know it numbs any sort of humanity while demons are cut off from Earth. Maybe he doesn't even know Drake used my life as a power play, and now I'm the one who's going to have to break the news. Maybe it's better finding out this way instead of upon Ezekiel's return to me not being there.

"Feel what?"

"Ezekiel, I died." There. That was easy enough. "I underestimated the hellhounds intent, and it was never really about me. It was about Dad and Kristin. It was about using me to get what they have to offer. Since I refused to help..." I can't say it.

He inhales a sharp breath. "Faith, you—"

Tears spill from my eyes. "I'm sorry I didn't fight harder. I just—they threatened Kristin and Cadence, and then—" I lick my dry lips. "Please tell me this is how my eternity will be. Please tell me I can still pretend everything's okay."

Ezekiel grabs my chin to peer into my watery eyes. "Listen to me."

I start sobbing, my shoulders shaking, and I rest my head on his chest. "I should've never carried the hope that everything would end with Mary's death. You had me so worried about Heaven, nothing else crossed my mind." I dig my fingers into his soft shirt. "The angelic army was never truly my enemy."

"Faith, stop. You're not dead. I'd know. I'd have felt your life end like I can feel your life right now as you sleep. Now, listen to me. If what you say is true, the hellhounds still have you. You have to wake up," Ezekiel says, rising to his feet. He reaches out to grab my hands to pull me to mine, but I shrug away.

Gasping, I try to compose myself. "What?"

I've grown so used to people trying to kill me, it's hard to grasp I'm alive. Drake threatened me in an attempt to draw my demon out. He could've killed me. He could've ended my life right in the middle of the parking lot to prove to Dad that he and his pack surpass him in power and will take the night. But he didn't. He has bigger plans for me.

"Oh, God," I say.

Ezekiel frowns. "Faith, pull yourself together and wake up."

"They want to use me to guarantee their existence on Earth," I blurt. "You have to warn Dad what will happen if he forces me to descend."

He releases a breath. "That's what all this is about?"

I glower. He shouldn't act so relieved. "How can you not think it's the end of the world?"

"Because it's not, Faith. Deals can be made. So what if some unleashed hellhounds want to secure their eternity outside of Hell."

"Do you hear yourself? This is what we fought against."

He shakes his head. "We fought against Mary and her need to make you bow."

It's like he's forgotten or he can no longer see the destruction from the hellhounds' wakes. All he sees now is an opportunity to shift power in the changing world.

"This will be good for you," he adds. "For us. Raphael has been searching for a way to use the beasts to our advantage. With them, you won't have to fear living eternity with me."

In this moment, I know the hellhound woman was right. I do basically own Ezekiel, though it's he who holds my soul. He'll do anything for me and this existence we're supposed to have that he created in his mind. Because before his fall, I was his purpose. His whole existence revolved around me and still does. The idea of being his only purpose was sad to me before, and now? I don't know how I feel. My whole being is battling it out—my demon seeing reason in his desire for me to descend.

"Stop looking at me like that," Ezekiel says, his sharp tone softening.

"Then maybe stop making me feel all the sacrifices I made to assure the hellhounds wouldn't rise was for nothing," I snap. "You lost your wings because of their alliance with Mary."

He sighs, picking me up off the ground to pull me into his arms. Pressing his forehead to mine, he whispers, "Your purity and goodness pains me. Kills me. I just—damn it. Faith, please, let's not do this now. I need you to wake up. Don't let them think for a second they can use you. You hear me? If you can handle your dad and me, you can put this pack of hellhounds in line and show them their place if they want to rise unbound. Make them prove their worth. Make them think you're doing them a favor."

"I don't want to make a point."

"Faith, you need to take this seriously. I know you're unsatisfied with how things turned out, but you have to see I'm trying to fix things for you. Those hellhounds could hurt you to gain the upper hand. Demonic affairs usually only benefit one side, and it has to be ours."

His words send a blip of fear through me. "They already have the upper hand. I'm pretty sure they'll kill me if they don't get their way."

"I will destroy their whole damn town if they so much as to—"

I cut off his threat with a kiss. The last thing I need is for Ezekiel to get the attention of the universe on my behalf. He reacts to my closeness, our very beings merging as one instead of coinciding, and he holds me closer like if he pushes against me hard enough he could walk through the veil to wherever I'm held captive.

I yank away from him, my eyes widening with the thought. "Ezekiel, the veil," I say. "I can cross the veil and take away their chance to barter."

He grins, kissing me again. "That's my smart and sexy Demon Spawn. Show those damn hellhounds who you really are."

I force myself to smile. "They'll definitely regret it." Because no one should ever have to experience the wrath of my inner demon.

"Now, wake your powerful ass up. I'll get your dad. We need to prepare for nightfall."

Before I can ask what exactly needs preparing for, Ezekiel releases a shock of power into my chest, stealing my breath. Gasping, I snap my eyes open and peer around a disgusting, feces-ridden room. Scratch marks peel the dark paint from the walls. A ratty, burned blanket sits piled in the corner near a bucket with mysterious, gag-inducing liquid. An empty dog bowl rests upside down near two thick chains bolted to the floor.

The hellhound pack of Sunrise Cove has done this before, though I'm probably the first demi-demon they've locked away. From what I know about werewolves, packs don't take kindly to traitors or those who turn against pack ways. And this room must be where the pack punishes and puts those who dare try to leave.

If the hellhounds thought this would win my demonic side over, they're sorely mistaken. Maybe if I were a mid-level demon.

Howls rise through the air, sneaking in through the crack under the door. Sunlight drifts through the curtained window, so I know I'm not underground in some basement. If I can manage to unbind my hands, I'll have a fighting chance to thin the veil. I don't know exactly how I crossed through before without breaking it, but I know I'm capable with my connection to Dad and Ezekiel on the other side. If only it didn't take such a toll on me. Better to hallucinate my demon running wild than wait for Dad to agree to any of the hellhounds' demands. Because if he does, I won't have a chance to save myself from a descent. It would nearly guarantee it. Kristin can easily take Mary's place to the hellhounds. She would do something so crazy on my behalf.

Like the female wolf said, I have a witch.

It really puts a twisted, yet true, perspective on all the relationships in my life. Dad, Ezekiel, and Kristin all strive to protect me one way or another like it's their purposes, like I'm their reason for being. Thinking it sounds crazy and conceited, selfish, but it's true. Their lives revolve around me. If I'm gone, they'll have to find new purposes. And the last time their purposes changed, they all nearly lost themselves. But I'm losing myself under their influence.

Sucking in a deep breath, I attempt to yank my wrists apart. Pain sears through my skin. The hellhounds aren't taking any chances of me escaping before Dad comes to find me at dark. Sharp wire slices deeper and warmth trickles down my hand to disappear in the bucket of water.

"Unless you don't mind losing your hands, I wouldn't do that again, Faith," a masculine voice says from behind me.

I blink, confusion and recognition washing over me. The voice sounds so familiar, stirring something good inside me for once. "You know my name," I say. "How?"

Chains clank against concrete as someone bound moves behind me. "Damn, I thought I had made a better impression. Guess Hell takes it out of you. You reek like demon, you know. You kick your angel to the curb or something? Damn, Chris would be so..." The boy's voice trails off.

I crane my neck, shifting as best as I can to look behind me. I meet the warm gaze of a young, filthy, familiar werewolf shackled to the floor behind me. Dread sends a cool wave down my back, and I blink a few times to make sure I'm not imagining things.

"You look like you could use a drink. Maybe a punching bag," he says, a ghost of a smile softening his sallow features.

I swallow. "More like blow things up."

"How in Hell did you even end up here? I thought that watcher would never leave your side unless...Zeke?" Malik asks, adjusting the short chain around his ankle. Dried blood coats his bare foot like he's tried more than once to yank himself free or change into his wolf form.

I suck in my bottom lip. "He can't be with me until sundown."

His mouth falls open. "Oh, shit. What the—"

"It is what it is," I say, cutting him off. "But what I want to know is how you're here? I thought you died in Mary's sacrificial ritual."

"I wish," he mutters. "Hell's probably nicer than this. The damn witch didn't want to waste a soul on a failed plan."

I grimace. "God, Malik. You've been here all this time? Kristin's going to flip—"

"She's okay?" he asks.

"Yeah. Misses her Traitor Pack."

"Same."

Commotion breaks out on the other side of the door. Fear

blossoms through my sadness at the reminder of everything we've both lost. Hell power automatically erupts in my hands, burning me as it fries in the holy water, but I don't release it. I keep summoning it, searing my own flesh in the process.

"Faith, stop," Malik whisper-hisses from behind me. "You're seriously hurting yourself."

"I don't car—"

The door swings open, the muffled howls growing louder in pitch. The female hellhound stands in the doorway with a chain hanging from her hands. She flicks her gaze to me for a second before training it on Malik behind me.

"I need to go to the bathroom," I say, struggling against my bindings, still gathering more power as fast as the holy water burns it.

The woman rolls her eyes at me. "So go."

If I could kill her with a look, she'd have died about ten times over. And they say demons are inhumanly awful. "My dad's going to break you come sunset. He'll make you bow. Just let me go."

She raises an eyebrow. "Highly doubt he will. But you can still make things easier. Swear loyalty to our pack and tell him you want us to rise with you."

"I'm not descending!"

"We'll see. I think you won't be able to refuse once you see what a powerful world we can create."

She struts past me and to Malik. The whoosh of something cutting through the air whispers to my ears, and Malik hollers as metal snaps against something soft—his stomach maybe.

I wince. "Don't hurt him!"

A shadow falls over me, and a hot hand touches my chin. The woman jerks my head up so I have to look at her. "Don't deny you like to break wolves. Consider this one a present. The wolf breaker, just like your daddy. You'll thank me later."

I sneer, jerking my body back and forth hard enough through the pain that a wave of holy water sloshes over the side of the bucket. The woman yells out, jumping back. The putrid smell of burning flesh wafts through the room, assaulting my nose.

"You little bitch!" the woman screams. "I'm trying to be nice."

She's trying to tempt my demon is what she's doing.

She kicks the side of my chair, knocking it over with me in it, sending the rest of the now power-tainted holy water across the disgusting floor. My shoulder screams with pain, the side of my face splashing in the liquid, nearly making me throw up. She drags me to my feet and throws me into the wall, pressing my face against it, roaring in my ear.

"I hear Heaven's Traitor's weakness lies in you. He might appreciate it if I toughen you up. Get you to shut that humanity of yours off. You can survive a lot, you know," she growls, grazing her teeth along my earlobe. "Your daddy might even appreciate if I help you look more like him in his true body."

I stiffen, expecting her to tear my ear from my head. "Please, don't. I'm sorry." Ezekiel was right. Being here, even letting the hellhounds think they're in charge, brings out the worst in them. I can't stay here and even humor them a minute longer.

Closing my eyes, I think about all Dad taught me about dealing with Hell, and how demons control people through fear—the hellhounds don't seem much different from demons now that their nice approach wore off. So I can use the same approach with them. If someone's scared enough, they'll do whatever you want. But Dad also taught me that you can use your own fear against demons. They think they have all the power. They underestimate you. And that's what I'm doing. It's time to show this pack what I'm made of—which is a whole lot of Hell power and the desire to get out of here.

"Drake won't even stop me if I gnaw on you until sundown—"

Summoning power into my still damp hands, I flick my fingers, sending beads of liquid power into the woman's stomach. She obviously has never dealt with a demi-demon, because if she had experience, she'd have known not to stand so close to my hands.

She screams, shoving me into the wall before flailing back. I spin on my feet and charge the woman, knocking her back to the wall. She scrambles out of the way and to the door. Instead of trying to fight me, she exits, leaving me ready to burn the whole place down.

"Faith, hurry. Let me help you," Malik says from the spot he's still chained to.

I rush to him, and he manages to loosen the razor wire around my wrist enough to pull my hands free. Growls echo from the other side of the door, and I summon more power into my hands. These monster hellhounds would be stupid to rush back in here now, but I hope they are.

"Can you get the chains?" Malik asks, shaking his ankle to rattle his bindings.

Nodding, I carefully drip my ruby power onto the anchors of the chains, melting them enough to pull them free. I slide them through the spilled holy water, sending sparks and smoke into the air, but it cools them off quick enough that they wouldn't do any more damage to Malik's ravaged skin.

The werewolf scoops me into his arms, hugging me so tightly he might crack a few of my ribs, but I don't complain. A mixture of emotions runs wild through me, and I laugh and cry at the same time.

"I'm so sorry, Malik," I say. "Had I known—"

"There wouldn't have been anything you could've done, Faith," he says.

"But my dad—"

"Knew I was alive. My soul is contracted to him. If I died, he'd have had to release it."

I blink the anger away. It's possible Dad wasn't aware of Malik's situation. He's been so concerned with everything else that his contracts have fallen off his priority list. Personal demonic affairs don't impact our lives. They're not made as a power play. They're convenient in getting things done in the human world. Dad's power came from his descent not like how demons born from Hell rise in ranks.

"But it doesn't matter," Malik adds, hugging me again. "Because you're my damn miracle. I always knew Chris had great taste. He was right about your bad luck being everyone else's good luck. Sucks you're here, but I'm glad you are."

More sadness washes through me. I try not to think about Christopher and any sort of future we could have had if he survived Mary's attempt to bring an eternity to the werewolves on Earth. I know it'd have never worked out. I ruin everything I touch.

I release a small laugh. "I guess my life is good for something, huh? If only everyone would stop trying to make me descend."

Malik releases me, smiling again, making my heart swell with the first happiness that hasn't felt forced in a while. He peers past me at the door, the hellhounds suddenly growing quiet. Dragging his broken chain across the room, he moves to yank open the curtain over the window. Metal bars block us from the outside world, but I'm not letting anything stop me.

"Think you can melt these?" he asks, stepping back.

I nod and raise my hands in front of me to summon power. If I don't have to cross the veil, I won't. I can't now that Malik is here. Shadows edge my vision at the sight of my burned and blistered hands, at the deep cuts around my wrists from the wire now oozing with black, demonic blood.

Malik twists his face in revulsion. "That's nasty."

"They hurt like Hell, too."

Taking a deep breath, I ignite demon power into my palms, thankful it doesn't scorch me since the holy water dried completely. I chuck a ruby orb at the window and cover my eyes to protect my face from the explosion of glass flying through the air at the force. Ezekiel and Dad stand a few feet away on the other side of the Veiled Realm.

"About time," Dad says, stepping forward to close the space.

Ezekiel follows behind him, rage marring his features. I half expect him to reveal his true body to me, but all he does is ignite blue liquid in between his palms. "I'm breaking every last one of those hellhounds who don't comply for thinking they could control you, Faith."

Dad holds out his hand. "Come on, hurry."

I freeze, staring at his outstretched hand. Shaking my head, I say, "I can't cross now."

"What?" Dad and Ezekiel say in unison.

Without waiting for them to make me see things their way, I drop my hands from my face. Arguing with them will steal the precious time I have left to escape. As much as it freaks me out to remain on this plane without the safety of Dad and Ezekiel, Kristin even, I can't walk through the veil and leave Malik behind—he might possibly be the only being who doesn't want me to descend. Something Dad and Ezekiel wouldn't understand.

"Do it again," Malik says, motioning to the broken window. I'm not sure he heard my one-sided conversation. If he did, he's choosing not to mention it. It wouldn't be the first time I've had one. But this time, Ezekiel remains behind the veil and not his angelic shield.

Growing the orb the size of a basketball, I jerk my hands forward, sending it at the bars over the window. They erupt in a sparkle of flames, shaking the foundation of the house. Pieces of drywall rain on us, but the bars remain intact. Blessed. The whole place doesn't hum with the energy of holiness, so I know I'm not in a sacred place, but the werewolves must've managed to bless my only way out that doesn't involve facing a pack of hellhounds. I bet it stops confined hellhounds from escaping, too.

"Damn it." Malik crosses the room and shakes the bars. "Guess we'll take the hard way out."

"You sure?" I shift on my feet, listening to the muffled sounds outside the door. The pack isn't storming in here because they knew we were trapped and the only way we'd exit was through the main door.

"The sun's setting soon. Odds are better now."

He's right. The second the sun sets on the horizon, all of Hell will release in this house. Dad and Ezekiel lie in wait for the veil to thin, and the pack of hellhounds probably ready themselves for the coming night, knowing demons will attack in full force for me. But they must have some sort of plan. I doubt they'd risk kidnapping me, knowing how powerful Dad and Ezekiel are without thinking things through.

The hellhounds know I'm a bleeding heart for people I love. They know I risked my life time and time again for my family. They knew the risk of me not complying from the goodness of my heart. They also knew if I didn't, Dad wouldn't have given them a chance. Drake mentioned he's appealed to my demon, but I think he realized that wouldn't work either.

A familiar clicking sound echoes into my ears from behind the other side of the door. I'd recognize Cadence's footsteps anywhere, even if they're erratic and heavy, scraping concrete like someone half drags her.

Of course they'll use her against me. It's the only reason I didn't fight harder and let them take me. I should've never trusted a hellhound's word. It's why demons use contracts to protect their assets.

The door flings open, and Drake stands in the doorway, hugging Cadence to his chest with his arm around her throat. Her eyes widen when she sees me, a mixture of confusing emotions crossing her face.

I tense. "Cadence."

Drake uses his free hand to comb the hair veiling Cadence's face out of the way. "Did you know Cadence and I go way back? Lost my chance the first time because of damn demons. I always knew she had a thing for them. Nearly threw up when I heard she was scre—"

Cadence stomps her heel on Drake's foot, causing him to yell out and squeeze her tighter where her face reddens to a color I've never seen on her.

He releases a growl. "Do that again, and I'll mess up your face, babe. I don't want to hurt any of you, but I will. I've tried to be a decent guy, but for some reason you can't appreciate that I'm trying to help everyone."

Power automatically ignites in my hands, a red haze clouding my vision. "Just let her go, and I'll do whatever it is you want."

"You're going to even if I don't," he says.

"No, F-Faith," Cadence huffs out. "Kristin told me everything. Just go to Raphael. They'll kill me anyw—"

Drake squeezes her tighter, stopping her from saying any more. My heart races, my inner demon begging to break free the lower the sun hangs in the sky. I thought Cadence only draws out my humanity, but it's my demon, too. It's all of me.

I have minutes to figure out how I'm getting us all out of here before the pack can draw power from Hell and get Dad to comply with whatever demands, but Cadence is right. If I stay, I'll give the hellhounds a chance to ruin the universe. But if I leave, my world will implode.

Covering my eye with my hand, I peer through the veil, watching my demonic power shift from red to orange. The demon within strolls away from me, standing in front of me to peer in my direction with soulless eyes. Firelight burns in the edges of my vision, and I turn my attention away from my demonic self and to the Hell beast barking and snapping, circling where Cadence hangs from Drake's arms in the Earth realm.

"Faith, hurry." Ezekiel's words whisper through the veil,

and I jerk my attention to him waiting for me next to Dad where I left them.

And then a horrible, universe-threatening idea hits me. I don't need to cross the veil and sacrifice Cadence and Malik's lives. I can still save them. All I have to do is the one thing I'm not supposed to.

The one thing that will surely repay me with the fire of Hell.

Training my gaze along the hazy veil in front of Dad and Ezekiel, I whisper, "Please, forgive me."

But it's not to them.

It's to the rest of the world.

My demon dances, jerking back and forth in front of me, lighting its orange power in its hand to mirror the power growing in mine. Tensing, I release the orb at the same time as my demon self does, shattering the veil between us.

"Faith, no!" a masculine, musical voice yells through the air.

Heat rushes over my skin as my inner demon disappears before my eyes. I broke the veil to the daylight prison realm, and now Dad and Ezekiel cross through before the hellhounds can transform with the night, giving Dad the upper hand. I've unleashed demons on the world before the sun has set.

The angelic army was right about me.

"Forgive me," I whisper. "I had to."

All I see is light.

EXIST FOR HUMANITY

OOL FINGERS HOOK around my wrists, yanking me into the daylight prison realm. Dad and Ezekiel don't get the chance to even touch me. By letting them out, I've been forced in by my watcher, and I don't think he'll forgive me for this.

I hit my back on the onyx path, losing my breath. Massive wings unfurl above me, haloed in the brown haze of the setting sun. More bright light stings my eyes, the sudden growls and yells filtering from Earth now cutting off completely as my Demon Watcher seals me away from the Earth realm.

My stomach heaves, and I roll onto my side, coughing and

spitting black blood into the dry dirt. Power buzzes over my skin. I blink my eyes, glimpsing my inner demon lying on the ground, mirroring me, its white eyes boring into my own as it takes me in.

"Oh, God," I say, drawing in air so hot it's hard to catch my breath. "I'm sorry. I'm so, so sorry."

My Demon Watcher drops down on his knees next to me and surprises me by rubbing his hand over my back as I throw up more black bile.

"I need to go back," I say. "This realm is killing me."

"You can survive a minute more. The sun's about to go down in three, two, one." The brown haze transforms into cool mist, draining the heat from the air, making it easier to breathe. "See? That's better, isn't it?"

I shudder, rolling away from him to press my aching, burned and bleeding hands into the ground. "I still need to go back."

"And risk dropping you in the middle of a demonic power play? You're still mortal, Faith. You could get yourself killed," he says.

I groan. "Isn't that what you're supposed to want?"

"No," he says, expanding his wings to send a gust of cool wind through my dirty hair. "No one wants you to die. Plus, I made you a promise."

"I think breaking the veil kind of voids that," I mutter.

"This isn't a demonic negotiation. My promise still stands," he says. "And after you saved me today when you had no real reason to, I'll do what I can to see you succeed if you let me."

"I don't understand what your purpose in all this is, watcher," I say, finally managing to sit up.

"Call me Jess," he says. "And I'm still discovering what my purpose is. You've changed it for me. Who knew you had such capabilities."

I groan. "Not again. I swear if you start telling me you exist for me I'll—"

"I exist for humanity, Faith, not you." He offers his hand to help me to my feet. I wince at the iciness of his fingers on my hot skin. "That's the difference between me and your former guardian."

"You mean apart from Hell in his veins?" I ask. "By your flaming sword."

Frowning, he slumps his shoulders. "I'm sorry. It had to be done. It was how his purpose was supposed to end."

"His purpose was supposed to end with me!" My voice rips through the mist, startling him, and he flaps his wings, jumping a foot in the air. "You ruined him."

"*Me?*" he questions, landing on his feet. "He abandoned his duties. He should've never hid you. If he had returned and warned us about the witch, we might have never been in this position. You would be at peace."

He means dead.

Summoning power, I blast it at his feet. He launches into the air again, and I take the opportunity to cover my eye with my hand to peer through the Veiled Realm at the calamity my watcher yanked me from.

I'm greeted with eerie silence, the room the hellhounds kept me captive in now empty. Crossing the room, I waltz straight through the door and into the hallway of a not surprisingly beautiful mansion. Werewolf packs must have homes to accommodate the sheer number of pack mates, and the Sunrise Cove pack is comparable to the one in Moonlight Shores.

"Where is everyone?" I ask out loud.

"I don't know. Time passes faster here, remember. They're all most likely out ruining the world," Jess says from my side, trailing next to me.

I drop my hand and turn to face him. "That's my destiny, remember?"

He chuckles, his hardened features softening. "I don't need the reminder."

"Me either." Sighing, I stroll through the first floor of the mansion, taking note of the scorch marks burning across the wood floors. A curtain over one of the front windows still smolders, and the front door hangs broken on its hinges like it was bashed open.

"They can't be far." Exiting the house, I enter the well-manicured front lawn. Black oil burns from the sidewalk in a hot trail leading to the desolate street.

"And what do you expect to do when you find them?" Jess asks, strolling in front of me to block my way. His brilliant white wings unfurl, and heavenly light radiates from every feather. "It's better if we go somewhere far so everyone can stop trying to use you."

I place my hands on my hips. "Only the hellhounds want that."

He lifts an eyebrow, glaring at me like I'm an idiot. "Do I need to remind you how demons think? Raphael will ask you to break the veil again."

"I won't do it."

"Maybe not for him, but what about Ezekiel? I can feel your love for him so deeply that it literally pains me. And his love..." He shudders, ruffling his feathers.

"Ezekiel doesn't love me anymore," I say quietly. It hurts my being to say the words out loud, but I feel like Jess should know I'm not some heartsick, clueless girl reacting because of my humanity. I know what my life has come to, and I know Ezekiel is incapable of loving me like he used to. He can only remember he did.

"Why do you think that?"

I frown. "He's a demon."

"Your father's a demon. He loves you."

"That's different. I'm made of his heart."

"And Ezekiel's made of your soul. I can feel it consuming him. Why do you think he won't let it go? Demons love deals. He should've found something to trade for it already, yet he hasn't. You know why?"

I roll my eyes. "He has found something."

"He won't go through with it," he says, already knowing

that I'm implying the deal Dad was trying to arrange for my descent as a full-blooded demon.

"Why not?"

"Because he knows you wouldn't want him to. He might be a demon, but he's not a monster, even if Hell runs through his veins. He can still feel the light if you make him remember."

"So, our love is not only messing with the world, it's ruining me. Great. You angels. You should warn people how poisonous love is."

He grimaces. "Faith, love is full of light and goodness."

"Unless tainted by Hell."

"That's not love you're referring to. Obsession, maybe. Need. All I know is if you pushed Ezekiel hard enough, made him feel how he should with your soul, he might realize the truth of what he's doing to you and willingly return it. No strings or deals attached. And then we can see where your soul falls."

"What is it with angels dishing out relationship advice?" I ask, despite the warmth blossoming through me—heat not from the demonic blood in my veins but the spark of hope Jess ignited in me. Hope that feels so painful yet amazing. Hope I know better than to hold.

He shrugs. "I've been watching the world for a long time."

"Watching is different than experiencing it."

"Maybe so," he says. "Won't ever find out."

"You sure? Haven't you heard? No angel stands a chance against my demonic lovable self." I laugh and nudge his shoulder with my burned knuckles. "At least that's what Dad tells me."

He purses his lips, giving me a once over. "I won't deny that you're lovable, but you'll be thankful I'm immune to your mortal charm."

"Is that so?" My cheeks burn. Am I flirting with the avenging angel who tried to send a flaming sword in my chest? Yup. Not because I like the guy—sure he's cute in an I'll-save-your-ass-from-an-eternity-in-Hell type of way—but because I can't resist pushing boundaries.

He pokes my nose. "Definitely. Your Hell-bound soul is quite off-putting. Also because I can feel my brother's wickedness coursing through you."

"He's not your brother," I say.

He shrugs. "I suppose not anymore."

Sadness glasses his golden eyes for a moment before he blinks it away, hardening his features to me once more. He peers at the moon rising overhead, the world moving at a faster pace here than in the Earth realm.

"Are you going to make me leave with you?" I ask, covering my eye with my branded hand to peer through the veil once more. We haven't walked far, but we're already near the motel I was kidnapped from this morning. The Veiled Realm distorts everything. What's the Pacific Ocean on Earth is nothing more than an endless desert here.

Jess presses his lips in a line. "I want to, but there's a little something called freewill. I'm going to highly encourage you to stay with me at least until dawn. We can get to know each other, bare our souls, whatever. Could be interesting."

I gape at him. "That sounds intimate."

He releases a loud laugh, startling me. "Intimate? You're joking, right?"

Turning my gaze to the ground, I hold my tongue as to not react.

His laughter tapers off, and he reaches out and nudges my shoulder with the back of his hand. "Hey, there's nothing wrong with getting to know me or allowing me to get to know who you are apart from this whole destroy the universe persona you now carry around like a ticking bomb."

I step back out of his reach. "I can name hundreds of reasons."

"Go on."

"People around me die."

He shrugs. "I'm immortal."

"Then fall."

"Won't happen."

"You'll prove yourself right about me," I say, putting more space between us.

"That you deserve a chance?"

I sigh. "Then because I have a thing for purity, and I'm afraid I'll fall in love with you."

His smile falters.

It's my turn to laugh. "Well, I guess I know what you're scared of."

He doesn't respond, glancing past me. The strange look on his face causes me to shift and stare in the direction he's looking in. All I see is the mist reflecting the silver moon overhead across the onyx path.

"What is it?" I ask, automatically raising my hand over my eye to peer through the veil.

Jess snatches my hand from my face. "Don't look."

"I thought you can't see through it?" I ask.

"I can't, but I can sense a darkness on the other side. We should go. I'll bring you back by morning."

I frown. "What? I have to see."

"Faith, don't."

Ignoring him, I bring my palm to my eye. Jess reaches for me again, trying to hook his arm around me so I have to focus on him, but I summon power. He gathers angelic light to combat my power.

"Please, Faith. Stay. I'm begging you. Give me a chance."

I shake my head. "You never gave me one."

"Forgive me."

Instead of responding, I turn my back on him. "Thanks for answering my prayer earlier. I appreciate it."

"Don't forget, you answered mine, too," he whispers.

I peer over my shoulder. "You're lucky I have a soft spot for angels."

"I don't feel so lucky."

I grimace. "You're probably right since you got assigned to me."

"You mean chose you." Flapping his brilliant white wings, he blows my hair out of my face.

"Whatever. Try not to let my dad catch you again."

He nods, and I shift away from him once more. Taking a deep breath, I slowly bring my hands to my eyes to peer through the veil. A shiver rushes over my skin as cool hands touch my back.

"Brace yourself, Faith," Jess says from behind me.

The world spins, shadows and light flashing in my eyes. My stomach twists. I stumble away from my watcher and spill to the asphalt, catching myself on my tender hands. A flicker of firelight to my right draws my attention away from the pain coursing through my arms.

I don't get a chance to look at what it is. Hot hands hook under my arms, scooping me from the ground. I scream out, thrashing, igniting power in my hands. Everything happens so fast—the shift between the Veiled Realm and Earth—my mind barely has a chance to catch up.

Then my stomach heaves and someone spins me around and sets me on my feet. My knees hit the soft grass, and I throw up black liquid everywhere. I gasp, tears burning my eyes, fear clenching my chest. A guttural growl sounds from nearby, and I'm pretty sure the moment I stop puking, I'll be mauled to death by the putrid smelling hellhound.

"Please," I beg. "Please, don't kill me."

A hot hand rubs my back. "You're the last person I'd ever kill. You know this, Faith."

A sob wracks my chest, fighting against my twisting stomach. "Ezekiel, oh, God. You're okay. I thought the hellho—"

"You don't have to worry about the beasts."

I groan, thinking of a million reasons why I wouldn't have to worry about them. "Cadence? Kristin?" I heave again, slamming my palms on the ground. "Don't tell me they're—"

Ezekiel kneels next to me, continuing to gently rub my back. "Just take a breath. The bastard angel should know better than to rip you back and forth through the veil like that. I'm going to break his damn wings."

I cover my face with my hands, sniffling. Jess stands a few feet away, staring at me from his side of the veil. Ezekiel pulls my hands from my face and removes his shirt to clean off the blood and other nasty liquids from me.

I suck in a breath. "Please tell me what happened. Where is everyone? Are they—"

"They're all fine."

"So that means the hellhounds—"

Ezekiel cups my face in his hands. "It's complicated, Faith. I'll explain everything once you get cleaned up." He reaches for my hands to help me to my feet and hesitates seeing the condition of my skin.

I tug my hands away. "They look worse than they feel."

"The beasts do that?"

I shake my head. "I did."

He narrows his eyes. "You are not protecting them after every—"

"Ezekiel, please. I don't want to fight. I just want you to hold me."

A strange look crosses his face, something indecipherable, almost familiar clouding his eyes. I remember Jess's words about Ezekiel still being capable of love if I can prod at the humanity he carries through me—if I can open him up and get him to remember.

He blinks his eyes, the firelight burning away whatever I saw. He nods. "Anything for you."

I hobble forward, the events of the day taking a toll on me. Ezekiel wraps his arm around my waist, taking some of my weight from me without picking me up, though I'm sure he's considering it. And resting against his muscular bare chest is about the only thing I want to do now. We continue to walk together because carrying me would give most demons the wrong impression. I'm strong enough to stand on my own and against any threats.

When we reach the parking lot, Ezekiel motions me toward a black Audi I've never seen before and opens the door. "Raphael insisted we relocate."

I slide into the passenger's side, feeling the cool leather against my hot skin. "Figures. He buy you a car?"

Ezekiel scratches his neck. "No, it was a gift."

"A gift."

"The hellhounds."

My eyes widen. "What?"

"I told you it's complicated."

"They're alive?"

"For now."

"How?"

"They couldn't pass up a deal with a demon—well, make that two demons."

A TRUCE

"FAITH, ARE YOU okay in there?" Ezekiel's voice drifts through the bathroom door.

Swiping my healing hands across the foggy mirror, I stare at my reflection. My damp hair drips water down my shoulders and into the fluffy towel I hold around myself. My white eye shines against my flushed cheeks, a hard contrast against the blue of my normal eye. I consider raising my hand to look through the veil to see Jess, but Ezekiel knocks.

"Faith, Kristin dropped by with a salve to heal your wounds more quickly," he says, turning the knob. I never locked the door so he opens it a crack and peers at me in the mirror.

I motion for him to come in. "Where's my dad? Shouldn't he have been the one to come by?"

"Demonic affairs, remember? He promised to be back in time for the sunrise to check on you." Ezekiel strolls up behind me, opening the glass jar of whatever concoction Kristin made that suspiciously looks like blood.

I tilt my head back, resting against his chest, letting him slather the strangely cooling liquid over my hands while hugging me from behind. "Tell him I don't need him to check on me."

Ezekiel sets down the bottle on the marble counter of this thankfully luxurious bathroom. "He knows that."

The Sunset Cliffs Plaza is a hundred times better than the motel just off the highway we were in. I have a balcony with a view of the night ocean on a floor far too high for hellhounds to surprise me.

"Then tell him I don't want him to check on me, not until one of you tells me what the Hell the demonic deal with the hellhounds was about," I snap.

His hands slide higher up my chest and comb my damp tresses away from my collarbone. He kisses the skin below my ear. "He's going to accuse you of being unfair to him."

I flick my gaze to his in the mirror. "Good. I know whatever it was came solely from his demented head."

"You sure about that?"

Spinning in his arms, I face him head on and press my

hands to his chest, leaving red handprints on the light fabric of his T-shirt. "Yes. My dad never passes an opportunity for power. I'm sure Heaven's already planning his descent to Hell. And this time, I'm not stepping in to save him."

"You're hot when you're angry."

I roll my eyes. "You haven't seen my fury."

"Show me," he says, smiling.

I take his bait and shove him back toward the door to the room. Power ignites in my palms, and I fake glare, closing the space between us faster than he can step back. I chuck a small burst of power at him, hitting him in the stomach. He laughs, ripping off his smoldering shirt as it reddens his bone-hard abs now wanting to capture my full attention.

"All you had to say was you wanted me to take off my shirt," he teases.

I grin, a smile overtaking my whole face making my cheeks hurt. "I like doing it this way, though."

"Oh, really?" Ezekiel summons blue liquid in his hands, tossing it between his palms.

I bite my lip. "Yeah."

He grows a bit more power in his palms without a word, his muscles rippling in his arms.

I hold my finger out to him. "But, I like doing it this way, too."

Ezekiel's eyes darken as my towel hits the floor. I like hiding my fear behind other emotions, and right now? I'm afraid of the deal Dad arranged. I'm afraid of how much Ezekiel is a part of it. I'd rather think about Ezekiel in a way that makes both our hearts beat wildly.

Heat blossoms up my chest to my neck under his scrutiny, his eyes traveling over every inch of me before stopping on my eyes. I don't know what's come over me, but after today, all I want is to lose myself in everything he is.

He sucks in a breath, his heart pounding so loudly I can't even hear my own heart anymore. "You're beautiful, you know."

Closing the distance, he drinks me in again, his eyes lingering on the feather imprint across my heart. He grazes his fingers along the edges of it, tracing it with fire lighting something in his dark eyes. It's not the same fire I usually see in them, burning at the humanity he suppresses. This is something different.

"I love you, Faith," he whispers, his voice soft and breathless. "I love you so much it scares me. I wasn't sure the watcher would bring you back to me."

I draw my hand up to his face, closing the space between us, pressing my hand into his skin. "You said you shut off my humanity because it's torture? But I think you're more afraid than anything."

He shuts his eyes. "Among other things."

"Well, stop." I stand on my tiptoes to kiss him. "Because I want you to feel every little thing however good or bad it is. I think it's a fair request on my part."

"You don't understand," he says. This wasn't the conversation I had planned to have in this moment, but I'm not missing the opportunity to prod against his softening demeanor, something he only ever does when we're alone. Because he can only do so with me.

"Understand what? That you shut me out because you're afraid you've ruined your eternity for someone who'll slip through your fingers and fade into a memory? Or how awful I make you feel denying what you want from this? Or how you question why you're in this position, fighting a cause you think I'm purposely losing? I do understand."

Flicking his gaze away from mine, he glances at the moon lowering in the sky with the coming dawn. His eyes flash green when he brings his attention back to me and says, "Some of that might be true, but I mostly do it because I see how you look at me. It reminds me I'm not the same person you fell in love with. It kills me, Faith. If I don't, I feel every bit of you through your soul, and I don't like the way you sometimes feel about me."

I frown, bowing my head against his shoulder, feeling the heat of his skin warming me from outside in. "It's not how I feel about you. It's how I feel about me. You want to know how I truly feel about you?"

He swallows, burying his face into the crook of my neck. "I do. Tell me."

I lean away and cup his face. "Open up and I'll show you instead."

Fire blazes his eyes, and he tilts his head, a mixture of emotions crossing his face as he considers my words. Jess told me

Ezekiel is still capable of loving me. He's still capable of being who I fell in love with. I just have to show him. I don't know a better way than pleading with him to open up to me in a moment where my world isn't exploding. In a moment where it's just him and me and the sound of our hearts beating.

He sucks in a shuddering breath, losing himself in my eyes. For the first time ever it's him who's lost, locked, captured in my gaze. My whole body hums with both love and desire, with the vulnerability of opening myself completely to him.

His serious expression morphs, his hard mouth curling into a smile. "Oh, Faith." My name sounds like a plea on his lips, like he's begging me to confirm all these bottled up feelings I hold in the depths of my humanity to keep them safe from the tainted world around me. "I love you. I love every achingly beautiful part of you."

I kiss him, devouring his words, stealing his breath. Because I can feel his love radiating from him. The intensity buzzes over my skin, making my body and mind react. My heart races, and I swear I feel almost whole again, my soul so close to me through his skin. His hands travel down my arms and scoop me up, spinning me toward the bed.

I slip my tongue in his mouth, kissing him deeper, pressing against his body while running my fingers through his hair. He moans into my lips, sitting on the edge of the bed with me on top of him.

"Faith," he whispers.

I kiss my name from his mouth, cutting him off. "Less

talking, more corrupting."

He chuckles, flipping me onto my back to peer down at me. Framing me with his arms, he holds his body weight above me, hesitating to make the move I've imagined dozens of times before. Fire courses through my veins, my inner demon and my humanity setting itself aglow for Ezekiel, sending wave after wave of my desire to him.

"Are you sure, Faith? I'm a demon. What if I accidentally—"

I interrupt his words with a kiss, arching up to try to close the space between us. "Yes, I'm sure. I'm not a glass trinket. You won't hurt me. I know you'll be careful."

He nods, lowering himself on top of me, breathing his dark chocolate scent into my hair. His hands dig under me, pulling me closer, mapping my back like he needs to remember every inch of my skin as his fingers lower to my hips.

Fire crawls across his eyes, his skin reddening as his true body flashes through his beautiful façade. I kiss him harder, trailing my own fingers over his face and across his horns that disappear under my touch. Because even though Hell peeks through in our moment of passion, Ezekiel is still Ezekiel to me. I didn't fall in love with his wings. I didn't fall in love with his good grace, the grace that sometimes made me feel like the worst being in existence. I fell in love with him and all his flaws. I fell in love with his light that still burns through to me, even if it's now fire. And I know I'll continue to love him, regardless of whether or not we see things the same way, because my new watcher was right. Ezekiel's made from my soul, now split between us.

I lose myself in Ezekiel's touch, feeling his own emotions pour to me from him. I never thought I'd feel his love again, but it's washing over me in a wave of warmth soaking into my bones to carry with me as the sun rises.

It lingers with me even as he breaks away to lie next to me, cradling me in his arms, kissing my temple, holding me like he'll do so forever. If the world would stop spinning. If the sun would freeze in the sky, I'd let him. I'd live right here where the universe feels right. Where everything about me and Ezekiel feels right.

I close my eyes, resting my head on his chest, listening to his heartbeat.

"Dawn's coming in a few minutes," he whispers, shifting on the bed next to me. He gets dressed, but I don't move.

"I wish you never had to go." I extend my hand to him.

Someone knocks on the door, threatening to ruin the last few minutes until the sun steals Ezekiel away for the day, and I'm not ready. I'm never ready.

"Go away!" I shout.

Ezekiel glances between the door and my outstretched hand.

"You promised to hold me," I whisper.

A smile lights his face, and he turns from the door and climbs back into bed with me. I fall asleep in his arms, listening to his breathing, just soaking up everything he makes me feel until it fades away with the rising sun.

But the new day feels different. Better.

For once, I can feel the light.

Ezekiel's light.

I'll never let it go out again.

"I need your blood." Kristin stands outside my door, shifting her leather bag on her shoulder.

"And I need to eat and go for a run or something." More like eat and sleep the day away until Ezekiel crosses the veil. It's taken everything in me not to peek through a dozen times. The last thing I want is to confront Dad, and I'm sure he'll return to Earth with a lot of lame excuses—maybe some Hell fire to intimidate me with. Most definitely fury if he discovers I ignored his knocks because I was...

She sighs. "Give me your blood first." The last thing I want is to start the day with bloodletting and spell casting. Witch magic has done enough to me, and even though I love Kristin, and even though she'd risk her life for me, she's still Hell-bound and contracted to work for Dad. After yesterday, I'm sure she has some sort of role in a hellhound deal.

Hiding my hands behind my back so she can't surprise me, I say, "Maybe if you tell me about the deal and how Dad managed to save you all and keep the beasts back."

"You saved us, Faith. He only assured a truce. You shouldn't worry about it. Raphael will handle things." She extends her hand to me. "Now, your palm please."

"No." I slam the door in her face and lock it. Turning back to my bed, I cross the room and flop onto it, hiding my head under the downy pillows. The scent of dark chocolate lingers around me, and I will myself to shut off the world so I can fall back to sleep and call for Ezekiel to keep me company in my dreams.

A beep rings through the air, and the door clicks closed. I ignore Kristin as she struts across the floor to the bed. She rips the comforter away from me, tossing it on a chair in the seating area near the balcony door.

Flipping over, I glare at her. "You're going to have to fight me if you want my blood."

She rolls her eyes. "I'm not fighting you. If you want to get taken by hellhounds again, that's on you."

I tip my head into my pillow. "That threat isn't going to work. The deal, remember?"

"Hasn't been fulfilled yet."

I groan. "No blood. I'll take my chances."

"Raphael's going to flip out."

"Whatever. Let him. Dad's not exactly on my good list. First he works on negotiating a deal for *my* eternity. Then he attacks *my* watcher. I'm afraid of what he'll do if he found out that Ezekiel and I—"

"You better say went out for ice cream. Anything else will put me in the line of fire because apparently I'm supposed to be your babysitter," she says, looking at me more intently.

I grin, blushing. "It was the best ice cream ever."

She pales. "Careful, Faith. You're walking a dangerous line. I know you love Ezekiel, but he's still very much a demon. He can't help all the bad that comes from his nature. You might get hurt."

"I'll heal," I say.

"I meant your heart."

"You sound like Dad." I sigh, not wanting to have this conversation with her about Ezekiel. Because I'm not stupid. I know what it means to love a demon. I know what it means to have opened myself up like I did with Ezekiel and the possible consequences. But I also know that he might be a demon but he's also more than that. He's half of my being.

"Who knew Jess would be better at these kinds of conversations?" I mutter, turning on my side.

"Jess? Is that—"

"My self-appointed Demon Watcher." I can't believe he let me tell Kristin his name. Maybe he can't stop me since she saw him with her own two eyes when she used magic to break his shield for Dad.

She sucks in a breath. "Oh, Faith. You mustn't let that angel get so close to you. That's as dangerous as eating ice cream with Ezekiel."

I laugh. I can't help it. "We're definitely not bonding or baring our souls or whatever. He just promised not to kill me until I get my soul back."

"And if you don't?"

"I will. Ezekiel loves me and will understand."

Her eyes glass over, her sad stare threatening to snuff out all the hope both Ezekiel and Jess gave me. "Faith…"

I close my eyes and hold out my hand. "Will you leave me alone if I give you my blood?"

She twists her lips to the side. "The blood can wait."

Annoyance clenches my chest. "Why can't I ever have a day where I'm not worrying about my life or death or heart or descent? I know you're a big picture type of person, Kristin. But I need the little things to survive."

"You deserve more than that."

I groan and cover my face with my hands. Brown haze blurs the room as the daylight prison realm overlays my hotel room. I sit on a dry hill overlooking a forest of gnarled trees with screaming faces.

"Even if that's true, I'm going to appreciate whatever I can get. And right now, I appreciate the fact that I can peek in on Ezekiel especially after he let me in."

She touches my shoulder. "Just be careful and remember he can't access humanity there."

"I know what I'm doing."

"I have to agree with the witch," a familiar voice says, materializing next to me on the other side of the veil.

I listen to Kristin sigh and leave when she realizes I'm done talking about what my life has come to.

"Jess, you shouldn't be here," I say. "Ezekiel will show up at any second."

"He won't. I'm shielding you."

"What? No. You can't do that."

"The witch's magic is bound to Earth, not here. Here, I can shield you if I want to. If you're going to insist on stalking your boyfriend, risking the very fabric of our existence, I'm going to help you do it safely. I can't have another break in the veil, Demon Tamer." He stretches his legs out in front of him while expanding his wings, brushing them against my back.

I lean back against them, a flash of memory about touching Ezekiel's wings flitting through my mind. "You're getting more annoying by the second. You're the one who encouraged me to remind Ezekiel who he was."

His gaze bores in the side of my face, but I refuse to look at him.

"It's really none of your business, though," I add. "And I don't need any more advice. I'm good."

"You're good?" he questions.

I nod. "The best."

He groans. "Seriously, Faith? That's not what I meant."

Oh, my God. And I thought Kristin was bad. "I—"

"You're sure about this?" Dad's voice echoes through the air, drawing my attention from Jess and the uncomfortable situation he put me in.

Reaching out, Jess sticks his arm across my stomach like Dad sometimes does when he's driving like a maniac to keep me from sliding around the seat or jerking against the seatbelt. But Jess is doing it to keep me in place without restraining me, just holding his arm in front of me while I use his wing as a backrest.

"Absolutely certain. There's nothing I won't do for Faith," Ezekiel says, strolling next to Dad as they come into view from the trees. They never wander far from where I am in the Earth realm.

"Except return her soul to her," Dad says.

Ezekiel lifts and drops his shoulders, turning his gaze in our direction. I half expect him to wave with the way he's looking at me, but I realize he's probably imagining this is where I'd be, since this is the place he left me in the Earth realm.

Ezekiel shoves his hands in his pockets. "You'll thank me one day."

Dad scowls. "What's that supposed to mean?"

My chest tightens, the edges of my vision darkening. Jess's block turns into a half hug as he folds his wing to curl around my shoulder.

"It's between me and Faith. I know that's not what you want to hear, but she's not a child anymore, and she doesn't need you getting in the middle of things."

I release my breath. I don't know why I doubted for a second that Ezekiel would tell Dad about Jess's promise to me once I regain my soul. And I will get it back. I have to.

Dad's eyes flash red, and he releases an orb of power at the screaming trees. "You better not try to turn her against me."

"Only you can do that, Raphael."

"And that's why you better make good on your word. You mess up this deal, and I'll send you to Hell myself."

"Not with Faith's soul."

Dad growls.

"I won't mess up," Ezekiel adds.

Dad throws another burst of power at the trees. "Good, because the last thing I need is to have Heaven threatening my eternity."

"I'm not worried about the angelic army. Because I have Faith. She'd destroy the world for me. I felt it."

I frown, but I don't get up. I suddenly can't breathe.

Meeting Jess's eyes, I say, "He doesn't mean it. He's saying it for my dad's benefit."

Jess tightens his jaw. "I was afraid of this."

"He's not a threat."

Jess shifts. "And if he is?"

"I won't let him use my love like that. I won't."

The angel releases a long breath through his nose. "For your sake, I hope you're right."

For the world's sake, I hope I'm right, too.

DEMON TAMER

"**Y**OU'VE WASTED YOUR day here in this miserable realm. Want to waste your night here, too?" Jess asks, bumping me with his shoulder.

I wouldn't say I wasted my day, considering I haven't been here more than a few daylight prison realm hours, but with how quickly the sun crosses the sky to dip into the horizon, I suppose he might be technically right.

"You'd love that, wouldn't you," I say. "Must get lonely having to stalk me in this world."

"You peek in on me more and more, so it's not so bad. Though, I really wish you'd consider convincing your witch to break her spell. I hate this place."

"Not a chance." I flick his arm. "Don't think I forgot your damn flaming sword."

He sighs. "It's not as scary as your demonic power."

"Angels don't get scared."

He smiles. "Most angels haven't met you, Demon Tamer."

"Probably for the best. I can only take so much purity."

"Obviously."

I glare.

He raises his hands. "Kidding. Relax, don't blast me. You make me nervous when you summon power while concentrating on the veil. Don't think I won't drag you through again."

"I should blast you for that. It was awful coming to you. You know, it didn't feel so bad the time I walked through to my dad."

"Because you used his demon blood, and he's anchored here. But me? I do things a little differently."

I shudder, knowing it's why I felt so bad when Kristin sent me through, too. "So, the answer is still no. I need to face my demons anyway. Find out about this stupid deal I have a feeling I won't like."

"And then you can tell me," he quips.

I grimace.

He huffs. "So, that's a no?"

"Thank your flaming sword for my lack of cooperation. I don't want anyone ending up on the receiving end of that blade."

Jess doesn't respond to my remark. Instead, he leans back on his arms and peers at the setting sun before us. Dad and Ezekiel emerge from the trees, peering around the area. Ezekiel's attention draws to mine, and he surprises me by raising his hand to wave. I glance next to me and startle, Jess now gone from my sight as he releases me from behind his shield.

Ezekiel jogs from my dad to meet me still in my spot on top of the dry hill where my hotel room comes in and out of view while I blink. I meet Dad's ice blue eyes for a second and turn away from him, anger still pulsing through my veins.

Ezekiel's fingers hum over my skin as he presses against the veil. "Have you been here long?"

I suck my bottom lip between my teeth, contemplating on whether or not I'll tell him the truth about being here long enough to overhear part of his earlier conversation with Dad about relying on my love to keep him safe. Because I'd kind of be a hypocrite. I'm alive because of his love, but the consequences from it are less than ideal.

"What's the matter?" he asks, intently staring at me because I'm too slow to respond. "I can't feel you right now, but I know you well enough to see something bothers you."

"I—" My throat tightens, my body refusing to let me spill my heart out to him. Because really, yesterday was horrible until I returned to Ezekiel, and I want to survive on the rush of how my day started, soak in everything he filled me up with for a little while longer. I'm afraid to test his demonic nature with my admittance.

"Ezekiel, I'd like a moment with Faith," Dad says, coming up behind him. He pulls Ezekiel back, not giving him a choice in whether or not he's going to give Dad a moment with me.

I pout, nodding to Ezekiel. Confronting Dad prolongs any sort of fight I might have with my fallen angel regarding what the Hell he's doing making deals with hellhounds on Dad's behalf. Deals that'll surely leave him on the opposite end of Heaven's vengeance.

Dad stands before me, his arms open, expecting me to hug him through the veil. I stare at him, trailing my eyes from his pristine shoes to the glittering diamond pin on his lapel. He's as handsome and unchanged as the first day I met him when he showed up to take me away from the miserable life I had after Grandma died.

"You're angry with me," he says, his eyes narrowing as his gaze bores into me. "But not with Ezekiel."

"Yes." The sound of my sharp voice makes him wince. I don't think he's ever responded to me in such a way. It opens a cut on my heart, filling me with enough guilt to drown me.

Even though I straighten my shoulders, burning him a look, steeling myself from his charm, he steps closer and touches my shoulders, not letting me dig under his skin. "I didn't want to negotiate with Hell beasts, but my options were quite limited. You might not believe me, but I cherish the lives of not only you, but of Cadence and Kristin. They've been loyal to me, honest, and brave. I'd rather give the beasts something they can't refuse than lose these precious souls too soon. I'd have done the same for your mother, you know."

"You think this is about the deal? I already knew it was bound to happen. Ezekiel made it quite clear what a supposedly awesome opportunity this will be."

Ezekiel meets my gaze. "It is. Everyone wins."

"Except me."

Dad clenches his jaw. "This is about you? You can't seriously be mad at me for being your dad and wanting to do what's right. Mary was right about one thing. Hellhounds make great allies if things are negotiated properly."

He doesn't get it. This isn't about demonic affairs or the hellhounds. It's about my life and eternity. About how he tried to ruin my new watcher like he doesn't believe I can handle things myself.

Weeks ago, I thought I couldn't. I thought I needed to hide in Dad's shadow. Behind Ezekiel's wings. But now? I'm not hiding or afraid. My demonic birthright as the daughter of Heaven's Traitor changed things.

I puff a breath through my lips. "I can forgive you for making a deal, Dad. I know who you are and don't expect less. I also don't want to see Cadence or Kristin hurt in your crossfire. But like I said, this isn't about that."

Fire lights in his eyes. "This better not be about the wa—"

The hazy air around us clears with the disappearing sun, startling me, and I spot Jess standing behind my dad among the white mist of the Veiled Realm safely out of a demon's reach.

"But it is," I snap. "You can't go around breaking angels."

Dad's eyes widen. "Faith, reel it in."

"No! What you forced Kristin to do, breaking my guardian's shield like that, was the worst thing you have ever done, and you've done a lot."

"I'm trying to save your eternity."

"You're ruining it. You *have* ruined it, Dad. Look at what happened to Mom. And then Aria. And the Traitor Pack. Ezekiel. Me. Everything falls back to you, and I'm tired of paying the cost of your wrongdoings that you keep adding to. I should've known you could never really be more than what you've become. A monstrous, self-absorbed demon." Tears burn my eyes as Dad's gaze bores into me, his face completely emotionless.

I brace myself for him to react and reveal his true body. Because I've basically announced the worst moments of my life and threw all the blame on him because of who he is. I couldn't stop myself, and I know it was unfair, because Mom made her choice—and Aria, the Traitor Pack, Ezekiel. Me. But I can't stop the consuming agony coursing through my demonic blood, my dad's blood, because none of this would've happened if he never fell.

Dad straightens his shoulders, and Ezekiel opens the hotel room door behind him. I'm sure the whole universe heard me, the world holding its breath like I am in anticipation for all of Hell to release at any second.

"Dad," I whisper, the edges of my vision shadowing. "I—"

"Stop, Faith," he says. "I know you didn't mean any of it,

but you are right. Everything bad in your life is a consequence of my existence as a demon, and I'm sorry you're wrapped up in the aftermath. But I'm trying the best I can to fix things. Sometimes I must act on my nature, but I never do so without good reason. And you can be pissed off at me. Blame me. Turn your back on me. I'll accept it. I'll accept it if you can never forgive me. But none of this will ever change how much I love you or how I'll do what it takes to assure your existence outside of Hell. You will not spend your eternity there because of me no matter the cost. Do you understand?"

I shake my head. "Nobody's eternity is worth more than mine. Try to hurt Jess again an—"

Dad hugs me, cutting off my words. "My sweet, pure daughter. Heaven already regrets forsaking you. I can feel it."

"You can?"

"The angelic army already knows you're not ruining the world. You'll save it."

I frown. "I know." Just not the way he thinks. I'll save the world by leaving it intact the best I can. If only Ezekiel didn't stare at me like by saving the world, I'd be obliterating his. And how can I continue to destroy him after everything? I guess I'll figure it out.

Dad releases me and steps back without taking his hands from my shoulders. "Good. Don't forget that. Now, if you could please put on something more appropriate, we have places to be. We've lost enough time as it is."

"Dressed? I thought I'd stay here."

Dad shakes his head. "We have a deal to complete."

I blink. "I thought it involved the hellhounds. Not me."

Fire lights Dad's eyes. "We're doing this for you and no one else."

"But why do I have to go?"

"Because you're the only one in the universe I trust, Faith," Ezekiel says, speaking up.

I turn to face him. "What is this supposed deal even about? Certainly not giving the hellhounds the eternity they want, right?"

Dad shrugs. "It's a compromise."

I groan. *Unholy Hell.*

"You're wearing a tuxedo." I hover in the hallway of the hotel, taking in Ezekiel standing before me. He styled his dark hair away from his face with product, sharpening his features, a new seriousness overtaking his face. Something in his eyes makes me hesitate, and my heart sputters in erratic beats, threatening to break free from me to run in the other direction for the first time. It must know I can no longer protect it from the force Ezekiel transformed into.

Ezekiel adjusts his bow-tie, curving his mouth into a smile. "Like it?" He strides closer, sliding his hands over my hips to rest on my lower back.

I release a shuddering breath, feeling the heat of his skin even through our clothes, reminding me of the moments before dawn. "It's different."

He chuckles. "I hate it, too."

"Gowns have always been my least favorite," I say, lifting the skirt of my dress up to reveal my glittering heels. "Try wearing these."

"You look amazing, though. Just like the first time I revealed myself to you," he whispers, leaning down to kiss me. "I couldn't help myself then." His finger trails over my collar, brushing my hair away. "Still can't resist you now."

I close my eyes, soaking up the heat of his fingers gliding down my arm. "So, if I asked you not to go through with the deal, would you?"

He stiffens in my arms, releasing a puff of hot air against my neck. "Faith."

"What if I asked you to go back to the room?"

His mouth hums against my neck as he groans. "You're trying to use my love for you against me."

I trail my hands to the hem of his jacket and slide my hands over the muscles I can feel through his shirt. "Like you can talk. I heard you earlier."

Pulling back, he locks me in his dark gaze. "I thought I sensed you peeking through, and the damn watcher helped you spy on us."

"I wasn't spying. I wanted to reveal myself, but he wouldn't let me. And I'm glad."

"Glad? This is a game to him, you know. He's playing with your humanity, Faith. He's trying to turn you against me."

I pull away, my heart seizing in my chest, splitting apart.

"He's not."

"But now you doubt me."

"You said I'd destroy the world for you."

"You would," he says, like it's a simple fact everyone knows.

"Ezekiel!" I step back, tears burning my eyes, threatening to ruin my mascara.

Lacing his fingers behind his head, he turns his back on me, staring at the elevator. "Faith, you know I don't lie to you, and I'm trying really hard not to right now as much as I want to, but you shouldn't be upset. It was just a thought. I don't want you to destroy the world for me. I like it here, especially with you."

"That's beside the point." My lungs clench, and I gasp, trying to breathe despite feeling like I'm drowning. How could everything be so perfect one second and ruined now? Our love winds a treacherous path, and just when I thought we evaded danger, we come to a cliff neither of us are capable of climbing. If only Ezekiel still had wings.

"Can we discuss this later? Raphael's expecting us." He turns back to me and holds his hand out.

I extend mine to take his, to fall in place by his side, but something dark snakes over me, and I cross my arms. "No. I'm not going."

"Faith, come on. You're not thinking clearly."

I scowl. "*I'm* not thinking clearly? Ezekiel, you're putting me in a terrible position."

"Faith," he repeats my name like saying it over and over again will suddenly make me see what he means, agree with him. But I can't see anything through the sudden mist steaming against my skin. "Faith, please don't."

Jess appears behind Ezekiel, staring at me through the mist. His wings expand on his back, blowing the scent of rose in my direction. I inhale a long breath through my nose and blink tears from my eyes. Jess says something I can't hear through the veil.

He lifts his hand pointing behind me and rushes forward, using his wings to thrust himself at me.

"Blood to blood from red to black. Stop her sight. Hold her back." Kristin's voice cuts through the sound of my heavy breathing, my heart pounding in overdrive, the sound of my world exploding around me.

The Veiled Realm blinks in and out of view, and Ezekiel tugs on my wrist, trying to pry my hand from my face.

"No," I whisper, struggling to break free.

"Faith, please. Just stop. Don't make me do this," Ezekiel says.

Jess lands next to me and locks his fingers around my free hand, but sparks erupt between us, sending him stumbling back.

"A demon's daughter bound to Hell, hear my words, hear my spell."

"Faith, please," Ezekiel begs. "Stop looking through the veil. Stop trying to leave me."

I summon power in my hands. "I can't stay. I'm sorry."

"Faith, we don't have to leave, okay? We can finish the conversation now. Just stop looking through the veil. Stop summoning power." Ezekiel's words burn through me, smoldering my heart, setting me ablaze. The fear in his voice wraps around me, restricting my ability to move.

I drop my hand from my eye and the Veiled Realm disappears. "I can't go tonight."

"You don't have a choice, Faith," Kristin says from behind me, surprising me. She locks her hand around my wrist and slices my palm without warning.

I yelp, stumbling back into Ezekiel's arms.

Kristin swipes the bloody blade across Ezekiel's outstretched palm. "From light to dark and dark to light, bind Faith's soul to the night."

My world blurs. "What are you doing?"

Ezekiel hugs me from behind. "I'm sorry, Faith. We can't risk him pulling you through the veil tonight."

"I won't. Just let me stay here," I beg, struggling to yank my hand free.

"Please, forgive me," he whispers.

The world flickers in and out of view, sending panic through my very essence. "A demon's fire and love's pure light, cut the link, suppress her fight."

My body slackens, my legs giving out on me though I know I should be able to stand. "Don't, Ezekiel."

"Trust me, Faith. It's going to be okay."

"It's not. You know you're putting me in a terrible position." My voice barely sounds above a whisper. The fight I had in me seconds ago washes away with Kristin's spell. It's like I'm being slowly lowered into gel, my whole body giving out on me.

"I'm not. You'll see." He sounds so certain, wrapped as tightly in his convictions as an angel.

"You're breaking my heart, Ezekiel. Please, don't go along with this. You said it yourself. I'll destroy the world for you." Pain expands in my chest with every beat. I've never felt so helpless in Ezekiel's arms in my life. Even when the world was falling apart around me, he kept me together. But now it's he who chips at my crumbling pieces, ripping them away faster and faster until the only thing left is my tainted soul, wrapped in the chains of his darkness.

He leans his head to mine like it'll somehow force his reason upon me. "Faith, you won't do such a thing. I meant you'd protect me if it came down to it. That's all."

I shake my head, even if he didn't mean it the way he did it doesn't change how I feel. "I can't be in this position. I can't be forced to make that choice."

"Faith."

"Ezekiel, I will destroy the world for you. I will! I know I will. So, I can't be with you here. Not if you're going to risk me having to make that choice."

Jerking my arm back, I elbow him hard enough that he loosens his hold on my hand. I cover my eye and peer through the veil, still struggling for Ezekiel to release me completely.

Jess's bright light casts beams of rainbow color through the Veiled Realm, and he grabs my arm to tug me away.

But Ezekiel grips me too tightly. If Jess pulls any harder, I'm sure they'll rip me apart.

"A demon's power you cannot fight, he will hold you in the night. Heaven's light will not win, shut him out, don't let him in."

"Jess, help me," I say, running my hand across his wing, looking for something to hold onto as Ezekiel rips me away.

The Veiled Realm disappears, and Ezekiel stumbles with me in his arms, taking the blunt force of the fall onto him. My stomach heaves from the struggle between Jess trying to rip me away from Ezekiel and through the veil.

Ezekiel sits up, gently lifting me in his arms instead of throwing me off him. The world spins again, and I groan, but thankfully don't puke all over the place, though I kind of wish I did because it'd buy me more time.

"Faith, are you crazy?" Kristin asks, closing the space between us. "We're not the bad guys. Have you forgotten that?"

Tears blur my eyes. "Then why does everything feel so wrong all the time?"

"It's not that things feel wrong." She turns to Ezekiel. "Lean her back."

"No," I whisper as the world flips.

Kristin stands above me with a glass vial in her hands. "What you're feeling is the shift Ezekiel went through. Hell doesn't feel good, I know, but it doesn't suddenly turn us into bad guys. We love you, Faith, and I need you to accept that the only thing different now is that Ezekiel doesn't hold Heaven's light. You need to control yourself and adjust before you let your emotions take over and make you do something you'll regret."

I squeeze my eyes shut. "That's not it and you know it."

Kristin runs her finger across my eyelid and then pries it open, forcing me to look at her. "It is. I don't care if that watcher swears your existence is bad for humanity. You're not. You're the best thing for it because things do need to change. That's how the world grows and thrives." Without warning, she pours the red liquid into my eyes, blurring my vision.

I scream, my eyes stinging. "Stop!"

The world turns dark as whatever Kristin did steals my vision away. I know my eyes are open, but all I see is the absence of light. It burrows deep into my heart, extinguishing the flames that burned for the people I care about. Now, I'm cold and empty. Destroyed. If they loved me like they claimed, they'd never do something as horrible as steal my sight and cut me off from the only person who gave me an ounce of hope. Because Kristin and Dad—Ezekiel—they leave me hopeless.

"I hate you," I whisper.

"Don't hate the spell caster," Kristin says. "Hate the demon who suggested it."

"Dad's going to—"

"Not him. Ezekiel."

Hot hands hold me tighter. "Forgive me, Faith."

I don't respond, his horrifying demonic act splitting through me in a way I never thought possible. "I'm not so sure I can."

13

STOLEN SIGHT

"FAITH, THIS ISN'T permanent," Kristin says, touching her cool hand to my cheek.

I don't answer her. Betrayal runs hot down my cheeks, my tears searing across my skin to drip onto my aching heart. Without my sight, I can't access the veil. Without access to the veil, I can't pray for divine intervention from Jess. I never thought I'd ask for it again, but I feel so lost and hopeless, trapped by the darkness of my stolen vision in a world I no longer trust to care for me.

Ezekiel shifts me in his arms, breathing his dark chocolate breath in my hair. From the sound of it, at least five hellhounds slink around somewhere nearby. A car door slams at the same time the whoosh of the door to a building, possibly a house, opens. Two sets of footsteps thud in my ears over the sound of Ezekiel breathing, Kristin's heart racing, and the rush of blood through my pounding head.

I clench my fingers, holding onto the single feather I accidentally pulled from Jess's wings, trying to summon him to break through the veil to find me. I've contemplated igniting power in my hands a dozen times to burn it, because I know the dangers of angel feathers in my dad's witch's hands, but I'm afraid if I do, I'll lose the last thing connecting me to Heaven.

"I was hoping it wouldn't come to this," Dad says, inhaling a small breath. His dress shoes crunch across the parking lot, growing in volume the closer he gets.

"Raphael, what's going on?" Cadence's voice cuts through the air, and I listen to her strut from the direction of the building. "What happened to Faith?"

I must look asleep as I hang helplessly in Ezekiel's arms, refusing to even hold on.

"Her new watcher threatens her wellbeing with his need to yank her through the veil. She's been through enough, and the only way to prevent this was to temporarily blind her." Dad touches my face. "She'll be fine come sunrise."

Cadence gasps, clicking her heels across the ground as she moves closer. "What? Are you kidding me? Look at her. Something else is clearly wrong."

Ezekiel tenses.

"Faith, Faith, can you hear me?" Cadence asks. Her footsteps stop. The subtle scent of her flowery perfume wafts through the air on a wave of her fear. "Why won't you let me go near her, Raphael? You must know how hard these last few weeks have been on me thinking the angelic army killed her. I need to see her for a second. Please."

"No," Ezekiel says, answering for Dad. "I don't trust you."

"Ezekiel," Cadence says.

Ezekiel shifts me, and Cadence gasps. The hum of his power buzzes in my ears.

Fear clenches my chest, and I suck in a breath and whisper, "Cadence, I don't want you to see me like this. Please, stay back. I'm fine."

I don't know if she believes my lie, but she doesn't persist, falling silent. I'm thankful she doesn't because I'm useless in this state, and I'm not sure even Dad could protect her from Ezekiel—my treacherous fallen angel, no longer holding the light I felt this morning. He closed himself off again, unable to withstand the pain he inflicts on me in his twisted way to keep me supposedly safe.

Growls, along with eerie howls, sneak into my head. Without having to see, I can hear the hellhounds, some in all their hellish glory and others still remaining in human form, as they slink in our direction.

Panic seeps through me. I can't even properly protect myself if I need to. I could accidentally hurt Cadence in the process. Kristin, too. I might be pissed at the witch, but I don't want her to get hurt.

"Faith, you're safe with me. I won't let anything happen to you," Ezekiel whispers. He's so in tune with my body language that he doesn't even have to read my mind.

"More than you've already done?" I ask.

He stiffens. "I'm sorry."

I tilt my head back toward the sky, imagining where the moon shines overhead. "You're not. You don't even care anymore. You shut yourself off from my humanity."

"I had to."

"You're a coward." Because he knows what he suggested was wrong. But Dad's beyond doing what I want and demonic protection comes at a price I never agreed to. It's sad that I'd rather risk my chances with the angelic army. They'd at least show me compassion. They'd suffer with me.

He intakes a sharp breath. "Maybe that's true, but I need a clear head right now, and if I open myself up, I'll drown in your darkness."

"I'm drowning in yours." It's turning all consuming. Ezekiel's darkness not only surrounds me, it drags me under farther and farther with no chance of ever finding light again.

"Faith, please," Ezekiel begs. "I want you to understand."

"I understand clearly. You're okay with hurting me as long as something falls in your favor and you think my suffering is worth it."

"I'd never. This is temporary, Faith."

Tears burn my dark vision. "To you. I'll never forget this.

I'll never trust you. You want eternity with me? This isn't the way."

"I—"

"Stop. Your demonic reasoning doesn't make a difference. I know you don't feel bad. You can't now. And if you can't handle my humanity, if you can't see how brutal you are as a demon, then you don't deserve my forgiveness." More tears drip down my cheeks. "You don't deserve to care for my soul. Because what's the point?"

"Don't say that," he whispers. "I love you."

I ignite power in my free hand not holding Jess's feather. "And you don't get to say that." Shoving my energy orb at him, I give him no choice but to drop me. Except I don't land on the asphalt. I land in another pair of hot arms.

"She's going to make a pretty little demon one day," a gruff, masculine voice says in my ear. I stiffen in Drake's arms, terror cascading over me. "And hopefully a good ally to have."

"Oh, God," I whisper. "Please, set me down."

"From what I've heard, darlin', Heaven can't find you, which means no one can hear you," he says. "I didn't expect that type of language to come from a demon's daughter's mouth."

"Drake," Dad says, his voice commanding attention. "Do as she says or there will be no deal."

"You should thank me for catching her," he retorts.

Power buzzes through the air, and I can almost feel the heat from both Ezekiel's and Dad's power.

Drake shifts me and sets me on my feet, giving me a little push. I stumble, flailing my arms out, and release a scream loud enough to make both Cadence and Kristin gasp. Someone grabs the back of my gown, stopping me from spilling onto the ground.

I jerk my arm back, elbowing Dad in the stomach. Summoning more power, I hold it up, spinning around, listening for anything identifiable to give me some sort of sense of direction.

"Faith, calm down before you hurt someone," Dad says.

I thrash my head back and forth. "Stay back. I need everyone to stay back."

The soft taps of Ezekiel's shoes close in on me, but he's not charging. He cautiously steps one foot at a time toward me, knowing I'll attack if he tries to restrain me again. I cover my eye with my hand, still clutching the feather in my fingers despite my inability to see.

"Jess," I say. "Help me. I don't want to be here."

I shudder, a cool sensation crossing my skin. I swear I smell the faint scent of rose, but I know I'm still on the Earth plane. I think even without seeing things with my vision, the veil thins for me.

"What's in her hand?" Kristin asks from somewhere to my right.

Dad growls. "Is that a—"

"Stop her!" Kristin screams. "The feather connects her to her watcher."

Howls erupt through the air, digging into my head. The world hums with power. With a dozen strange scents. Too many sounds to keep track of except for...

"Jess," I whisper. The sound of silk rubbing silk, the whisper of feathers, drifts through the noise consuming me.

"Faith, please. Don't leave me," Ezekiel says.

His hot hand latches onto my arm the same time cool fingers touch my shoulders. The world spins around me, turning from dark to light to dark again, and I fall forward, turning to land on my back because I'm too afraid to remove my hands from my eyes.

Silence falls upon me, and I release a breath.

"Jess," I whisper again. "Are you here?"

A gust of wind blows the strands of hair from my face. "I'm here."

Cool fingers touch the backs of my hands, gently tugging my fingers from my face. I heave a breath, my stomach twisting, and he rolls me over while I adjust to the sudden shift between worlds. He rubs his hand between my shoulder blades, pushing away the shudder rolling through me as I release a sob.

I groan, sniffling. "I lost him, Jess."

"Come here," he says, grasping my hand, pulling me from the ground and into his lap. He smears my tears away with his fingers, and I blink, staring into his golden eyes.

I bring my hand up and touch his face. "I can see again."

His lips twist in a grimace. "Oh, Faith. They didn't."

"They couldn't steal your sight so they went with the second best thing by blinding me." I blink more oncoming tears away. "Why did I expect more from them?"

"Because you know they're capable of better," he says.

I sigh, rubbing my hands across my cheeks. "I hate this."

"I know."

The pain in my chest makes me release another sob. "It kills me."

His feathers encase us. "I know that, too."

"I don't want to go back."

"Now, you're lying."

I sigh, shifting in his arms to pull myself away. "You say that like you want me to go back."

"Well, not right this second. But—"

"Blood to blood from dark to light, thin the veil and give me sight. Heaven's Traitor with the soul, summon Faith, make her whole." My skin buzzes, Kristin's voice drifting through me.

"Oh, no," I whisper.

Jess slides his fingers through mine. "A summoning spell."

"A demon's daughter, bound to Hell, hear my words, hear my spell. Use the light to beat the dark, feel his power, feel his mark. A rush of heat, light your skin, thin the veil, let him in."

The edges of my vision darken, fading the Veiled Realm around me. Jess pulls me back to him, unfurling his wings to wrap them around us like he can somehow protect me from Kristin's summons. But something's different. I'm not forced to move from my spot. I'm not dragged through the veil. But something burns across my chest, sliding up my throat, to bloom in my face.

"Faith." Ezekiel's whispers tickle my ears over Jess's soft breath. "Please, let me see you. I know you're here."

"You can fight it, Faith. Just hang on," Jess says.

But I can't. The mist fogs the air, blurring the world around me. And then Jess's light fades.

Ezekiel's darkness shadows over my vision.

Our darkness consumes me.

A hot hand cups my face, brushing strands of hair out of my eyes. "Please, help me. I'm losing myself. I'm losing Faith. I've lost sight of my purpose. This isn't me."

I've never heard a demon pray before.

Fluttering my eyes open, I stare at Ezekiel's pouty face as he looks at the glittering stars above us in a world of his making. I've been summoned by Kristin, but instead of being ripped from the Veiled Realm, I've been tugged into the one place I've always felt safest, entangled in Ezekiel's very being.

A tear drips from his dark lashes and splashes across my face. My breath catches, my own eyes welling up with tears, because in this moment, Ezekiel is the angel I fell in love with despite his missing wings.

I reach up to wipe the glittering trail away with my finger. "You're not losing yourself, Ezekiel. You're still very much you."

He cups his hand over mine, pressing my fingers into his face. "But I'm not. You were right about my darkness. It's extinguished all the light I used to feel inside me. And without the light, things aren't so clear."

"You still carry light. It's just different now, but you can't see that because you've turned your back." I shift up in his lap to face him. "And I'm standing behind you, staring at this achingly beautiful light that warms me unlike anything in the universe, screaming at you to face me, but you're too scared to look."

"Because I'm afraid of what my shadow does to you, Faith," he whispers. "Look at what I did to you tonight. You gave me every beautiful, soulful, incredible part of you, and I ruined it. Even if you manage to forgive me, I can't promise you something like that won't happen again. I'm a demon. I have Hell coursing through my veins."

"As do I, Ezekiel," I say. "I know what it's like. I've seen my demon self."

"It's not so bad, Faith."

"And neither are you. Even Jess thinks there's still something good in you—"

He groans. "Jesaiah stole everything from me without giving me a chance. He's stolen you, Faith. You know how crazy that makes me? I can sense him now. His light reflects off you. It hurts me and not just physically."

His jealousy snakes around my chest, squeezing the breath from me. How can I even blame him? If our roles were reversed, I'm sure I'd want to blast Jess away as well. I still want to sometimes.

"He's manipulating you. You see that, right?" Ezekiel adds. "All angels do it. They can't force you to do things against your freewill, but they'll do whatever they can to sway you in the direction they want."

I can't deny it. I've been played with by angels as they use my humanity against me. The idea has been ingrained in my thoughts for years by Dad. Even Ezekiel did it as an angel, but it's different. Angels have a lot to fight against with how strong Hell is. And it's not like demons aren't manipulators. They're better at it. Better at negotiating. Better at turning things in their favor. Like with whatever Dad is doing with the hellhounds. Dad's power derives from his ability to align with those who benefit him. But if it came down to it, and he was face-to-face with an army of angels, he'd put up a helluva fight, but in the end, he'd probably lose.

Dad can't rule the world, but he can help someone else to. Always the right hand.

I grip the front of his tuxedo shirt between my fingers, absently playing with the fabric. "I know Jess is. He's not my first watcher, Ezekiel, and he's not a bad guy."

"The wings make it obvious, but he's still not someone you should entrust your well-being to."

I sigh and rub my hands on his shoulders. I'll get nowhere defending an angel I'm not even sure deserves it. "Ezekiel, I'm tired. I don't want to do this right now. Whatever I say, you won't agree with me."

"Just come back to me, please," he says. "Kristin broke the

spell already. The hellhounds will wait another night."

Wait another night for what? As much as I want to ask, I'm also terrified of finding out. Drake commented on my descent toward a demonic eternity, but Dad wouldn't do something so rash without a vessel, would he? Of course he would. "I'm sorry, Ezekiel. I can't."

"Why not?"

I release the front of his shirt and peer at the button I unfastened. "You know why."

"But I need you."

I pull myself away from him. He reaches out and laces our fingers together, not letting me get far. It takes everything in me not to fall into his familiarity. This small piece of Ezekiel doesn't reflect the demon he's hardened into outside of this private world. Here, he's touching my humanity—mingling with my soul. The moment I wake up and return to him in reality, he'll remain closed off behind the fiery armor I can barely crack without hurting my heart in the process.

"And I need you. Like this. Always," I say.

He grimaces, spinning away from me, and links his fingers on the back of his neck. "Faith, I know what you want, but I can't open myself up like this all the time. Raphael has kept you so far removed from demonic affairs that I don't think you realize the danger I face for showing any signs of weakness. I might have fought for an eternity on Earth against Heaven's warriors, but I have to stay on guard and continue to fight if I want to keep my place. And I will do what it takes to assure you don't end up in Hell by my doing. So please, understand."

But I can't. Dad manages. He always has. "Dad siphons my humanity. It makes him stronger."

Ezekiel takes a few steps away, putting more space between us. "Filtered through demonic blood. We're different."

I fold my arms across my chest. "Then I guess I'll see you through the veil at dawn. I can't handle being thrown in the middle of demonic affairs."

"Faith."

Fury laces around me, winding so tightly my vision shadows. A dozen thoughts cross through my mind, reminding me of the position Ezekiel put me in. "I can't do this! What you had Kristin do was—"

"Unforgivable. I know. I'm not going to give you an excuse, either. But I hope you come around. I never thought our eternity together would turn to this, staring at each other through a veil because of how toxic I am as a demon."

I can't stand this. My soul splits at the seams in front of me as I rip Ezekiel apart. I've wanted my soul back so desperately, but looking at him now, feeling everything he's experiencing as if I'm experiencing it too, snuffs out my longing. Because without my soul, he will cause irreparable damage to the world. But if he keeps it, he'll cause irreparable damage to me.

The universe must hate my existence.

If I give up on Ezekiel, I'll hate it more.

I open my mouth to respond to him, to come up with something more to say, but he disappears from view, abandoning me to turn back into the demon he prefers to stay as—unfeeling, unaffected, forged from Hell.

The world around me clouds with cool mist, and I blink, suddenly back in Jess's arms, encompassed within his brilliant white wings. He offers me a weak smile, knowing the last thing I want is to smile when I'm losing Ezekiel, and he's losing me.

"I don't know how to get through all his fire without it consuming me in the process," I say.

"How do you handle your dad, Faith?"

"Like a demon."

"I think that's where you'll find your answers," he says.

I hate to admit he might be right. I've been trying to get through to Ezekiel using my humanity, but I can't use something he clearly struggles with. Something that reminds him of everything the universe ripped from us.

I need to charge right into his fire and let it set our world ablaze.

And I know exactly how to.

I'm going to make a deal he can't refuse.

At least I hope.

Moral Support

STARING AT JESS'S outstretched hand, I watch the fluff of the feather in his palm flow in the breeze created by his beautiful wings. He raises his eyebrows, his golden eyes catching the last beams of moonlight as it sinks into the horizon.

"I can't take it," I say, wringing my fingers together.

He grabs my wrist, rubs his finger across my skin until I open my hand, and then sets the feather in my palm. He smiles, curling my fingers around what feels like a grenade in this moment. I've collected dozens of angel feathers over the years, but I've never held onto them. I had always felt the need to destroy them because Dad hated any traces of Heaven floating around.

But I had no idea that a single feather in the wrong hands could be used against an angel, or how it could save me in a moment I needed divine intervention.

"It's just a feather, Faith," he says, eyeing me so intently I keep my gaze trained at the ground.

"That Kristin could use against you," I say. "Not to mention holding it somehow allowed you to portal me through the veil."

He purses his lips. "That was all you. You thinned the veil on your own and my feathers had nothing to do with it."

"Kristin acted like it did."

He shrugs. "She freaked out because you used my feather to concentrate on me in your mind's eye. That's all. Objects aren't magical on their own. You used it to focus on your own ability even without sight. Your power far exceeded my expectation to be honest. Probably hers, too."

Even if that's true, I still don't like it. "So, if it's useless, why give it to me?"

"An angelic reminder when you need it. Unless you'll get Kristin to break the spell, you could use a little light. Think of it as moral support," he says, smiling.

I roll my eyes. "What I'm about to do has nothing to do with morals."

Reaching out, he messes up my already tousled hair. "It has everything to do with them. Now, be careful, Demon Tamer. Remember not to leave anything open for interpretation."

Who knew an angel would go along with a demonic deal? "I heard Dad negotiate thousands upon thousands of deals over the years. I can manage one little one with my boyfriend. It's not like I have my soul to lose or anything."

"Your heart is pretty important, too," Jess says.

"It's a good thing mine is made from my dad's. Otherwise..."

I let my words trail off as the veil thins around us. Jess disappears the exact moment Ezekiel appears in front of me through the veil long enough to run his fingers across my cheek before the Veiled Realm spits me out into the Earth plane and pulls him into the daylight prison realm for the day.

Bright sunshine glows from the east, turning the purple sky blue with hints of gold on the lazy clouds drifting over the ocean. Waves crest toward shore, and my bare feet sink into the powdery sand.

I inhale a cool breath of the morning sea breeze and spin around. The empty beach greets me, reminding me of the home I dearly miss back in Moonlight Shores. But instead of my beach fortress of steel, concrete, and bulletproof glass, a looming hotel cuts a shadow across the beach, hiding the morning sun.

Without Kristin hovering nearby to act as my babysitter, I meander forward toward the water to stroll along the waves. I know better than to wander in an unfamiliar area without the protection of my witch, especially with the presence of local hellhounds tainting the day in their Hell-bound werewolf forms, but I haven't had a moment alone in the open outside of unpickable locks for a while.

And I desperately need some freedom to do something familiar that doesn't involve spells or demons, angels even.

Sauntering down the beach a bit farther, I head toward the path that'll take me into the small downtown area in the center of town. Dread washes over me as I enter the sidewalk in front of a small stretch of stores, because unlike in Moonlight Shores where humans lived and went about their days in blissful ignorance, this town seems nearly abandoned. Haunted even.

A howl rips through the air, and a wolf darts from the shadows to stop on the sidewalk in front of me. Its hackles rise on its back as it bares its teeth with foam dripping from its jowls. Seeing a wolf right in the center of town out in the open sends panic crashing over me.

I summon power and cup it up in my hands. "Stay back or I'll melt your face off."

"Better think twice about what you plan to do next, Faith."

I spin around to face Drake in all his vomit-inducing glory. If I didn't think an entire pack of werewolves would jet from the shadows to tear me apart, I'd thrust my power at him until he turned into a pile of guts on the ground.

"And you better stay away from me," I snap.

"Didn't your daddy tell you downtown is off limits? This is Sunrise Cove pack territory and you need my permission to be here."

Taking a breath, I snuff out my power and turn away from him. "Fine, whatever. I'll go back to the hotel."

A warm hand grips onto my shoulder, twirling me around. "All you have to do is ask."

Dozens of responses flit through my mind—from screaming at him that I'll never resort to begging him for permission or flipping him off while shooting demonic power at his boots—but instead, my mind pleads for me to play nice because I'm not in the mood to risk my life again or in the mood to return to the room where I'll die of boredom.

"May I please stay and explore town? I promise not to cause any trouble." My voice comes out sweeter than I expected it to, but it does the trick.

Drake's narrowed eyes soften, and he smirks. "See? That wasn't so hard." He rocks on his heels and shoves his hands into the front pockets of his jeans. "And yes, you're welcome to roam until sunset."

I twist my lips to the side, studying the man who was hell-bent on using me to get Dad to comply, who now seems to be coating his nicety on thick enough to make my stomach roll like at the restaurant where I first saw him in his human form. Raising my hand to my eye, I peer at Drake as he morphs between werewolf and hellhound through the veil, his inner beast revealing itself to me.

"Thank you," I say, dropping my hand back to my side before Dad or Ezekiel confronts me. There really isn't any hiding from them. Even if they can't see me unless I thin the veil, they can sense my presence.

Drake nods. "I'll see you tonight, kid. Maybe this time

you'll listen to your dad like a good little girl so we can get this truce in place."

He struts away, his words digging under my skin to open up a wave of fire to explode from me. Without thinking, I charge after the hellhound and snatch the back of his shirt to pull him back. Swinging his arm, he nearly elbows me in the stomach, but I let go and scramble out of the way.

I summon more power. "What do you mean a truce? I thought Dad was negotiating some sort of deal."

Straightening his shoulders, he puffs out his chest. "Not your father. Your boyfriend. You're lucky he makes some valid points or you'd all be spending the rest of your days in Hell." He says it like he could possibly make that happen. He's the one who sought me out to help him.

Instead of pointing it out, I narrow my eyes. "Like what?"

He releases an annoyed growl in his throat. "Why don't you go enjoy your day and let the rest of us worry about the night? Raphael made it clear you're not to be involved due to those damn featherheads taking an interest in your life."

"Seriously?"

"It's a demonic affair, Faith, and until you let that pretty demon inside you out, the terms of the truce are clear."

I toss my power near his feet, my vision turning red. "That's not happening. Stop saying it like it is."

Drake raises his arms up. "Don't blast the messenger. You're low on allies during daylight hours unless you plan on smashing through that veil again, which I'm told will bring more attention from the angelic army. The last thing I need is the damn alliance acting as if they control the world like you made them do back in Desertville. Ruined my damn home."

I hate seeing reason in his words, but an ally? Never. No way. "*You* ruined your home."

He snarls. "I'll get it back. Raphael guarantees it."

"How?"

"Like I said, demonic affairs."

I open my mouth to argue, but howls from an alleyway don't give me the chance. Drake nods once to me and leaves me standing outside what used to be an old diner according to the sign. Now only an abandoned building with wood boards over the windows remains. Another beautiful town ruined at the hands of Hell beasts.

My mind whirls with the little information he gave me, and a sinking feeling settles in my stomach. After everything I've gone through, after everyone I've lost, I hate to believe Dad—or Kristin for that matter—would finish whatever Mary had started. An action so vile would have dire consequences. I've managed to assign excuse after excuse to my dad's demonic behavior—I have to if I'm to live with myself—but something like that is unforgivable.

But I don't think he realizes it.

He's going to now after I have a word with him.

Covering my eye with my hand, I peer through the veil into the sunlight realm, searching around while strolling back toward the Sunset Cliffs Plaza. The gnarled trees scatter around the desert landscape along the onyx path, and I pass a house where flaming hellhounds on the other side of the veil sit in the front yard at the feet of the werewolves watching me on the Earth plane. I probably look like a weirdo, shuffling along with one hand over my face, but I dare someone to mention it.

A shadow casts on the dry brush next to me, and I jerk my attention to Ezekiel. With how the veil mutes the world, I had no idea he had been following me. He's probably been near all along since the beach, watching me like he always has, except now instead of behind an angelic shield, he's just beyond the veil.

Picking up pace, he stands in front of me, walking backwards. "You should be at the hotel." Staring at his pouty lips saying the words without hearing them clearly makes me give him all my undivided attention, but I don't stop walking. He's not who I'm on a mission to find.

"Where's my dad?" I ask, pushing against the veil when he slows. My skin buzzes as our presences touch, teasing each other without being able to actually feel.

"Business," Ezekiel says.

"But you're not there," I say.

He stops completely, and I press harder into him. My whole body buzzes with a welcomed heat that rushes from the tattooed feather on my chest to my stomach and down my legs. If I push any harder, I'm afraid I'll walk right through the veil. And right now? Being in a world purely made for demons isn't where I want to be. Seeing my possible future step out of my body in all its demonic, soulless-eyed magnificence really messes with my head.

"His demonic affairs aren't mine."

I cross my arms. "But yours are his?"

He tips his chin down, staring at me intently, trying to capture me in his gaze. "Faith."

I don't let him. "You know, you don't have to do whatever my dad says. I talked to Drake and—"

Fire flashes in Ezekiel's eyes. "If he breached our con—"

I tap his mouth through the veil, stopping him from finishing his sentence. Standing on my tiptoes, I lean closer and into his face, holding his dark gaze. "He didn't tell me anything, but don't think I won't try to blast it out of him when there aren't dozens of hellhounds waiting to rip me to shreds."

A smile crinkles his eyes in the corners, and I drop my hand from his mouth to see it light up his face. I can't help myself. Smiles are so rare that when they happen, I have to brand it into my mind to remember Ezekiel's capable of more than piercing my very being with serious intensity.

He closes the distance, surprising me with a whisper of a kiss. My lips hum with static, the shock sending warmth through me. "I'd like to see that," he says. His eyes darken but still manage to shine. "Prove Raphael wrong."

"What's that supposed to mean?"

"He has the hellhounds convinced you're harmless—acting out as a form of rebellion. But I know you, Faith. Better than your father."

"Then why don't you tell him what's going on with me?"

"My demonic affairs aren't always Raphael's despite what you think." He sucks in his bottom lip between his teeth, his gaze making my heart race. "And you won't always be his devoted daughter. You're more. Kristin sees it. I see it. That bastard watcher of yours sees it. And I'm going to be the one here for you when you're not."

"Ezekiel," I whisper. It's hard to separate my feelings for him, especially when he says things like this. But he's not saying them out of love. His words come from a darker place cut off from my humanity.

He touches my face through the veil. "What is it? You don't believe me? You know I still have never lied to you."

"Only refrained from telling me anything at all." Before I can lower my guard and accept his excuses, I step around him and dash in the direction of the hotel, the world zooming by me, flashing between Earth and the daylight prison realm.

I'm so concerned about returning to my prison of a hotel room, hiding away behind walls that will supposedly protect me, that I don't see the curb in the Earth realm. I stumble forward and flip on my back. The air whooshes from my lungs, and I gasp a breath. A figure stands over me, blocking the sun from view. Wings expand out, shading my face, and Jess stands above me in the daylight realm.

"If you drop your hand, he can't bother you, remember," Jess says. "I'm going to assume you failed to negotiate a deal."

I groan. "I didn't even try."

"Why not?"

"I ran into Drake and he—" I snap my mouth shut. "No way. I'm not spilling my soul to you." Angels make it extremely easy to talk to them, and despite Jess's friendliness and company, I haven't forgotten who he is. The last thing I need is to drag Ezekiel and Dad into the heavenly light of the angelic army to broadcast the trouble they're getting themselves into.

Jess frowns. "How many times do I have to tell you that you can trust me? I technically never leave your side. I can't make a phone call or anything to give anyone a head's up of the mess Heaven's two traitors are making."

"I'm sure you would if you found out they...never mind. You'd love it if I accidentally said too much." I offer a fake smile. "Now, if you'd excuse me, I have a demonic dad I need to share a piece of my mind with."

"And a fast approaching boyfriend who'll stop you the moment I lower my shield," Jess says.

I get to my feet, and he dusts off my arms like he could really touch me through the veil and pokes my nose. I bat his hand away, making him step back.

"Then I better hurry," I say, peeking behind me. Ezekiel peers around the area, stopping next to me though he can't see me.

"Or I can follow you," Jess says.

I sigh. I think he'd follow me regardless, so at least I can take advantage of what Dad calls an angel's most annoying talent. "Fine, but I swear on unholy Hell if you try anything stupid or open your mouth, I'll burn that ugly shirt off your back."

"You'd like that, wouldn't you?"

I smirk, giving him a once over, zoning in on his stomach. I bet he has abs like Ezekiel considering he's Super Angel. "Very much for several reasons."

He laughs, shaking his head back and forth. A slight blush warms his cheeks, sending another bout of uncontrollable giggles from me. Stupid blushing angels. I can't help that embarrassing an angel happens to be on my list of favorite things to do, and it's been forever since I've poked fun at anyone's purity.

"I flew right into that one," he says, nudging me to walk next to him with his wing.

We stroll together the rest of the way to the hill where the hotel looms in the Earth realm. Peering behind me, I glance at Ezekiel as he gives up on following whatever presence he feels of me. He sits at the base of the hill, leaning back on his arms to stare at the hazy air.

"And I thought Heaven's Traitors did everything together."

I lift and drop my shoulders. "The only thing they have in common apart from falling from grace is me. Luckily for me, they're not suddenly best friends forever. Dad holds a grudge against Ezekiel for the whole soul thing, and Ezekiel holds a grudge against Dad for—well, everything else."

"Must be awkward," he says.

"What's awkward is hanging out with the angel who severed the wings on my boyfriend's back."

"You're never going to forgive me for that." It's not a question.

I peek at him in my peripheral vision. "Never. Some things are unforgivable."

"I don't believe that."

"I hope it eats away at you that I do."

"Such a demon-tainted mouth."

"You say that like an insult."

Jess freezes in his tracks, jerking out his hand to stop me in place. His feathers ruffle, and he drags me toward the closest twisted tree, nearly pressing me into the trunk. Closing my eyes, I concentrate on the veil, pushing away the hum of Earth noises to focus on whatever caused Jess to stop and hide. After breaking it so many times, it's become easier and easier to listen through if I concentrate hard enough.

"What are you doing?" I ask. "Demons can't see you."

He motions for me to lean forward and presses his lips to the veil near my ear. "But angels can."

The hum of his lips to the veil sends a shiver through me, and I step back and cross my arms. "Angels? What are they doing here, and why are you hiding from them? Doesn't that break angelic law or something?"

He expands and retracts his wings, making them disappear. "It's complicated."

"I can follow."

He turns his gaze from the trees to me. "I can't lie to you so I'm not going to say anything at all."

I shove my hand into his chest, the force enough to knock

him back through the veil. "You're such a hypocrite accusing Ezekiel of doing the same thing by hiding me from the angelic army. This is why I'm not telling you anything."

He raises his hand to my mouth. "It's not the angelic army. Now be quiet."

"The angel can hear me?"

Opening and closing his mouth, he struggles to form words. "I don't know. I only know I can see you because you're my charge, and I felt your soul in Ezekiel. I basically have a two for one deal with you two, but I'd really prefer to only have you."

I ignore his jab at Ezekiel. "What would happen if they see me?"

More silence. He has no idea. And why would he? Angels fly blind, following whatever their angelic instincts tell them. If there was a handbook, I'm sure Ezekiel might have broken fewer rules—but maybe not.

"Are you sure you have it under control?" a familiar voice rings through the air, drawing me away from Jess. Panic rushes through me, and for a second I think I've crossed through the veil, but I realize Cami's raising her voice. "I do not want to deal with another disaster. I have enough problems as it is with people gathering."

"Don't forget the alliance," another familiar masculine voice says.

"And the alliance is basically threatening to start a war on demons again. You know what'll happen if they do. It took years for them to rebuild. So, I need you to tell me if you really have the hellhounds under control, Raphael."

"You have my word, Cami. They are falling into line as expected."

Jess grabs my hand, stopping me in place. "Don't, Demon Tamer."

I tug away and stroll right through the gnarled roots toward the black onyx path winding through the trees. A mixture of emotions collides through me, starting a war with my insides, at the sight of Cami with her own Demon Watcher. Zach's black wings remain hidden from sight, and I never thought I'd be thankful for that. With Jess, it's easier, his wings a stark contrast to Ezekiel's.

"I hope so," Cami says. From my position, I get a direct view of her flawless face framed with chocolate curls that glitter in the sunlight overhead. Her emerald eyes sheen over for a second before she blinks and says, "You've been distant the last few weeks, and rightfully so, but if there's one thing I've learned from life is that the world never stops no matter if you need it to."

Heaven still hasn't told her, and from the sorrow clouding Zach's face, he doesn't know, either. Somehow, Dad managed to stop Cadence from cluing them in on my supposed miraculous resurrection. But it still leaves me wondering why. Cami walks the fragile line between Heaven and Hell, maintaining the balance. She doesn't pick sides often, trying to keep everyone working together.

Maybe the world wants to protect her. She'd deserve it. If only I could figure out how to get the universe to protect me. But I doubt it'd protect someone who could destroy it.

Dad reaches out and touches Cami's shoulder, surprising me with an act of comfort. "What you feel is distance is me keeping busy, Cami. I assure you everything's under control. I'm quite familiar with hellhounds, and there will be no need for the alliance or angelic assistance."

She nods. "If there are any problems, you'll call me, right? The last thing I want is to send entire packs to Hell, but if they want to roam the night, they must abide by the rules. No exceptions."

"No exceptions," Dad repeats.

"Good." She puffs a breath of air through her lips, blowing a curl from her face. "Now, if you'll excuse me, I have a long flight ahead of me. Tell Cadence I'll call her as soon as I can. And you better keep her safe or I'll—"

"She's perfectly safe and happy, enjoying her day in the honeymoon suite of the best hotel in Sunrise Cove," Dad says.

"The honeymoon suite, huh?" Zach says with raised brows. "I can hear Aston Dubois now. He'll accuse you of attempting to conceive another child if he were to ever find out."

Cami groans. "I swear, Raphael if you—"

Dad chuckles, one of the first times I've heard him laugh in weeks. "Don't worry, my queen. Like you said, I've been distant. I'm only trying to make it up to my little huntress so she doesn't rip my heart out."

"She still might. So you be careful, too." Cami laughs and hugs my dad before hopping into Zach's outstretched arms. A gust of jasmine-scented air wafts through the veil to me. I stare at the hazy brown sky, watching the silhouette of wings block the sun and then disappear.

"You should be in your room, Faith." Dad seemingly materializes in front of me, startling me. I rock on my feet, nearly falling back onto the sidewalk. Jess must be upset I ignored his pleas and got as close as I did because he pushed me out of his angelic shield.

"That's really the first thing you're going to say to me after last night?" I ask, sucking in a breath.

His jaw tightens. "Yes."

Power erupts in my fingers, glowing orange through the veil as my inner demon peeks through, thriving on the heated emotions Dad pulls from me. I shouldn't expect anything more from him in this realm, but even if he can't feel anything, he knows what he did to me.

I tense, readying myself to chuck my power at him, but a cool hand touches mine, Jess appearing next to me, still hidden by his shield. His simple touch sets me off like he doused me with a bucket of ice water, cooling the heat in my veins. Now I'm drowning, struggling to breathe.

"Faith, drop your hand," he whispers. "I'm begging you. You're too upset."

Tears burn my eyes, and I turn away from Dad, but I can't drop my hand. It's like some otherworldly force holds it in place, forcing me to confront my personal demon manifested in front of me in a man who's changing before my eyes—or maybe this is how he's always been and I was too blind to see. Too immersed in good grace to realize who he truly is as a demon.

"Do you remember what you promised me the first day I met you?" I ask, keeping my back turned, knowing he might not hear me. "You said you'd always protect me and keep me safe. But you're failing. You don't feel like the man who told me he was my dad."

Dad's shadow moves, and his shiny shoes stop in front of my bare feet. "I haven't changed, Faith. I'm still your father, and I'm doing everything to protect you. But you have to understand how difficult a task it is when you're fighting me every step of the way."

I roll my eyes, releasing a strangled laugh. "Of course you blame me. Because I'm the rebellious daughter who needs to get whatever you think I have in my system out. But you know what? I'm not a little girl, and I'm not going to be the perfect demon's daughter. Not when you treat me as what I really am to you—a vessel. A possession."

"You're not only those things," Dad says, touching my chin to get me to look at him. "You think I like being in this position? Making these kinds of decisions for you? I don't. But you don't get it. Your eternity is at risk. Hell, Faith. Hell. I fought to stay on this plane for a reason. You will not pay for my sins that way."

"You keep saying that, but I don't believe you. You're still using me. Like whatever the Hell truce you have with the hell-hounds," I say, more anger flooding through me. "I don't understand. You have Heaven to help with them. You're powerful. We're no longer pushed into a corner, facing a deadly pack. We don't have to go through with whatever it is you want."

Dad reaches out and slaps his hand across my mouth, sending a shock through my lips. "Not here."

"Afraid of divine intervention?" I ask, automatically summoning power.

Dad's jaw clenches. "Faith, I mean it."

I shake my head. "You don't get to tell me what I can and can't say. If I want to shout to the universe you're making some kind of deal with Drake and his pack, I will."

Dad ignites his own power in his hand. "Faith!"

A cold hand pinches my shoulder, yanking me back. "Drop your hand, Faith. I mean it."

I stretch my arm back to throw power at Dad.

"Do it or I'll rip you through," Jess says.

I don't. I release my power at Dad in one huge burst. Hands shove me from behind, and I fall forward, the world spinning around me, sending shadows across my vision. Pain twists my stomach, and I scream, curling my knees to my chest. A figure jerks above me, swaying smoldering arms over its head in a slow dance. Two white eyes stare at me from my own burning face.

I scream again.

The world turns white.

DEMONIC INTERVENTION

LIGHT FOOTSTEPS DRIFT to my ears. "Whoa, what happened to her? Is she okay?"

"Pick her up. We need to take her inside to Kristin," another voice says.

"This is messed up," a third voice says. "Twice this week we've found her looking like she was on the verge of death. I can't believe Ezekiel lets this kind of thing happen."

"Shut up. She might hear you." It's Greg. The rogue wolf pack's voices pull me from the world of light, and my eyelids turn red.

Lola releases a soft growl. "She should. She needs a demonic intervention."

Cool hands dig under my back, and the world shifts as unfamiliar arms lift me to my feet. I've never been picked up by one of Kristin's familiars before. They're also cautious around me, especially now that Ezekiel has fallen.

"Faith? Can you hear me?" Calvin asks, his warm breath tickling the side of my face as he leans close, probably listening to me breathe.

I swallow, my throat burning, my stomach still reeling from Jess yanking me through the veil before I could break it and then shoving me right back out. I'm afraid if I open my eyes, I'll throw up whatever evil twists through my insides.

"She's regaining consciousness," Greg says, his looming presence shading me from the light overhead. "Hey, Faith? Can you open your eyes for me?"

I don't right away. Opening my eyes will jumpstart my world again. Cami was right about the world continuing to spin when all I want is for it to stop. If I could get a moment to think, to make a plan without having to worry about everyone else's plans, I could fix the things people are constantly breaking for me.

"Come on, Faith. Tell us you're okay."

Slowly, I flutter my eyelids and meet the concerned gazes of the rogue pack. Lola takes my hand in hers and squeezes my fingers. Calvin shifts me in his arms, letting me rest my head against his chest. Greg peers around the beach, tense and ready to fight at any sign of threat.

"You shouldn't be here," I whisper. "It's not safe. Drake,

he—"

Calvin chuckles, the light tone of his voice poking at the darkness threatening me. "We find her half drowned on the beach, and here she is worrying about us. Heaven really messed up with her."

Lola jerks our clasped hands and hits Calvin on the shoulder. "We're not supposed to talk about that. You want me to go buy a muzzle?"

Greg releases a low growl. "Knock it off, you two." He steps closer, tilting his head to search my face. "Faith, you don't have to worry about us. We're only stopping by to pick up a new pack mate."

I blink a few times. "Malik?" I've been through so much that I hadn't thought about the last remaining wolf from the Traitor Pack that I found in the Sunrise Cove pack's breaking room.

He nods. "You know him?"

A sob wracks my chest, and I can't stop the strangled cry from coming out of my mouth. This tiny moment of light sets me off. I didn't know how much I needed to hear that someone is finally escaping the damage of my life—limping and hurt but at least alive.

I tip my head back. "Thank God."

"No, you should thank your father," Kristin says, her voice sounding from behind me. "He's agreed to release Malik from his contract early come dawn."

"He did?" That doesn't sound right. Dad never breaks contracts from the goodness of his heart—and now? I can't find much good left in him.

Calvin turns me toward Kristin, and she motions for him to bring me closer. "Is that so hard to believe?"

"Yes." My stomach convulses at the jostling movement, and I breathe through the pain. At least I haven't puked on Calvin, though it's not like he hasn't experienced my grossness before. He did help Kristin with my poisoned skin.

Kristin presses her lips into a line. "Come on, everyone inside. We have things to do before sunset."

Bucking my legs, I surprise Calvin from my jerking, and he drops me on the sand. I launch to my feet, not giving anyone a chance to move. Hot power erupts in my palms, and I cup it between my hands, my fingers shaking from nerves and anger.

"I'm not helping you with anything, Kristin." I'm still so upset that she even agreed to perform a spell against me like that.

She steps forward, and I thrust power at her feet, making her freeze.

I burn her a look, my inner demon probably shining fire in my eyes. "I mean it."

Narrowing her gaze, she reaches into the bag that never leaves her side and pulls out her ivory dagger. I expect her to rush me to cut my palm, to spill my blood to cast another spell to keep me in control, but all she does is flip it in her hand and aim the hilt at me.

I stare at the jewels on the dagger in the sunlight. "I'm not participating in any more spells."

She waves the athame. "Just take it. It'll assure you that I won't make you. I've had a lot of time to think about last night, and you're as right to hate me as you are everyone else. I'm not going to excuse my actions, but I do want you to know how sorry I am for betraying your trust. I just—it's easy to get wrapped up in darkness because the light reveals how awful things truly are. But, I'm going to make it up to you, Faith."

"How? Are you going to get my soul back from Ezekiel? Are you going to cast a spell to return him his wings? Are you going to convince Dad that there's another way to save me than forcing me to descend? What about the hellhounds? Are you going to reverse their self-imposed curse? Tell me, Kristin, how are you going to make things up to me?"

She tightens her jaw, a look of sadness crossing her face for a split second before she composes herself. "Come dawn, I'll break the demonic shield blocking you from your new watcher."

I blink, tears burning my eyes. "You're going to what?"

"I want so badly to protect you, but the only way I'm capable of doing so comes at a cost you shouldn't have to pay, Faith. Your father and Ezekiel can't see the aftermath they leave behind in the day. And your watcher made you a promise he will keep." She steps forward and takes my hand to make me take her dagger. "I know he will. He revealed himself to me the second he took you into the Veiled Realm, and I could just feel everything. He's not the one I need to worry about. He's not going to kill you to avenge the world. He's here to avenge you and what Hell's done. That's why he left his promise open ended."

I bring my hand to my face to clear my tears, peeking at Jess hovering through the veil next to me. He offers me a smile, but all I can manage to do is pout and drop my hand. "How are you so sure that's his reason?"

"Because you're clutching his feathers," she says. "That's a sign of his loyalty. Why do you think Ezekiel always left them behind?"

My heart falters at her revelation. "I thought he was molting"

Kristin releases a loud laugh, filling me up with her soft voice, so pure and full of everything I miss about the world since Ezekiel fell. If only I could bottle up the good feelings to give to Ezekiel, it might sway his demon side to embrace my humanity.

She extends out her hand to me. "Angels really do love their secrets, don't they?"

"Not as much as demons," I quip.

She bobs her head, turning to glance at her rogue pack of wolves. "Come on, let's go find Cadence. I think it's time I catch everyone up to speed before Hell starts burning the night."

Surprise lightens the weight of Hell pressing down on me. "You're going to tell me about the truce?"

"I realize keeping it from you isn't protecting you like

Raphael thinks. He's grown even more overprotective the last few weeks," she says, twisting her lips. Her eyes cloud with her thoughts, and I know she's noticed the change in Dad as well. It wasn't in my head after all. Ezekiel's good grace didn't blind me before.

I run my hand through my messy hair, strolling next to Kristin while the rogue pack follows behind like quiet shadows. "He acts like I can't take care of myself."

"Why do you think he's going overboard now? He knows you can. But he's afraid if he doesn't prove his worth to you, you'll leave him."

I blink a few times at her revelation. "I can't stay in his demonic shadow forever."

She pulls me toward the door to the hotel. "You're right. I just hope all this mess is over when he realizes."

I take one last look at the sun sparkling on the ocean. "I'll be forever the disappointing daughter."

Nudging my shoulder, she says, "Your mom would be proud."

"Talk about room service," Calvin says, devouring the steak on his plate, barely taking the time to chew.

"Order everything you want and everything you don't," Cadence says from her spot on the bed. "Raphael's taking care of it."

"He must've pissed you off," Greg remarks, taking a bite of his grossly rare meat. He smiles at Cadence, and she rolls her eyes.

"It's a lucky day for anyone staying in this hotel," she adds, smirking. "Raphael should appreciate he still has a beating heart."

"You don't have to refrain because of me." My voice barely sounds over a whisper. The longer I remain in this room with the others, the more anxious I get about the coming night. No one except Kristin should be with me. I'm afraid of the danger they're all putting themselves in, but especially Cadence. She's human and less resilient than all of us. "He deserves it."

"You're right, he does," Cadence says. "He knows it. He even opened his shirt for me to cut his heart out. But then—" She sighs. "I'm losing my touch. All I could think about was the disaster he'd leave behind, and none of us deserve to clean up after his mess. So, I thought about it long and hard all day, and I decided to see to it that he picks up after himself."

"That's why you haven't told Cami? Apart from being unreachable," I ask, wondering how much Cadence will put up with. I wouldn't blame her if she picks up everything, asks one of her angel friends to relocate her to the holiest place on Earth, and just forgets about everyone else. But she'd never do that. She has a higher tolerance for demonic chaos than I do.

Cadence clenches and unclenches her fingers. "Loving demons is hard, and they do some questionable things, but we're here to never stop reminding them that they're here because they're better than Hell. Just a little too hot for Heaven to handle, though those damn angels are a hot..." She lets her voice trail off as she loses herself in her thoughts.

"Don't you wish you'd have stuck with humans?" Greg asks, grinning. "Possibly werewolves?"

Cadence throws her hairbrush at the wall mirror, shattering it. "Definitely not. You know I once went out on a date with Drake when I was fresh from the Hunter's Academy? He was nice for all of a second before he accused me of being a demon sympathizer." She darts her gaze to me, a smile playing on her lips. "But I guess he was right. I don't know why I was so offended, really."

Kristin snickers from her spot at the table in the small dining area. "Only the purest souls can survive your lifestyle, Cadence. It's not because you love evil or can excuse demonic tendencies. You don't sympathize with Hell. What you do is slap the Hell out of Raphael and remind him he's capable of using his demonic streak for the greater good."

"I still want to shove my dagger through his heart," she quips.

"Good, you'll remind him he still has one."

Covering my hand over my face, I tune the Earth realm out and focus on what lies on the other side of the veil. If I listen to Kristin and Cadence talk about my dad for a moment longer, I might purposely cross to the daylight realm just so I don't have to hear them.

Cadence might claim to want to send Dad to Hell, but she wouldn't. Even if her life was in danger, she'd still try to force reason onto him. Jess was wrong about me being the demon tamer. I'm certain it's Cadence, and I'm an imposter, pretending to know what I'm doing. Because like Kristin said, one needs a pure soul to combat demons, and my soul might be ruined beyond salvation.

"You came back." Ezekiel's voice drifts to me through the veil, now sounding louder than before.

Reaching out, I touch my hand to his knee, half expecting to feel his heat, but my fingers buzz with the cool energy between us. "I'm finding it harder and harder to stay present in the Earth realm," I admit. Because it's true. There's something about looking through the veil, during moments of pure devastation and also in moments where I can just breathe that helps me make sense of things.

Or maybe it's because the people who've turned into my whole existence remain here, in a world where they can't do anything to hurt me by accident—or on purpose. I can no longer tell. The veil separating blurs so much that I've adapted to living in a constant haze of uncertainty.

"As much as I know I should worry, I can't," Ezekiel says, "I like you here with me."

"But I don't belong here."

He traces his finger over my hand, grazing the air between us. "You're right. You don't."

"You don't belong here, either." I stare at our hands, at how it's so easy to soak up his presence no matter how toxic it sometimes feels because he still manages to make me feel okay in moments it's only us. Maybe I'm too lost to even pull myself away, addicted to Ezekiel's darkness because I deserve it.

"But I do. You're safer away from me." His admission stirs something inside me. He's never said such a thing before. He's always been so adamant that he protects me, but maybe last night shattered that part of him, and he sees the damage. But I can't get my hopes up.

I bump against his presence. "You're right about that. The whole world is safer if you're away from me."

He smiles. "I should be offended."

"It only means I love you too much." Which I do. Jess was wrong about love being all good and light. It really is danger-ous. At least for me.

He brushes his fingers on my cheek, though my hair doesn't move from my face. "We all have our faults."

Sighing, I lean on my hands, remembering the dozens of times before where it felt like it was only me and Ezekiel in the world. And like then, I still feel I'm counting down the minutes until the universe unveils my fate, proves that as Heaven's Trai-tor's daughter, I'm destined to live a short life.

I stare at the sun speeding across the sky, dipping toward the horizon, which means I'm running out of time to make my deal with Ezekiel. If Kristin's good on her word about breaking the protection spell she cast to hide me from the angelic army, I need to be prepared.

"I miss this. I miss just sitting and being together away from the world," I say to fill the oncoming silence.

Ezekiel tilts his head closer, making me wish so badly I

could test my luck and enter the light prison realm. "I can steal you away from Raphael. He'll be too busy to chase us."

"What do you mean?" I couldn't imagine Ezekiel taking me from Dad, but there's no doubt he's scapable.

He wags his eyebrows. "You'll see. Things are changing again, Faith. What better way to assure your safety than with a pack of hellhounds devoted to you?"

I scrunch my face. "I don't understand."

"Heaven's not giving up on you, and we all know that if you reach your full potential, you'll face an uncertain eternity, so we've come to an agreement with the hellhounds."

I groan, the perfect, calm moment slipping away from me. I should've known not to let my guard down. "So, this is all about me?"

He shakes his head. "It's about creating a new balance in the world."

Closing my eyes, I cut him off from my view, though the veil remains thin with my hand over my eye. "Shifted toward Hell?"

I can almost feel his excitement, his pride that he's messing with the universe. "No, shifted toward you."

"I don't want that."

He releases a low sound that reverberates through the veil to buzz against my ears. I'd think I'd have offended him for denying his demented idea of a gift. But this isn't someone giving me a candy I hate or an ugly shirt. I can't accept it graciously and thank him for the thought. "You say that now, but—"

I slam my fist into the ground feeling the soft, cool grass instead of the hot sand I see through the veil. "Ezekiel, I said no. Cami's doing a great job. She has Heaven on her side."

"She's tired. She never asked for this."

"And I'm not either." He's playing with my humanity, poking at my bleeding heart for the people I care about. He knows I'll do anything for him. He knows how fiercely devoted I've been to Dad, risking even my own soul for him. And as for Cami? He might be right about her desire to live a peaceful eternity helping others like she always has, but even if she stood back and let the balance shift, what would that mean for me? I'm not all powerful. I'm a dangerous mess.

"Faith," he says. "Just think about it. You'd have a lot of fierce support and loyalty. We could even make it so that the veil is no longer needed."

"What?" I peer round the desert landscape, half expecting the whole angelic army to erupt heavenly light before my eyes. "How could you say that? You sound like Mary."

He shrugs. "The witch made a good point."

"Ezekiel, no."

Reaching out, he rests his hand on mine, his body heat breaking through as the sun fades. "What if I made a deal with you?"

Fear slides through my veins, coursing through my body in a cold rush that puts out the flames smoldering from my inner demon trying to sway me to see reason in his words. Because if the veil wasn't here, I could be with the people I love all the time.

But it's about more than the people I love. Without the veil, demons will rule night and day. Heaven and humanity would never get a break. I'd never get a break—except, I would be who the world needs a break from. I'd be a demon. "I don't want this. You know I don't want to be a demon."

Ezekiel forces me to stare into his fiery eyes. "I'll return your soul to you if you agree to cooperate."

I blink, my breath catching at the sound of his words. In the last few weeks, I never in my wildest dreams imagined Ezekiel would be willing to give me my soul. But the cost? Oh, God. I'm still lost regardless.

Jess appears in my view, his glowing wings bathing me in his light. I expect him to yell at me to run, to ignore Ezekiel, to slap him even for suggesting such a deal, but Jess surprises me by saying, "Take the deal, Faith."

I tilt my head to my watcher standing before me, hidden from Ezekiel behind his shield. "I—I can't." Because if I take the deal, Ezekiel will no longer possess my humanity. If I take the deal, the hellhounds get what they want. If I take the deal, I'll descend and arise as a demon.

I'd still have my soul, but Hell would ruin it. Ruin Ezekiel.

"Faith, this might be your one chance to get it back," Jess says, unfurling his wings. "We'd still have the chance to fix things."

"I'd be a demon. Forever."

Ezekiel touches my cheek, drawing my attention away from

Jess. His hot fingers graze across my skin, pleading with me to turn to look into his eyes.

"It's not so bad. You'd have your soul," Ezekiel says, leaning in to brush his lips on my cheek. "I know how much you want it and how afraid you are of descending without it, so I want to return it to you so you'll be like me, with me."

I glance back to Jess, now mingling in the cool mist of the Veiled Realm. I missed the sun setting, lowering the veil to leave me so close to Ezekiel that I can hear the thrum of his heart beating in sync with mine.

"I—I don't want it. You need it more." I compose myself, steeling against Ezekiel's demonic charm.

He frowns, tilting his head, boring his dark stare into me. "What is it you want then, Faith? There has to be something."

I inhale a breath through my nose, my chest clenching, my heart breaking, knowing that Jess was right. This might be my only opportunity to get my soul back, but everything in me screams my soul's not worth it. "I want to live, Ezekiel. I want to feel good grace again. I want to touch your wings one more time. I want to go home to Moonlight Shores. I don't want to constantly feel betrayed and cheated. I don't want to feel like I deserve this for the sole reason I was born a demon's daughter." Tears splash on my cheeks, the weight of my life swelling around me as I remind myself of all the things I'll never get.

"Faith," he whispers, brushing my tears away. "I can't fulfill any of those things."

I meet his empty eyes, unfazed by my sadness. In what feels

like another life, Ezekiel would've hugged me. He would've done something more. But as a demon, he can't. And I'm so incredibly angry. I'm pissed at Ezekiel, at Jess, at Dad. I'm furious with myself.

Snatching his hand from my face, I smack it against my heart, feeling the weight of his hot fingers jolt a different kind of pain in me, but it does nothing for the agony of having to reject his deal, reject my soul, my one chance at falling back into good grace.

Because even if his choices led to his fall, I'm to blame. Just like my mom blamed herself for my dad. Dad was right. I am my mother's daughter. I used to think it was a good thing, but now, I hate it. I hate her. The world would've been better off without me.

Ezekiel pulls his hand away at the thrum of my racing heart. "Think of something else, please. I can't lose you. What will it take for you to agree?"

I scream, sending an orb of power at the grass. Because what I'm about to say will still destroy me in the end. But how can I not ask it? If I can't find the courage to take his offer, to get my soul back and leave him as a soulless demon, I want the second most important thing to me. I want him to feel. I want him to feel what he does to me, especially if I'm forced to descend.

"I want you to feel my damn humanity!" My voice echoes through the air as I practically scream the words. "I want you to feel everything. Because if you don't, you'll lose me. And I know what it's like to lose someone. You're sitting here, but you're gone. It's awful. The worst thing in the world."

"You'd rather me use your humanity than get your soul back?" he asks, confusion puckering his brows. "But, Faith—"

Pulling his hand closer to my heart again, I soak in the heat from his skin. "I love you, and because I love you, I ruined you. I did this to you, and I don't know how to fix it. It's the only way I'll go through with this deal with the hellhounds, because I can't fix you the same way my mom fixed my dad. I—I can't. Not after everything."

"You're not responsible for my fall, Faith," he whispers.

I steel myself to his useless argument. "Even so, I carry that blame anyway. So, if you want this. If you want to damn me as a demon and damn me to an eternity I don't want, you will agree to never turn off the humanity my soul gives you. Ever."

He bows his head, running his fingers into his hair. "Are you sure about this?"

"You can say no to the deal." I expect him to. Because agreeing to the deal would bring his own personal Hell to Earth.

"You'd be a soulless demon, Faith," he says, his voice lowering.

I nod. "Exactly. You want me to ruin the world, then I don't want to have to care about it. Or care about my eternity."

"But I'll care."

I shrug. "This is your deal."

"Faith, I—"

"Take it." The voice sounds from behind us, stirring up all the negative emotions I carry toward my dad to spill them out in the form of hot power I toss at him from over my head.

"Stay out of it!" I yell. "You've done enough."

Dad holds my gaze. "I see what you're doing, Faith. It's not going to work. Ezekiel will take your deal."

The edges of my vision shadow. "You know nothing."

"This will be better for all of us. Taking the deal will assure Faith never feels what you've done to her soul. You can live with that Hell drenched turmoil ruining my daughter so she can rise from the depths of Hell and make Heaven regret forsaking Raphael Blackwell's daughter. So, take the deal, Ezekiel. You owe her that."

"Ezekiel," I whisper. "You owe me nothing."

Ezekiel swallows, his Adam's apple bobbing in his throat. He doesn't look at me or my dad, just staring at his hands before he tilts his head to the sky. "I—"

"Before you answer, turn it back on," I say. "You should feel what you're about to do to me."

Dad snarls from behind us, summoning power into his hands. "Take the deal my daughter offered you. This is her eternity we're talking about. She's too blinded by Heaven to see what kind of purpose she can fulfill. This is the only way to assure we never lose her. She can conceive a new vessel. Just make the deal."

Fire burns in Dad's eyes, shining red as his true body reveals the Hell in his veins. I tense, bracing myself for whatever he's about to do. I cover my eye with my hand, summoning my own power, power now different than my father's, brighter, hotter, more full of Hell than he could ever summon.

Jess appears between us through the veil. "Faith, stop. Give me your hand."

"Dad's changed, Jess," I say. "Something's wrong."

"He's losing you, Faith. Ezekiel has your soul, your humanity."

"Which means Dad's losing access to it." I should've seen the signs. I should've known better than to think I could possibly control the two demonic forces in my life.

"Oh, God," I whisper, dropping my hand.

Ezekiel ignites power in his hands, pulling me to my feet as we face Dad. He steps in front of me, blocking me from my dad's wrath. But Ezekiel isn't all powerful. He isn't invincible. And Dad looks ready to send him to Hell. He's lost control of himself.

"Faith, deal or not, you'll do as I say or I'll send Ezekiel to Hell," Dad says. "Convince him to take the deal. He deserves it."

My hands tremble, my power faltering. "You'll damn me."

"You're already damned, Faith. I'm trying to save you."

"Dad," I whisper. "Please."

"Make him."

My whole eternity presses against me, threatening to set my world ablaze. I knew better than to deal with demons because no matter what I came up with, I still lose in the end.

I shake my head. "No. The deal's off. I've changed my mind."

Dad summons more power. "Faith, this is your last chance."

Covering my hand with my eye, I meet Jess's wild gaze. "Agree to do it, Faith. Just give him what he wants."

"Why? This could solve the world's problem," I say. "I'm damned anyway. At least now the world would be safer without me."

Tears shine in Jess's eyes. "Just do what he wants, please. I'm not ready to give up on you."

I release a breathless laugh. "You angels. Always willing to fight a losing battle."

He expands his wings. "Please, trust me. Have faith."

I drop my hand, staring my dad straight on in all his true body glory. He summons so much power in his palms that the ground quakes beneath my feet. Ezekiel tries to grab my shoulders to pull me back, but I rip myself free to face Dad.

"I'll do it," I say. "Please, just stop, Dad. I'll do it."

He snuffs out his power. "If you don't, I'll guarantee you'll never see Ezekiel again, Faith."

I nod. "I'll do it."

Turning his attention to Ezekiel, he says, "You're lucky to have Faith. I hope you realize that. I didn't know how lucky I was to have her until you stole her from me."

SALVATION

I STARE AT the power in my hands, swirling like molten fire in my palms. Dad left twenty minutes ago to finalize the negotiations with Drake and his new hellhound pack. To my relief, the truce is set to occur in stages as to not draw attention from the angelic army or the Hunter's Alliance. So, I'll survive another night as a mortal until Kristin finalizes the spell to use Ezekiel to drag me back from Hell through the part of my soul tethering him to me. Who needs divine intervention when remnants of Heaven lie under the flames of Hell tainting his blood? Lucky me for being special.

"Faith," Ezekiel whispers from his position by the door. "It won't be so bad."

"It'll be worse."

Straightening his shoulders, he glances once through the peephole before striding across the room to me. He shifts on his feet, almost nervously, and sits next to me. Leaning forward, he rests his elbows on his knees.

"Faith, I—"

"Don't talk anymore." My low voice makes him turn to look at me. I slide my hand over his shoulders to rub his back. "Talking doesn't help me. Nothing you can say will save me now. Just be with me. Let me feel your love before I lose the ability to feel it forever."

"Why won't you agree to take back your soul?" Ezekiel asks.

"I said no more talking." I don't want to go there because this already devastates me enough. The only reason I wanted my soul was for my personal redemption, something that won't happen when I'm forced into the position I lost everything not to be in. Betrayal cuts through me deeper than my grief, and I'm not even sure I'm strong enough to survive. I won't survive. Not as the person I am.

Ezekiel clasps my hand, bringing it up to his face to feel the weight of my fingers against his warm cheek. A tear rolls onto my knuckle, and he shudders a breath, turning his head so I can't see him. He groans, tensing, and I tilt his head to face me.

I meet his shadowed eyes, untouched by Hell's fire in this moment. "You opened up for me. Why?"

"Because I love you, and I've failed you, and I don't know what else to do to make things right," he whispers. "I'm weak."

"Such an angelic thing to do—granting me a final request."

He sighs. "I'm not an angel."

"When you're like this, you still feel like one to me, even without your wings." I run my fingers over his damp cheek, brushing his tear away.

He rubs his shoulder, touching the spot his wings used to be. "Those are kind of important."

"Not to me. I hate flying."

He chuckles, his voice sounding low, raspy. Utterly human. "Even in moments of turmoil you still manage to bring me relief. You were always so strong. Stubborn as Hell."

I rest my head on his shoulder. "Enjoy it while you can."

I can't help it. Even after everything. Even after his demonic games. The torment he put me through. Even after shattering my heart and making me see the part of him I've tried so hard to ignore, I can't stop from wanting to melt into him. It could be some deep-seated part of me wanting to be near my soul, but I'm certain it's more. I want to be near my soul only in his hands. Hands that used to hold so much more—hope, faith, the light I could use right now.

"Because Faith Blackwell, demi-demon, lover of good grace, demon tamer, mortal—she's going to die and disappear forever. I'll forget her, and when I do, you'll forget me, too. I know it deep in my heart. The only part you'll salvage of me will be just my body, but even it will be consumed," I add.

Another tear drips on his cheek. One of the hardest things for me to ever witness was an angel crying, but it can't even compete with the misery drowning me seeing my beautiful demon cry on my behalf. He's lost in the only emotion left in my humanity, summoned from the looming brutal death of my hope for an existence in the only place I imagined spending my eternity.

I continue to trace my finger along his cheek, a small smile playing on my lips, though the world blurs through my tears. If I could bottle this moment up to hold with me—a moment that reminds me why I'll never regret my decision to let Ezekiel keep the one thing connecting him to humanity—I might still manage to find peace amid the tragedy my life becomes.

His forehead wrinkles, his eyebrows pinching together, and he says, "What am I feeling in your soul? You feel...serene, almost. How can you manage to feel that after everything?"

"Because at least you will still be capable of being you, even if you don't want to. It makes me feel better about the end." I close the space between us, caressing my lips against his so lightly the kiss whispers across my mouth. He reacts to the sudden bloom of warm emotions swirling through me, devouring my kiss like it's the answer to our unsaid prayers.

Running his fingers through my blond tresses and to my back, he links his fingers onto my side and pulls me to him, so I straddle his lap on the edge of the bed. My thighs squeeze his sides the tighter I embrace him, pushing against him until he falls back. I cage him in with my elbows, kissing him deeper, tasting hints of the dark chocolate of his demonic scent.

His tongue brushes mine, flicking lightly but hungrily, turning our kiss from sweet to desperate to something hot with passion only found in the fire in our veins. My guard cracks and fissures, splitting open to allow him in—stealing away the feelings that ruined us. Instead of tossing the broken pieces to the wind, to lose myself in the only thing I have left, I imagine gathering them up to repair the damage, surrounding Ezekiel with everything I am and everything we are together, keeping him so close that we're one being.

I lock the world away from us, protecting us. Because it wasn't us who broke each other. It was the world—the universe. But I know now the universe didn't leave us irreparably damaged. It wanted us to recreate who we are in a way to survive this life, whatever way we're forced to live, with the strength to withstand the catastrophic devastation thrust at us.

Ezekiel works his way from my mouth to kiss my jaw, his fingers exploring the skin of my stomach as he tugs my shirt over my head. The firelight in his eyes shines so brightly the rest of the room shadows as I'm consumed by the darkness surrounding us. Heat blossoms with every kiss that trails from my navel and up to the only thing I have left of Ezekiel as an angel—the black feather tattooed on my chest that sears my flesh with the reminder of his love at its purest.

I hook my fingers to his shirt and rip it over his head. I want nothing more than to feel the thrum of his heart against mine, crashing into my skin because it would prefer to be with me where I'll keep it safe.

But these feelings won't last.

I can't be responsible for protecting his heart much longer.

I'll destroy it.

I shudder a breath, the emotions I try so hard to suppress, to ignore while I'm in Ezekiel's arms, sneak through my heart, snuffing out the fire of my demon blood. Ezekiel tenses under me, and I blink to hide my tears, but they betray me and splash across his face.

He reaches up and smears my tears with his thumb. "I can't do this," he whispers.

I suck in a breath. "I'm sorry, I don't mean to cry. Just give me a second. I want this. I want you."

He pushes up on his elbows, cradling me against him. "Faith, I mean I can't do this—I can't lose you. I can't let you lose yourself."

"What choice do we have? My dad's lost, Ezekiel. I feel it. I can see it in his eyes. He will stay true to his words," I say.

"We'll run."

"We can't," I say. "His blood burns through my veins. He'll always find us."

His jaw tenses, his body turning rigid. "Then I'll send him to Hell."

Dad used to joke about waiting for the day for me to send a blessed dagger through his heart, claiming that's what has seemed to be the fate of all demonic fathers. But how could I? He may be a demon, he may have lost what made him the man

I felt safe with, but he's still my dad. My mom sacrificed her soul for him. How could I take that from her regardless of the damage it caused me?

"Ezekiel," I whisper. "He's my dad."

"He's a monster."

"We're all monsters. We're all the same," I say.

He shakes his head. "No, not you. You're not a monster. You're my faith and light, my hope, my grace. You're my salvation even as I burn."

His words touch me so deeply, stealing my breath while returning it with a gust of imaginary cherry-blossom scented wings. This is the part of Ezekiel I fell in love with—the part that fills up the empty void left where my soul should be. The part of Ezekiel I knew never vanished but stayed buried inside him, waiting for me to dig it out, dust it off, and reclaim it as mine.

"Even so—I can't allow you to send him to Hell. I can't damn you, either. I'll just—" I take a breath and cover my eyes.

Jess stands in front of us, his white wings flapping, swirling the silver mist around me in the Veiled Realm. He's been waiting for me to return since I denied the chance to reclaim my soul in exchange for being a demon. Disappointment crosses his angelic face, his eyebrows low over his golden eyes that pierce my soul through Ezekiel.

"You should've taken Ezekiel's deal. There's still time. Ask him again, right now, while he's still open," Jess says.

I shake my head, realizing Ezekiel stares at the side of my

face because I never finished my thought out loud. "I'll just accept my fate."

"No, I won't allow it," both Ezekiel and Jess say in unison.

I sigh. "How?"

"I'll pull you here and hide you," Jess says.

Ezekiel remains quiet, unable to hear Jess but also unable to answer me because he doesn't know.

"You expect me to hide in the Veiled Realm? How does that solve anything? Dad said he'd send Ezekiel to Hell if I don't follow through with the deal," I say. "I don't doubt he'll damn me. If I'm not here he can start over." Another vessel. I bet it's all his demonic self can think about as he loses me to Ezekiel.

Jess groans. "That blasted witch. If she'd just break the spell I could locate you and—"

I fist my hands. "No one is sending my dad to Hell!"

Ezekiel touches my chin, drawing my attention to him. "Faith, do you think Raphael would push you into this if he could access your humanity?"

"He'd trade himself for me," I say. I know it's true. He's accepted Heaven's smite on my behalf before.

Tightening his hold, Ezekiel rests his chin on my shoulder. "Then you know why it must be done. Don't give in to his demon. Don't pay for his sins. Don't waste your beautiful, irreplaceable, powerful life like this."

"I—I can't," I whisper.

A knock sounds on the door, dragging my attention away

from Jess and Ezekiel. I drop my hand from my face, blocking the veil from my view. I never thought my new watcher and Ezekiel would ever agree on something, and I wish they didn't agree on yet another thing that'll hurt me.

"Faith, open the door," Dad says, banging on it again.

I don't move from Ezekiel's lap, hugging him tighter. An explosion booms through the air, and the door flies off its hinges and crashes to the rug by our feet. Dad stands in the doorway with a ruby orb in his fingers, readying himself to throw it at Ezekiel.

He lowers his hands, seeing I'm blocking Ezekiel. "What the Hell are you doing taking advantage of my daughter's humanity?"

I glower and summon power in my own hands. "Stop, Dad. Control yourself. You're already getting what you want. I will not stand here and let you make Ezekiel feel guilty for granting me a last request—one I shouldn't need."

"You're going to make things harder on yourself, Faith. This isn't who Ezekiel is anymore. He's doing it to mess with your heart. He takes pleasure in your suffering," Dad snaps.

Anger sizzles under the surface of my skin. "He doesn't."

"It's what demons do!" he hollers, throwing his power in our direction, trying to hit Ezekiel.

I chuck my own power at his, and the two forces collide, sending a shower of liquid power across the floor and walls. Smoke pours through the room, clouding my vision, and I gather more power to threaten Dad with.

"Just get out. I'll be down in ten minutes. If you don't calm yourself, you'll leave me no choice but to not go through with it," I say.

"I'll kill him," Dad says, pointing at Ezekiel.

I summon more power. "I'll kill you before you could even try."

Silence falls between us, leaving behind only the sound of our power humming through the room. Dad glares at me long and hard, trying to see if I'm lying. But I don't even know if I am or how I'll react.

"Just wait downstairs. Ten minutes. I promise," I say, lowering my voice to stop it from shaking.

He composes himself. "Make it five."

Without waiting for my response, he spins on his feet and marches into the hallway, leaving me trembling in my spot. I close my eyes, shutting off the world, concentrating on my beating heart to calm my nerves.

"I can't stand by and watch him push you into this," Ezekiel says.

I turn to face him as he comes to my side. He wraps his arms around me despite the power still burning in my hands. The edges of my vision darken at the thought of losing Dad by Ezekiel's hands, by my own hands. I lost my soul in the first place to save him from an eternity in Hell. If I lose him like this, everything will have been for nothing.

Snuffing out my power, I rest my head on his chest. "Ezekiel, please. Just give me a night. I need time to think."

"You're running out of it."

"Please. A night. We'll set the truce in motion, get Dad to believe I'm on board, and figure something out."

He hugs me tighter like I'll fall to my knees at any second. "And if you can't?"

I swallow, steeling myself at the thought. "Then I'll fight."

"You'll send him to Hell?"

"I'll do what I have to. Because you're right. I can't lose myself. I won't be a demon."

LAST REQUEST

I NEVER IMAGINED I'd carry holy water on me to protect myself from my dad. Back in Moonlight Shores, I kept a few bottles under my bed, but those were always intended to keep me safe from other demons, though Dad would've disapproved. Human-made weapons make demons appear weak, since one could assume I lacked any power, but I'm not a demon. For now.

The Sunrise Cove pack's mansion buzzes with annoying sounds that make my head pound. From the blaring music coming from one of the bedrooms to the incessant howling from outside, this is the last place I want to spend the rest of my night, especially wearing a dress I'd have loved weeks ago—the way the bodice glitters in the chandelier and shows off my cleavage with the deep V-cut, how it hugs my curves, making me feel more like a woman than the dresses Dad used to buy me with capped sleeves in baby doll silhouettes. But this dress, while drawing a lot of attention from Ezekiel, sucks. I'd have to rip a side seam to run if I had to, something I've never done at a demonic affair in Dad's shadow, but it's Dad I'd need to run from.

A hot hand touches my shoulder, and I jump, sloshing holy water from my glass. It spills across the gleaming marble floor, and Ezekiel swipes a napkin from the table of hors d'oeuvres. I yank the back of his suit jacket to stop him.

"Ezekiel, don't," I say. "You'll burn yourself."

He straightens his back and raises an eyebrow to me. "Is that?"

I nod. "I'm sorry. I—"

Leaning over, he kisses me, freezing when our lips meet.

"I'm sorry," I repeat. "I forgot what it was and took a sip."

His bottom lip reddens from the hint of blessed water on my lips, but he only chuckles and touches his fingers to his mouth. "That was the hottest kiss ever."

I laugh.

He kisses me again. "And worth it."

I roll my eyes, setting the glass behind me on the table. Having it nearby is enough without having to worry about accidentally spilling it on Ezekiel as he keeps no space between us.

Explaining something like that to Dad in a time where I'm supposed to play nice with Hell isn't something I need.

Peering around the room, I spot Kristin standing in front of a makeshift altar, setting up for whatever spell she'll cast to put the truce in place. All I know is my blood's required, because I'm the only one the hellhounds can supposedly swear loyalty to without binding them to me completely since I'm only half demon. It'll maintain the blood rites Mary had performed even after my descent, allowing the wolves to never enter through the veil unlike completely broken wolves who follow their masters. Not like they'd have to worry even if I'm forced to descend. I doubt the veil could contain me for long.

Maybe that's what everyone's counting on, bringing the worlds together, making it humanly impossible to kill a demon. The veil regenerates any harm caused to their bodies apart from a fatal blow. It empowers them. It's basically a small slice of Hell to help them thrive. If the Veiled Realm and humanity merge, the universe will lose.

Ezekiel slides his warm fingers into mine. "Your emotions are all over the place. What are you thinking about?"

I twist my lips to the side. Dad's somewhere nearby, and the last thing I want is for him to overhear something I say to Ezekiel. He's probably already revoked his promise of privacy to never listen in on me with the state he's in. I don't want him to know about how I suspect things will turn out if I don't figure out how to save myself. I don't want to give Dad any ideas if he hasn't thought about that possibility yet.

"How much I want to rip this damn dress off," I say. Because really, I'm getting more nervous by the second. People will smell my fear soon, and fear brings out the monsters in everyone.

Ezekiel grins. "I could help."

My cheeks burn, and I playfully slap him. "Maybe later."

A flash of red light catches my attention from the top of the staircase, and I meet Dad's heated gaze. I was right. He was listening to me from wherever he's been spending the evening. Cadence saunters up next to him, touches his arm, and draws his attention back to her. Fire lights his eyes, and Cadence stiffens for a moment that I think only I catch, because Dad offers his arm to her and leads her out of sight once more.

Kristin waves her hand at me, drawing my attention from the staircase. I tug Ezekiel with me, afraid for him to leave my side. Kristin shifts her gaze between us. A thousand thoughts dance across her face as she tries to figure out what's going on. Ezekiel and I have been so hot and cold to each other that I can barely keep up.

"Ezekiel, I need a moment with Faith," she says, trying to tug me away from him.

He tightens his grip on my fingers. "No."

Swiping her ivory dagger from the table, she aims it at his white dress shirt. "Give me a minute or you'll be the reason tonight gets postponed. I don't know if you've noticed, but Raphael lost his patience. So, unless you want to test your power, you'll give me a moment with Faith."

I stand on my tiptoes and press my lips to Ezekiel's ear. "It's okay. It's just a minute."

With a glare aimed at Kristin, Ezekiel strolls across the room and near the front door. I turn my back on him to face Kristin. She messes with her ivory dagger and opens and closes her mouth like she can't spit out whatever it is she wants to say to me.

"Give me your hand," she finally says.

I hesitate but relent and give it to her. Instead of slicing my palm open to spill my blood into the onyx bowl on the table, she pricks my finger, gathering a tiny drop of blood on the tip and brings it to her mouth to smear on her bottom lip. She does the same with her finger and coats my bottom lip with blood.

I grimace. "What are you—"

She motions with her index finger for me to be quiet. "Blood to blood, from a demon to witch, lower our voices, mute the pitch. The sound of our words Heaven's Traitor won't hear, block the noise from his ears."

"Raphael is a mess," Kristin says. "I'm afraid he was right about Ezekiel stealing you from him. I should've paid more attention. I thought he meant your loyalty."

"I know," I say. "Why do you think I'm here tonight?"

"I'm sorry. I wish there was something I could do, but until dawn..." She sighs. "Do you still have your watcher's feathers?"

I scrunch my face. "I promised him I'd never give them to you."

"But I need them to break your shield against him."

"I don't know," I whisper. "Dad will murder you for—"

"I can handle a demon's wrath," she remarks.

Something about her voice, how she straightens her shoulders, leads me to believe she doesn't actually believe she can. She's been Dad's soul keeper for as long as I've been alive, but she hasn't had to deal with him in this state since my mom.

"You don't sound so sure," I say.

She shrugs. "I don't want you to worry about me. I'm the one who put myself in this position, so I'll deal with the consequences. But you, Faith? You don't deserve this. If I have to give up my chance at a bearable life for you, I will."

"I just—"

"Give me the feathers."

I don't move. If I give her the feathers, Jess will be free to find me. I know he made me a promise, but we don't exactly have a binding contract. Releasing him could have irreparable consequences. He wants to send Dad to Hell as much as Ezekiel, but unlike Ezekiel, he won't give me a day to figure things out.

"Faith."

I turn my back on her and raise my hand to my eye to peer through the veil. Jess stands before me, his brilliant wings unfurled and stretching to the silver moon above. Light shines from his golden eyes, and he looks ready to tackle me to drag me through the veil.

"I want to change my last request," I say.

Jess grimaces, his eyes narrowing. "You want to give up your chance at salvation?"

"We agreed you'd save me when I got my soul back, but I'm not taking it back, so please, just hear me out," I say.

He blinks a few times. "Go on."

"Blood to blood from dark to light, thin the veil and give me sight." Kristin's voice cuts through the air to me, trying to grab my attention from Jess.

The air around us quivers, and pain bursts through my palm.

"A demon's daughter will let me see, the avenging angel hiding from me." The air shifts, and Jess takes a few steps back.

"Leave," I say. "Hurry."

But Jess doesn't move. He stares at something behind me. Slowly turning, I catch sight of blood hovering like a ruby-tinted window in the veil. The crashing waves pulverize the beach behind Kristin as the glowing moon casts streaks of silver through her black hair. Her black eyes shine red, and she presses her hand to the veil.

I drop my hand from my eye. "Kristin, what are you doing?"

"Getting a feather myself," she says.

The world shudders around me, and it takes a minute to orient myself. A moment ago, I was standing near Kristin's altar inside, and now we're outside the mansion on the beach. Silence hushes the world around us, and I can't stop the fear seeping under my skin.

"What do you want one of my feathers for?" Jess asks from his side of the veil.

I try to wave my hand through the blood-coated looking glass, but my fingers spark, sending a shockwave through me to knock me onto the beach. I ignite power in my hands, growing the orb the size of a softball, and jerk my hands back to throw it at Jess to break Kristin's spell, but she steps in front of me.

I hesitate. As much as I want to break the connection she created to talk to Jess using me, I won't use my power on her, even if she wears a protection amulet.

"Faith didn't tell you," she says. It's not a question. I didn't exactly have time to before, and then I changed my mind.

"That you're about to doom Grace Blackwell's daughter all for a ruthless demon's desire to ruin the world?"

She sighs. "It would've never gotten to this point had you showed her mercy when Raphael asked you, but no. This isn't what it's about. I need a feather to break the spell I cast to protect Faith from you."

Jess furrows his brows. "And why would you do that?"

"She's not going to," I say.

"I realized that dooming Faith to an eternity she never wanted wasn't protecting her," Kristin says, ignoring me. "And I realized there was only one being in the universe that could truly protect her from such a fate. You."

"He'll send Dad to Hell, Kristin," I say. "You'll follow him. You know this."

She purses her lips, ignoring me. "My only request is that if

I break the protection spell, you'll assure me you won't damn Faith."

"You have my word, witch," Jess says.

Fury forces my inner demon to the surface, and I ignite an orb of liquid orange power in my hands. I jerk my arms back to thrust the power at the bloody looking glass, but hot hands grab me from behind, yanking me away.

I scream, thrashing in Ezekiel's arms, burning his hands as I attempt to throw the power. It explodes on the beach, sending sand raining down on us.

"You can't do this!" I yell.

Jess's image wavers in the air. "It must be done, Faith. I told you my purpose lies with humanity. I'm sorry."

"Ezekiel, stop them! He'll steal me from you. You'll have my soul, but he'll never let me see you again," I say.

Ezekiel holds me against him, breathing into my hair, his body rigid as he processes what's going on.

"Please, Ezekiel," I whisper. "Do something."

He holds me tighter. "Forgive me, Faith. This must be done. I'm not strong enough to protect you."

"I can protect myself," I snap.

"I'm not taking that chance," he whispers."

A sob wracks my chest, stealing my breath. How will I ever learn to survive in this world if no one will ever let me? Why can't anyone give me the chance to fix things? *Because you've only ever broken them.*

I sniffle. "You'll lose me."

"If it means I can save you, it'll be worth it."

"Try saying that after shutting off your humanity."

Ezekiel spins me around. "No. I see what I'm like without it reflected through the actions of Raphael. I'm never shutting you out again."

"Then I'll shut mine off. Because I can't stand by and watch."

"You won't," Ezekiel whispers.

A howl cuts through the quiet night, drawing our attention back to the house. Kristin closes her looking glass to Jess, and I rip my hand free to look through the veil by myself still locked in Ezekiel's arms.

"I know this doesn't feel like the right thing to you, but you'll see that it is," Jess says, still standing in front of me.

"I hate you," I whisper.

"Faith, please. Everyone makes their own choices. Your Dad made his long ago. Kristin made hers. Ezekiel, too."

"Then why can't I?"

He rubs his lips together. "Because they should've never been choices for you to make. Now, I'm sorry the world has been nothing but unfair to you, but I want to try the best I can to make it right. You mentioned a last request."

"Don't kill my dad," I say.

The look he gives me speaks volumes. "Faith, I—"

"Then intercept Kristin's soul. I know angels don't usually intervene with demonic contracts, but I know it's possible."

"Faith, you know that a soul bound to Hell can't always be

saved. And Kristin, she's been working with your dad a long time."

I scream in frustration. "You're useless! Ezekiel was way better at being my watcher."

"Faith," he says.

I shake my head. "No. I'm done with you. Don't expect me to cooperate when Kristin ruins my life and lets you near me."

All he does is glance toward the sky above us before bending his knees and launching into the air. White feathers scatter through the Veiled Realm, and I drop my hand from my eye to focus on what's really around me.

A single white feather drifts to the sand between me and Kristin.

Ezekiel lifts me in his arms, stopping me from rushing to it. Kristin picks it off the sand and cradles it in her hands. She peers around the beach for something, maybe a sign, maybe a miracle, but nothing is here.

"The ceremony will start in an hour," Kristin says to Ezekiel. "I trust you'll look after Faith until then."

Ezekiel nods. "Always."

BLOOD RITUAL

NOTHING GOOD EVER comes from a blood ritual involving hellhounds, but at least they're all in their human forms as they stare at me standing before them on a small platform. The bright moon shines light through the window, sinking toward the horizon the closer it gets to dawn.

Hot fingers rest on my shoulders, and I tense, knowing Ezekiel stands on the other side of the table with Kristin as she finalizes the contract. Deals with demons take many forms, but for something like this, a blood contract is in order. I've never seen one before, though I've also never gone through Dad's belongings. Kristin is his soul keeper and handles that sort of thing, and tonight, she's handling it for Ezekiel, too.

As for me, I'm merely a piece of the game. Ezekiel owns my soul. In the demonic world, that makes me one of his possessions, and because I gave it to him with no strings attached, he can do as he pleases, which includes making dozens of hellhounds swear their loyalty to me.

"I know you're upset, Faith, but look around. Look at all those who want to see you thrive in this eternity," Dad says from behind me, combing my hair behind my shoulders. "When has Heaven ever stood by our sides? They murdered your mother. They deprived you of the childhood you deserved."

"That was the old alliance, one you helped dismantle and destroy," I say, keeping my eyes trained on the eye branded across the back of my hand. It takes all my strength not to raise my hand to my eye to peer into the Veiled Realm to find Jess again, to plead with him for another night, another final request—something, anything, to give me a moment to think. Because time's moving too fast. It feels like the night speeds by like in the Veiled Realm, and if I blink, the sun will rise.

Dad leans forward over my shoulder to peer at me. "For good reason. But still, they were acting on the angelic army's behalf."

His blue eyes reflect green in the crystal chandelier. He doesn't move, waiting for me to look at him straight on instead of from my peripheral vision. But I'm afraid he'll lock me in a demonic stare down. I'm afraid to see the emptiness in his eyes beyond the fire I can't see lighting within him from my position.

"I don't want to talk about this now," I say.

He shifts in front of me, blocking my view of the hellhounds quietly talking among themselves. "But we need to. I know you, Faith. I'm the one who molded you into who you are, and I admit, I didn't always know what I was doing sometimes, and other times, I tried too hard to protect you, so much so that I couldn't bear to break your heart and tell you the truth about your mother or the alliance. I kept my entire past from you."

"But why? If you hated them so much, why not be honest?" I ask.

He sighs, drooping his shoulders, looking incredibly familiar. He reminds me of the man who raised me and promised to protect me. He reminds me he's not entirely lost to me yet. Demons don't have heartfelt discussions like this. They don't see reason. But Dad? He's hiding somewhere behind that true body of his begging to sneak out.

"Because they ruined enough, and I didn't want them to sully the only good thing I had left," he says. "Forgive me for wanting to protect the purity of the soul born from the one person in the universe who knew me as me—neither angel nor demon."

"You don't think I do?" I ask.

He offers me a ghost of a smile. "Not since Heaven's army

ruined me for you."

I open my mouth to tell him the angelic army didn't ruin him for me. That the only one ruining him for me is himself. But I don't fully believe that either.

"Dad," I whisper. "You're not ruined for me yet. But I can't promise you won't be if you force me into this."

"I'm not forcing you," he says. "We have no binding contract."

I run my hand through my hair, pushing loose strands from my face. "You'll murder Ezekiel if I do."

"But you're still free to walk out of here."

Raising my hand, I push him back and out of the way. My chest tightens, my heart aching as it fissures the longer I try to hold onto the memory of the man I want so badly to stand before me, who'd never give me such an ultimatum. He reminds me of true demons, born in Hell, come to Earth only to destroy everything in their wake. The ones who twist their ideals away from what the universe needs to maintain balance and instead fighting for power to maintain the eternity they desire. The type of demons Dad spent the last few years punishing and keeping in check, sending them back to Hell if he had to.

I saunter away from him and to Ezekiel's side. Dad swears under his breath, claiming once again that Ezekiel's stolen me from him. Kristin peers at me in the side of her vision, a new hardened look in her eyes. She looks ready to chuck her ivory dagger at Dad, but instead uses it to prick her finger to draw a rectangle on the scroll of paper intended to bind the truce between the hellhounds and us.

My stomach twists, and I suck in a breath and lean on Ezekiel. Mary's spell about Hell taking my body back swirls through my mind, the memory of it causing my knees to shake. She was right all along. She always knew it'd come to this—a pack of hellhounds for her pretty little demon. She's probably cackling from Hell this very moment. She might even be at the gate waiting.

Ezekiel slides his hands around my waist, practically keeping me on my feet so I don't curl in on myself in front of everyone. "It's only a contract." He sounds like he's saying it more to himself than me.

"It's only a contract," I repeat. "I'm not forcing anyone to do anything they don't agree with." I hate I have to give myself an excuse for not standing up to fight against Dad this very second. But I know I'd fail. Because I don't want to rise against him. I have too much to lose, including him.

"Where's my witness?" Kristin asks, glancing at Dad.

"Are you sure it must be her?" Dad asks, crossing his arms over his broad chest. "There are dozens of people present."

"Go pick up some unsuspecting human off the street if you'd like," Kristin says. "They might be less likely to try to dagger you."

Dad grins, a look of desire morphing his face into something even more familiar. It's the same expression he always wears in regards to Cadence. And thinking about her right now, knowing she put herself in harm's way by loving Dad, burns through me. She knew the risk of getting involved with a demon, but I'm sure she had no idea how far Dad has fallen. Even at their worst, an upper-level demon like my dad is still charming. Cadence might not have even seen his wrath yet.

"I hope she does try," Dad says, releasing a guttural noise in his throat. "I love a good fight with my little huntress."

I refrain from fake gagging.

He's admitted as much hundreds of times before, but something darker now hides in his words. And I fear for Cadence's life. Because bearing witness to such an occasion guarantees she'll never be free again. Dad nor the Sunrise Cove pack will allow her to return to her normal life amid hunters and her family and friends.

Dad struts away, leaving me alone with Kristin and Ezekiel. An idea sneaks into my mind, watching him disappear up the staircase. Jess couldn't help me with Kristin, but he can help ensure Cadence is safe.

I raise my hand to my eye and peer through the veil. "Jess?" I whisper when I don't see him standing in front of me.

My shoulder buzzes, and I turn away from my spot hiding against Ezekiel's chest. More hellhounds gather around, closing in as Kristin spreads the scroll across the table and daggers it down to keep it flat. My heart pounds in my ears while Ezekiel's remains utterly calm. Because he can't see what I see. Among dozens of fiery beasts stands my watcher with his glittering white wings outstretched from his back. He holds his flaming sword at his side, a fierce warrior unafraid of the beasts waiting for their human halves to release them.

I swallow the panic rising in my throat. "I thought of a new final request."

"You no longer need a final request. You are not going to die."

I blink oncoming tears away. "Please, Jess. I need to make sure Cadence gets out of here. If you go after my dad, she'll be left to face the aftermath."

He slowly nods his head. "Okay, that I can do."

I release a breath and drop my hand from my eye, bringing me back to the Earth realm. A small groan sounds through the air, and everyone, including me, turns their attention toward the enormous staircase where Dad guides Cadence down to join us. The overhead lights sparkle off the intricate beading weaving around the soft flowing tulle fabric of her black gown. She gathers it in her fingers, showing off her spiked stilettos pointy enough to stake someone through the chest. And she just might if she realizes what's really happening.

"I never dreamed I'd be in a room again with so many hellhounds," Cadence whispers to Dad, but I still hear her over every annoying sound made by the anxious hellhounds threatening to steal my attention. "At least no one's trying to eat me alive this time."

Dad chuckles and leans over to kiss her cheek. "Never. Never again after tonight, my little huntress. And you'll assure it."

"You're sure you got the terms in order? I can call Cami

and run them by her if you'd like," she says.

My mouth falls open at her suggestion. Dad tricked her. He's leading her to believe he's arranging the deal to see to it that the alliance and Heaven don't have to worry about the pack. I know it. I remember him telling Cami exactly that. And I know they'll let them believe it until everything is in place, until I descend—no, I'm not descending. This isn't happening.

But it is.

Dad raises an eyebrow. "You doubt my capability in deal making?"

"Of course I don't doubt your skills, Raphael. You're the most talented, handsome, powerful demon I know." Running her hand along the muscles bulging through his suit, Cadence manages to get Dad to smirk at her instead of roar in her face for even suggesting he is incapable of completing a contract.

"Tell me more," Dad says, leaning down to kiss Cadence's lips. "You seem to be the only one who appreciates me these days."

She laughs and rolls her eyes. Cadence leaves Dad's side when he waves her in my direction. She steps in front of the table and smiles at me. "Nothing like a creepy blood contract to bring peace, right?"

I don't smile. I don't react. All I do is drop my gaze to the gleaming floor. I could tell Cadence the truth about what's happening here tonight, but she's safer hiding in the lies and half-truths Dad told her.

Ezekiel pulls me closer to him, sliding his arm over my

shoulder, half blocking me. Dad struts by and peeks his head into a wooden door a few feet away from me, leading to where I think I was being held captive in the mansion not long ago.

Drake emerges, wearing jeans and a T-shirt, a casual contrast to the rest of us. His gaudy decorative belt buckle gleams in the light, and I shudder. It reminds me of Joshua, the man who started all this mess, because he had stolen one like it from Drake before ruining the Desertville pack and sending Drake here.

People holler and howl, some clap, and I squeeze my eyes shut, trying to push away the cacophonous racket hurting my ear drums. For basically stealing the pack out from under whoever was in charge before, Drake seems to be coveted among the hellhounds, kind of like I'd be coveted among demons if they knew the extent of my ability.

Kristin turns to Ezekiel. "This is your last opportunity to change anything on the contract."

Dad straightens his shoulders. "It's fine as is. I saw to it myself. The Sunrise Cove pack shall bow before my daughter and swear loyalty. If they prove their worth by her side, an eternity will be granted with her descent into Hell through a blood rite."

"And how will you prove your worth?" Kristin asks Drake.

Drake clears his throat, shifting in his boots. "Through a sacrifice. I offer one soul to break in exchange for loyalty through a contract and not in the form of a demonic leash."

I furrow my brows, turning to Ezekiel. "A sacrifice?"

Ezekiel doesn't look at me. Instead, he drops my hand and stands before Dad and Drake. Panic freezes me in place, remembering how Mary needed souls contracted to Dad when the gates of Hell opened to go through with her spell.

Dad pulls out a yellowing piece of paper from his pocket. "I have the contract for the soul, which I've exchanged with Drake for this lovely estate in a perfect town to keep my daughter safe."

Confusion washes over me. Dad made his own deal with the pack leader. He exchanged someone's soul for a piece of property. Demons rarely give up souls to another. It's hard to believe Dad loved this place enough to trade Drake someone to use for his sacrifice to Ezekiel when Drake has dozens of people in his pack to choose from.

"Please let me see the contract," Kristin says, holding her hand out.

Dad hands it to her, and I watch her slowly unfold it. Kristin pales, the color draining from her face. My heart races, ramming at my ribcage, threatening to break free. Whoever's soul is written on the contract must be someone important to Kristin to garner such a reaction from her.

"Raphael," she says. "This is—"

He glares at her, and she snaps her mouth shut under the weight of his fiery stare. "It's not open to discussion."

She opens her mouth to argue but decides against it and nods her head. "Do you agree with the chosen sacrifice, Ezekiel?"

His stare flicks over the paper. He stiffens and glances at me for a moment. I suck in my bottom lip, begging him with my eyes to deny whoever it is. Because if Drake wants this truce in place to protect his pack, maybe he should be the one to sacrifice himself, not someone who made a bad deal with my demon dad.

Ezekiel folds up the contract and pockets it. "Yes, the soul will do."

Kristin straightens her back and extends her hand to Ezekiel. "Give me your hand."

Ezekiel does as she asks, and Kristin pokes the tip of his finger. He smears his black blood over the pad of his finger and then presses it on a line Kristin had drawn with her own blood. The paper smokes as Ezekiel's fingerprint sets in, sealing his end of the bargain.

One by one, the entire pack of hellhounds make their way to the table, allowing Kristin to prick their fingers to sign the contract with a fingerprint. My stomach threatens to spill out in front of everyone.

I clutch the edge of the table, practically lying on it to keep me from falling to the floor. Each tap of a finger on the paper bangs through my ears in a rhythm like an erratic heartbeat. The edges of my vision darken, and heat rolls over my skin in waves. I can't breathe, the room filling with haze as each drop of blood sends the smoke from Hell through the air, searing the paper without setting it ablaze.

I cover my eyes with my hands, wanting to be anywhere

but in this boiling hot room with people who are dooming me to an eternity as a demon. This far exceeds a simple contract to gather allies for me. Each hellhound swearing loyalty binds my soul tighter to Hell. Even if I've decided not to take my soul back from Ezekiel, I never expected it to be sullied in such a way. Each Hell beast leaves his mark on my soul, snuffing out any possible chance of it finding good grace again.

This isn't only a contract like Ezekiel said.

It's far, far worse.

"Faith, it's going to be okay," Jess says, blinding me with the light of his wings. I'm already changing, my soul reacting to the contract, making him harder to look at. His sacred being will soon repulse me.

"It's not," I whisper.

He runs his finger across my shoulder, his skin buzzing over mine. "Dawn is approaching. Just hang on a little longer."

"I can't do this," I say. "Pull me through."

He shakes his head. "Not now."

"Please," I whisper.

"Faith, I can't. I can't risk what your father will do. Not yet." Jess reaches out, touching my cheek. My skin tingles under his fingers, my eyes watering from fear and disappointment.

"Faith?" Kristin asks, pulling me from my thoughts. "I need your hand."

But I don't want to give it. I want to continue to look at my watcher in all his heavenly light. I want to soak the good grace into my bones to combat the inky darkness of the hellhounds' loyalty now burning over my skin, threatening to drag my inner demon from me.

The world spins as someone lifts me off my feet. Dad yanks my hand free from my eye and locks his hot fingers around my wrist to offer it to Kristin. I thrash, struggling to free myself. I thought I was strong enough to survive the contract to put the truce in place, but now, I'm not so sure. I don't want to test my strength.

"Raphael," Cadence says. "You're hurting her. Stop."

"Shut up!" Dad roars at Cadence.

She draws her dagger. "Raphael, if she has changed her mind, I will not allow you to force her. It's not worth it. Cami will think of another way."

Growls sound through the room, and the sweet scent of Cadence's fear trickles through the air. It's enough to make me stop thrashing. A few of the hellhounds close in on us, focusing their attention on Cadence. She steps back behind the table where Kristin stands.

"Don't do anything stupid, my little huntress," Dad says. "This isn't the time to act high and mighty. Save it for the angels."

She narrows her eyes, lowering her dagger. Cadence is the bravest hunter I know, and she's also the smartest one and understands how demons work better than any human ever could. She won't start a fight, knowing there is no possible way she could win. I wouldn't want her to, either.

"Please, Dad," I whisper. "I don't feel so good."

He sighs. "Then I will help you finish what must be done."

Ezekiel stands in front of Kristin, blocking Dad's path. Fire shines in his eyes, and Dad stiffens, his muscles rippling under me as he unleashes his true body for the whole room to see. A deafening quiet settles around us. No one moves or breathes. I'm not even sure anyone's hearts continue to beat, but I can't tell through my throbbing head.

"I will take her from here." Ezekiel's low voice cuts through the silence, kicking my sputtering heart into overdrive. "I am negotiating on Faith's behalf, not yours. You will give her to me, Raphael. I'm more fit to take care of her than you are."

I cringe expecting Dad and Ezekiel to start blasting power at each other without regard to anyone in their way, including me, stuck in the middle. A demon's hold is far worse than blessed chains.

Dad growls and shoves me toward Ezekiel. I hit Ezekiel's taut chest, and my shoulder explodes with pain because he doesn't even waver to soften my impact. He wouldn't give Dad the satisfaction of seeing him unsteady on his feet—a vulnerability that could cause a demon in Dad's state to react without seeing reason. Dad takes a step away, lacing his fingers on the back of his head, composing himself to hide the horns ruining his human façade.

Ezekiel runs his hand over my cheek, peering at me with softer eyes than the glare he tried to sear my dad with. "Faith, I know you're scared, but I will help you through this. Please trust me."

I press my face into his chest. "Don't make me. I thought I was strong enough. But I'm not."

"Do you know what you're asking me to do?" he whispers. "Because I will try for you. Right now. And I'm not sure we'd survive." He's right. The only way to put a stop to this would be to break the contract before it's complete and face Dad and dozens of hellhounds. They'd tear us to shreds.

"We'd only have to survive until dawn," I whisper so softly, thinking over our chances. I could smash the veil and pull Ezekiel in with me. But then there's still Kristin and Cadence. Kristin can't undo her protection spell without us. We'd still have to survive another night, and Dad can find me anywhere.

Ezekiel hesitates, peering around the room. A million thoughts cloud his expression as he thinks through every dooming scenario he can think of. "It's just a contract," he says again for what seems like the millionth time tonight.

"Ezekiel." I hate thinking that a small chance at surviving is better than completing the contract, burning my soul, leaving Hell's residue so thick I can feel it just being in Ezekiel's arms.

He grabs my hand and holds it out to Kristin, taking our guaranteed survival over the state of my soul or my deep-seated need to remain unbound to the very species who ruined my life. "Forgive me, Faith. I can't risk it. But I will make sure you get through this and away from here." Ezekiel kisses the tears dripping over my temples.

"Please, help me," I whisper to no one in particular. Even if the entire universe listens, there's no help left for me in this moment. I can't even help myself.

"Faith, turn off your humanity," Ezekiel whispers. "Just do it. Please."

I sniffle. "I can't." What he asks would allow my inner demon to reign over my being.

"Please. Just until dawn. Block it all out. Protect yourself from the pain and devastation."

"No. I will not ignore or suppress any of this. I'm more afraid of shutting everything out than I am of letting everything in. Don't ask me again." I refuse to do it to save myself from feeling any of the evil coursing through the room with the blood contract. Because if I stop feeling, I'll stop caring. If I stop caring, so will Ezekiel. And I need to feel human for as long as I can. It keeps me fighting as much as I want to give in.

Because if I do, then we'll truly be lost. I'm afraid there's no coming back for me if I steel myself from the vile acts evil forced upon me through my dad's demonic blood, through the Hell beasts left behind by Mary. The vile acts Ezekiel believes I'll survive, and Jess thinks I'm strong enough to take.

And maybe I am. I have to be.

"This is going to sting more than usual, Faith," Kristin says, holding a strange golden athame I've never seen her use before.

I groan. "Of course it will."

"Ready?" she asks.

"No."

"Yes," Ezekiel says, hugging me tighter.

Kristin positions the dagger with the double sided blade against my palm. "Okay, your turn, Ezekiel."

"Take a deep breath, Faith," he says.

Before I have a chance, Ezekiel slams his hand on the top blade of the dagger, cutting us both at once while summoning power. Fire not unlike that from the depths of Hell burns my skin, sinking through the cut in my palm to course through my veins. The room hazes as agony washes over me, stealing my breath.

I scream.

SACRIFICE

MIST FOGS THE beach around me, and I dig my toes into the cool sand. The moon sinks toward the horizon, lighting a silver path aglow on the still water. I wish I could step on the ocean and stroll the path until I disappear within the pitch-black nothingness stretching before me, but pain burns through my essence, threatening to rip me back to the real world.

Ezekiel materializes in front of me, blocking the shining moonlight on the water. If I didn't know any better, I'd think his achingly beautiful black wings would unfurl and stretch toward the sky at any second. But he doesn't change. All he does is take a few steps forward to plop on the sand next to me.

"This contract is killing me," I say, leaning back on my hands to peer at the glittering stars strung across the midnight sky, though I'm sure it's purpling with the oncoming dawn outside my consciousness.

"Your part is almost over," he whispers.

"It's only beginning," I say.

He shakes his head. "I already told you, I will not allow Raphael to force you to descend. I will see to it Kristin breaks her spell and you can safely remain in Jess's protection away from the demonic world."

"And you. This stupid plan doesn't solve anything, you know. Say Jess somehow manages to send my dad to Hell, which I don't agree with, if I might add, then what? I'll be alive, but I'm mortal, and you need my soul to—"

"Creating a vessel is still an option," Ezekiel says. "I'm pretty sure we can manage to survive a few years until you're ready to—"

Warmth blushes my cheeks. "The angelic army would never allow it. Not to mention you keep making my existence sound like I'm a possession with this vessel crap. I'm a person. This vessel you keep imagining would be a person."

"If I still had my wings you'd agre—"

I huff. "Ezekiel, no." I can't believe I'm even having this conversation again.

He rubs his hand over my knee. "Okay. We'll think of another way."

"We're out of options. You've always known I was a losing battle," I say.

"Doesn't mean I'm going to stop fighting."

"Demon-bound, and Hell will burn, sear the flesh, make them turn. A mighty beast, now will bow, with the blood they will vow. A demon's daughter will rise with Hell, hear my words, hear my spell. Twist the bones, make them crack, let fire consume and take them back." Kristin's chant drifts through the air, tugging me from the only place I find reprieve.

I hug my legs. "No," I whisper.

"You must be conscious to witness the oath," Ezekiel says.

"I don't."

"You do."

"Blood to blood, a demon's kin, hear their words, let them in. From light to dark and dark to light, accept their flames that will protect your night. And with the sun, they will rise, in human form as their disguise. Unleashed yet loyal, they'll remain. Nothing but power you will gain."

The world shudders around me, flickering from the dream beach to the dozens of fiery beasts bowing before me. Pain steals my ability to do anything but watch Drake undress in front of me. If the edges of my vision weren't shadowing, I might try to turn away, but I've lost control of my limbs, the only thing my body allows me to do is bear witness to the final hellhound ready to bow.

"A brand mark will sear your skin, and you will let her demon in. Her blood will course through your veins, in its wake

Hell will remain."

Ezekiel steps us closer and raises my glowing hand to Drake's back. The hellhound's muscles tighten under my palm, now burning with blue liquid fire that doesn't belong to me. I cry out, my hand smoldering against Drake's skin. Ezekiel pulls my hand away, leaving a puckered, red handprint on the hellhound's shoulder. Fire ignites from my mark on his flesh, rolling over his skin as his body cracks and shifts. He ignites into a huge, fiery beast, larger than any of the flaming monsters lighting up the room.

Straightening his front paws while leaning forward, Drake bows.

A heat wave washes over me, blanketing the pain gripping me like lowering myself into a warm tub to ease my sore muscles. I release a soft breath and blink. The sinking feeling I had now pulls me from the darkness as the glow of my loyal hellhounds lights up my skin.

"Simply mesmerizing, isn't it?" Dad asks, a strange look lighting his face flickering with shadows.

"Yeah," I whisper.

He takes my still tingling hand and cups it between his without trying to yank me from Ezekiel's arms. "And how do you feel now?"

I flick my gaze to Ezekiel, his eyes reflecting the burning bodies of the hellhounds. His lips hide in a thin line, his jaw tense, but he doesn't meet my gaze or say anything. I'm pretty sure he's holding his breath, hiding his anticipation as he waits for my response.

I roll my shoulders and wiggle until Ezekiel sets me on my feet. "Confused. I was certain I was going to die, but now I feel—"

"Stronger? Powerful?" Dad tries to extract my feelings from my swirling mind.

I'd be lying if I denied the truth of his words. Because I feel better than I have in weeks. Comforted and unafraid. "Like I'm a better version of me."

Ezekiel sucks in a quiet breath but still doesn't speak. Kristin and Cadence remain utterly quiet, too, like shadows amid the dancing flames of the hellhounds.

"This is only a mere taste, Faith. Your suffering will be well worth it." Dad nudges me forward toward the bowing hellhounds. "Go on. Go feel what it's like to have such magnificent creatures on your side."

Slowly, I meander closer, extending my hand out to Drake, the nearest Hell beast. He stands on all fours, raising his head to me, so tall I can nearly peer into his human eyes—a sign that while Hell claims his body, he's unbroken and still carries humanity within him.

He nuzzles his nose into my hand, licking his black frothy tongue over my palm. I gently graze my fingers over his fiery head, a strange sensation crawling over my fingers. His flames dance against my palm, but his fire doesn't burn me. I've never experienced such a thing before. I've been burned dozens of times by hellhounds, especially when Dad used to break werewolves, and even demonic masters aren't always immune to their fire unless they can summon it, but here I am, feeling the flames like they're the softest fur in existence.

"Now can you see you have nothing to fear from this eternity?" Dad asks, sliding his arm over my shoulders to half hug me and to gaze at the reward of the demonic contract he put together for Ezekiel on my behalf.

"Dad," I whisper.

I can't get the rest of the words to come out. His hellish mood is long gone now that he's finally gotten something he wanted, and I don't want to mess it up with complaints. It'd be pointless. Might as well soak in his familiarity before everyone I love is torn away from me by a watcher who wants to protect me while getting his own vengeance for the wrongs Dad committed as both an angel and demon.

"Don't worry, Faith. I know you can't always see things as clearly as me, and you think I'm trying to create your eternity for you, but all I've ever wanted is for you to get the opportunity to make one yourself, even if it might not be exactly how you imagined." He kisses the top of my head. "Everything I ever do is for you. Always has been. Always will be."

Tears burn my eyes, so much doubt and anger threatening to steal the power Dad managed to give me when I felt powerless. "I love you, Dad." This might be the last time I get the chance to tell him.

"And I love you." He pulls me away from Drake and the rest of the hellhound pack and motions for me to take a seat near the table.

Kristin steps from the shadows, drawing my attention away from Dad's blue eyes, the same shade as mine even with the fire burning within them. "We have one final piece of the contract to complete."

Ezekiel turns to Dad. "I'd like you to take Faith out of here, Raphael."

Dad tips his head back and laughs. "Oh, but why? You can't remain on that heavenly pedestal she keeps you on forever. Don't you think she deserves to witness the demon she insists on allowing to keep her soul as who he really is?"

I swallow, remembering that a sacrifice must be made by the pack to prove their worth. Give one soul to strengthen the many, to strengthen me. And because Ezekiel's blood is on the contract, he's who has to take the soul and damn it to Hell.

Guttural howls echo through the room in an eerie song to cheer Ezekiel on. And he can't back down and risk breaking the agreement. My heart pounds in my ears, my breathing quickening as Ezekiel cracks his neck and heads toward the door leading to a pitch-black part of the mansion.

"I don't want to see this, Dad," I say, finally finding my voice. I get to my feet, hugging myself. "I'm really not feeling well."

He tilts his head, peering at me for a moment. His expression softens the longer he stares at me. "I think it'll be good for you if you do. Shouldn't take too long, though this is Ezekiel's first time, so he might savor the process since he'll rather enjoy it."

Knots form in my stomach. "Dad, please."

He sighs. "Fine. Let me escort you to your room. I think I've found one you might like."

I suppress a groan. Of course he already picked out a room for me here among my loyal hellhound pack. Dad guides me toward the staircase, his hot hand on my back, to lead me upstairs. I drag my feet up each step as much as I want to run into a room and jump out a window to escape.

The room falls utterly silent the moment I reach the top of the staircase, and I can't stop myself from glancing over my shoulder as the crowded room parts for Ezekiel and—

I gasp, covering my mouth with my hand. My head spins, dizziness threatening to throw me down the stairs. Dad steadies me on my feet, swiftly spinning me around with him to watch Ezekiel push Malik to the floor. I knew something didn't seem right when Kristin mentioned Dad would end Malik's contract. He only meant his contract to him.

Kristin's gaze darts to mine from below, and she covers her eyes with her hand before turning away to push Cadence against the wall before she even tries to lift her dagger. Malik rolls from his back to his stomach and presses his hands to the floor to get back to his feet.

"I don't understand. Kristin said Greg and his pack were taking Malik back with them to Desertville," I say, gripping the banister.

"Kristin sometimes gets ahead of herself and forgets her

place. She's *my* soul keeper and doesn't get a say in what happens to the contracts I make." Dad places each of his hands on my shoulders, locking me in place. He never planned on taking me to my new room. He probably thought it best to give me a better view without risking me intervening.

"Malik's my friend, Dad. Please, you have to stop this," I beg, tears burning my eyes.

"The wolf is not your friend. He's only ever used you to his benefit," Dad says. "He nearly got you killed and sent to Heaven."

I sneer and jerk to free myself from Dad, but he holds me tighter. "He helped me save your eternity. You should thank him."

"He wasn't saving me from the goodness of his heart."

"Dad."

"I don't want you letting your emotions get in the way, Faith. You've always known how our world works. Unfortunately, friends aren't a luxury we have. It's me and you against the world."

I lean forward, closing my eyes when Ezekiel's blue light sparkles through the room. Malik yells out, the fear in his voice cutting me deep enough to reopen scars I thought too thick to ever be split open again.

My fingers ache from my grip on the railing. "Can't you see that I don't want to be against the world?"

"You don't have a choice."

More howls ring through the air, mixing with low, fierce

growls. I snap my eyes open in time to watch Malik evade Ezekiel's power. The blue liquid hits the window, and glass explodes across the floor. Ezekiel shoots power at the chandelier, sending it crashing down on Malik, but he manages to roll away. The lights cut off with the shower of sparks, and we're left with only the flames licking the backs of the hellhounds, turning Ezekiel's stone-façade even scarier.

Malik slips on the glass, smearing blood across the gleaming tile. Hell power automatically ignites in my hands, and I thrust it forward at Ezekiel without thinking things through. All I want is to give Malik a moment to get up. He's resisted breaking against the pressure of his pack, against Mary, against all those who sought to put Hell in his veins, but none of those people were my beautiful demon, now made ruthless by the hands of my dad.

Ezekiel's jacket smolders, catching him off guard, and he spins in my direction, his true body unleashing from his once handsome face to tear the resemblance of the angel I fell in love with away from me. His dark eyes glow red, his fury aimed right at me, so hot I can feel my skin reddening like with the heat of sunburn.

"Please, Ezekiel, stop," I whisper so softly I'm not sure I said the words out loud. "Don't break him."

Ezekiel jerks his attention away from me and back to Malik without a word, aiming his blue orb once more.

Dad leans closer to me, pressing me into the railing. "See who holds your soul. Think he's worthy of such a possession?"

"My soul isn't a possession. It's me. And I—" I release a small cry at Malik's yells.

"He's not worthy of you. He can't be who he is and still be who you want him to be. You can hope and beg and pray for him to hold onto the angel he was when he ruined you, but he'll eventually lose, Faith. Sacrificing your soul to him will have been for nothing. You can't keep pretending he's worth saving," Dad says.

I elbow him as hard as I can, getting him to step back so I can spin to face him. "Like you?"

Dad's skin shudders at my words, his true body threatening to break free.

"You think I sacrificed everything for Ezekiel, but you're wrong. I did it for you. I jeopardized and lost my good grace because of you." I chuck power at the wall. "And you still blame him. You blame everyone else. And I do, too. Because even if you threaten me, hurt me, destroy everything I pray to keep safe, I still can't stop myself from wanting to protect you and keep you safe. But I shouldn't. I can't do it anymore."

"I never asked you to, Faith."

"Because you've never had to!" Summoning power, I ram it into my dad, sending him flying back into the hallway.

Spinning on my feet, I race for the stairs and head back down to where Ezekiel corners Malik. The hellhounds part around me, giving me space to race through. But Ezekiel spins to face me, Hell burning in his eyes, and he holds his hand up.

"Ezekiel, stop," I say.

He shakes his head. "Forgive me. It must be done."

I don't even have a chance to respond before Ezekiel chucks his power at Malik, hitting him in the chest, sending him crashing into the wall. The werewolf screams as Ezekiel's power sends him jerking forward on all fours. His back arches, his body twisting and cracking as his wolf form breaks free.

"Ezekiel," I whisper.

But he can't hear my pleas over the fire stealing away Malik's humanity.

He can't hear my heart shattering over Hell coursing through his veins.

"Help me," I whisper, covering my eye with my hand to peer at Jess standing tall with his white wings reaching toward the sky.

But no one, not even my watcher, can hear my prayers over the wolf breaking.

Over his yells turning into howls.

Then Malik, the last traitor wolf, bows to Ezekiel.

He bows to me.

THE DEAL

I THRUST POWER at the back door, sending it crashing onto the sand. Howls follow me onto the quiet beach as I make my escape. My heart throbs, my hands trembling with more power I expel toward the moonlit water. Fury squeezes me so tightly that it keeps my heart together as it struggles to fall apart. Bearing witness to such an atrocity at the hands of the demon I love leaves me bleeding black as my inner demon fights for control.

"Faith, wait," Ezekiel calls from the back door. "Please."

I don't wait. I pick up my pace, running down the beach. I can't stay and wait as the rest of my world explodes in Hell fire.

I can't face the coming dawn, waiting for Kristin to cast what might possibly be the last spell she ever does. If Jess fails to find vengeance, Dad will murder Kristin for releasing my watcher. If Jess does succeed, he'll damn Kristin to Hell with Dad, who has no choice but to follow the demon who holds her soul.

And Ezekiel? He'll have no one left to remind him of the angel he used to be. He'll have no reason to keep fighting his internal demonic battle.

So here I am, running away to try to salvage the burning pieces of my life until I can think of another plan that doesn't involve sending Dad to Hell, releasing my avenging angel, or procreating with my demon boyfriend to give him what my soul offers him. If I can make it to sunrise, those I love will remain protected in the very place that protects the world from them.

"Faith!"

"Stay away! I won't let you drag me back," I yell, kicking up sand while blindly shooting power behind me.

Firelight sears the edges of my vision, and a flaming hellhound jets past me and skids to a stop, trying to block my path. It launches at me, knocking me into the sand, and I freeze as the beast snarls at me. Its coal-like eyes burn in its head, the humanity the broken werewolf used to carry now gone.

I shove my hands into Malik's smoldering chest. "Get off me!"

Ezekiel whistles, calling off his new broken hellhound, making the situation even worse. I scramble to my feet, summoning power in my hands, and face Ezekiel. Malik strolls behind his back to take his place by Ezekiel's side.

I toss my power at the sand near their feet, a sob escaping my mouth at the sight of my fallen angel even now closer to Hell than ever, summoning evil to Earth in the form of an invisible chain to bind a soul to him for eternity.

"I need you to g-go away," I whisper. "I c-can't deal with this r-right now."

Ezekiel's hardened features soften, and the fire in his eyes sputters out. He doesn't back away, but he doesn't step closer either. "Please, Faith. Give me a chance to explain myself."

"I don't need an explanation. I get it. You couldn't break your end of the contract. I just—you shouldn't have agreed to break *him*!" My voice screeches over the ocean. "I know you don't care for those who contract their souls to my dad, nor do you care about those who you think deserve the consequences of their actions, but Malik wasn't Hell-bound before he needed help from my dad. He could've been saved when his contract expired."

I rub my hands into my eyes, smearing the tears from my vision. Jess flashes in and out of sight, and I drop my hands.

Ezekiel takes a cautious step closer. "Faith, you don't know what I feel or who I care for so stop turning me into some bad guy before I ha—"

"You're a demon. You feel nothing."

He glares at the ocean, tossing his own power at the sea. "I feel everything. I feel you. And your fury is burning me, stabbing at me, pissing me off because you won't stop and listen to me."

"Because you only have excuses that I can't stop accepting," I say.

Ezekiel roars, throwing more of his power at the beach, sending sand raining down on us. "Just listen to me! I broke your wolf because it was the only way to save him, Faith. I could've picked any damn one of those hellhounds to break."

I fold in on myself, dropping to the sand. "You should've. They'd deserve it."

"You don't think I agree? But when I saw the contract, I took the opportunity to claim one of Raphael's souls so I could do as I pleased with it."

I glower. "Ezekiel, do you hear yourself?"

He sits in the sand next to me, and his new hellhound settles not far from us, avoiding the waves. "Apparently you don't. I agreed to break Malik because if I didn't, someone else would have. He was already swaying. A soul can only take so much before they give in."

"But—"

"Faith, I know this is hard to deal with, and I know I don't deserve your trust or love or any part of you, but I need you to believe me that I accepted the contract and broke Malik with good reason."

Digging my fingers into the sand, I force myself to control the urge to blast him away because really, what possible good reason could he give me for breaking a wolf, stealing his freewill, damning him to demonic servitude?

"And why's that?"

He reaches into his jacket pocket and pulls out the yellowing contract. "So I could give him to you."

"I don't want another hellhound," I snap.

Taking my hand in his, he presses the paper to my palm. "But come dawn you can give him a miracle, Faith. I don't have any good grace left in me to help him, but you know someone who can."

I squeeze my eyes shut, tears blurring my vision. Such a gift as a broken hellhound was not something I ever expected or knew I wanted until Ezekiel handed it to me. But as for a miracle? That would mean I'd have to go back. I'd have to face the real aftermath caused by my love for Ezekiel and his love for me.

I'd have to brace myself for goodbye.

Ezekiel slides his arm around my back, hugging me against him. This isn't how I imagined our story would end. This isn't how I imagined my life would be like. But I guess asking for something as simple as walking a path of righteousness into old age was too much for a half demon like me.

"You know, Faith, you still have the most beautiful soul I've ever seen or touched or carried. I've been so focused on myself reflecting onto you that I forgot how brightly you shine and not with the glow of Hell. When I concentrate on you without me, I can remember things that slipped from my mind with my severed wings. It helps me deal with the idea of allowing Jesaiah to do the job I was incapable of doing."

"You think I'm better without you?" I ask.

He chuckles. "Yes. Even though I hate the thought and want nothing more than to swear to high Heaven, letting you go still gives you the chance to find good grace. You know, just because you suddenly don't want me to return your soul to you doesn't mean I have to keep it. We can make a deal."

"A deal? I swear if you try to mention children one more ti—"

Ezekiel interrupts my threats with a kiss so passionate I fall back into the sand, clinging to him, devouring each brush of his lips with a hunger I didn't know I had until I realized this might be the last kiss we share.

And it ends too soon.

He rests his head against mine, his eyes closed, his chest heaving as he regains control. "I wasn't going to suggest a vessel. You're stubborn as Hell, and I know everything is too much for you right now."

I snuggle against his neck. "So what kind of deal? If I'm forced to leave you, I can't do it if you don't have a soul. That would be damning you."

"If you go with Jess and live life the best you can, I'll return your soul to you upon your death, hopefully in many, many years. In exchange for keeping your soul for the time being, I won't get wrapped up in demonic affairs for the rest of time nor will I corrupt your soul any more than I have."

"But you'd still be soulless when I die," I argue.

"And a contract is binding. I think I'm smart enough to fulfill our agreement, even without a soul, because I don't know if you realize this, but self-preservation is a huge deal among demons. No second chances at roaming humanity. Hell's unforgiving of mistakes."

I let his deal sink in, imagining Ezekiel spending eternity locked in a contract where only I truly benefit. Giving up demonic affairs means there'd be no chance of him trying to rise to power. He'd be fulfilling his purpose as a demon, what Dad has been doing since he made his own agreement to secure his eternity on Earth—one he's ruining because he can no longer see things as clearly as he claims he does. The only thing he has thought through was how to preserve his eternity by having Ezekiel negotiate the contract instead of him—he can place the blame elsewhere.

"You'd really agree to those terms for me?" I ask. "Eternity is a long time."

"That's why I need you to accept the deal. It's the only way I know how to give you what you want. A lifetime where I can use your humanity and an eternity for you where you belong. You might have your father's blood, but you're not him." Ezekiel kisses me again, holding me tighter.

"Okay," I say, nodding. "I accept your deal. Do we need to find Kristin for the contract?"

He shakes his head. "Demons make deals without witches all the time. I only want your word and your mark."

"My mark?"

"I need the reminder, Faith. I need to feel it with every beat of my heart." Ezekiel unbuttons his shirt, revealing his muscular chest to me. "Now summon your power."

I ignite a small burst of power in my palm and swipe a small amount across the pad of my thumb. Ezekiel's dark eyes bore into mine, watching me slowly raise my hand to his chest. I press my thumb twice to his skin, searing his flesh with a mark I'll never give anyone else. It's not my handprint like with the hellhounds. This is my version of my heart over his. Just for him.

"My heart for you," I whisper, staring at the smoke wafting from his puckering skin. "Hopefully it doesn't cause as much pain as I do."

He grins at me, trailing his finger across my cheek to push my hair behind my ear. "Come on. We're running out of night. Kristin's waiting. I'm sure Jesaiah is, too."

I raise my hand to my eye, peering through the veil. Jess faces the horizon instead of me, watching the moon. "He is."

Before Jess can turn around, I drop my hand away. Ezekiel helps me to my feet, dusts the sand from my dress, and slides his fingers into mine. He tugs me along back to the beach mansion where music now hums from within as the Sunrise Cove pack celebrates the beginning of what they think is their rightful eternity on Earth.

I barely make it back inside when Drake scoops me up into his arms and twirls me around. Something has shifted in his demeanor already. Where he was cold and ruthless before now warms with new emotions fitting for his pack.

"My pretty little demon," he says, smiling at me in the fire-light of those hellhounds still remaining in their beast forms. "You ready to celebrate?"

I lift my chin, stiffening my back. "Yes, but don't ever call me that again."

He raises his eyebrows. "I'm sorry, Faith. I won't." Offering his hand out, he waits for me to relent and rest my hand in his. He kisses my knuckles, fire flashing through his eyes, and then he tries to hand me to another pack mate.

I force myself to smile and tug myself away. "Excuse me. I need to find Kristin."

"She's out front," Drake says.

"And my dad?"

He grins. "Probably fighting with the hunter."

I grimace at the stupid smile he gives me. I should find Dad, say goodbye to him in case I can't spare him one more night, but the sky lightens by the second. Ezekiel guides me through the crowd toward the foyer leading out front. Kristin motions for me to hurry through the glass door.

"Quickly, Faith. Raphael will come looking for you in a minute." She swipes her ivory dagger over my palm without giving me a chance to brace myself, spilling my black blood across the limestone steps she perches on. She pulls a white feather from her pocket, coating it with my blood, her heart pounding so loudly I'm sure even my dad can hear it.

Kristin tips her head up. "Ezekiel, I need you to keep him

away. I need the universe to hear my words for it to work, so he'll hear the start of my spell."

My chest tightens at the thought. "Kristin, maybe we shouldn't. Your life—"

"Blood to blood from dark to light, thin the veil, show the night. Heaven's warrior can now see through. He will watch over you."

A familiar yell cuts through the air from somewhere inside. She was right about Dad hearing her, and he's running in our direction fast. Ezekiel ignites power in his hands and blocks the door, threatening anyone who tries to step a foot closer.

"A demon's shield will break for you. With dawn you can come through. An avenging angel full of smite, with Faith's grace take back the night."

The veil thins around us, revealing Jess on the other side, his flaming sword glowing in his hand as he prepares to take the second he needs to send Dad to Hell in an attempt to save me from descending by Dad's doing. My hands tremble, and I can't stop myself from getting to my feet. The glass door explodes behind us, raining debris over the ground. Kristin tumbles forward down the steps, but I manage to clutch the pillar to support myself.

"Kristin!" Dad roars. "What are you doing?"

Ezekiel charges Dad, power cascading from his hands, knocking Dad back. They slide across the floor, throwing power and punches in a fight unlike anything I've seen between them. This isn't some fight for power, it's a feud running far deeper as they wage a war for me.

And I'm frozen in place, watching the room flash in bursts of red and blue. Because how can I pick a side? How can I even hope for one of them to win? No matter what, I lose.

"Stop," I whisper, inching forward.

Hell runs too hot between the both of them that they don't hear me.

"Demon-bound and Hell born, your body and soul will now be torn. The highest angel from Heaven will rise, light will hide you from demon eyes. From black to red and red to black, Heaven will take your body back. Grace will light up the skies, and you will sever your demon ties. A demon's kin will now be free, so Heaven can now watch over thee."

I draw my attention back to Kristin as she finishes her spell. The bloody feather erupts in a flash of light, blinding me. A cool hand slides into mine, jerking me back from the entrance to the pack's mansion. Jess portals through the veil and stands before me, his brilliant white wings extending out, sending the scent of roses through the air. Seeing him in all his avenging angel glory freaks me out, and I yank my hand away.

Frowning, he glances from me to the chaos inside. "Faith, wait out here."

He struts forward, hidden in his angelic shield. I ignore his command and run behind him. It's then I realize he's already shielding me from everyone's view because the hellhounds don't react as they watch Ezekiel and Dad fight. Racing ahead of Jess, I hold my hands up, summoning power between my palms. I don't know what I'm doing, facing him and his flaming sword, but something comes over me, catching sight of the emptiness in Dad's eyes while seeing a new light in Ezekiel's.

"Don't!" I yell. "Please. You can protect me. You can shield me, and they'll both never find me."

Jess's heavenly light intensifies, making it incredibly hard to look at him. "He'll never stop searching for you, and I can't guarantee he won't ever break through my shield."

"Then I'll fake my death again. I know it's possible to trick him."

Jess raises his sword. "He'll tear the world apart, Faith. Look at him."

I don't turn away from Jess. "I don't have to see him. He's still my dad. He's in there somewhere. I just—I need time. I can bring him back."

"You can't."

Something explodes behind me, shaking the foundation of the house like an earthquake. I spin away from Jess to face Dad as he crashes into Ezekiel, pressing his hands to his chest. My breath catches at the sight of Dad in his true body, ready to punch his power through Ezekiel's heart.

"Dad, no!" I scream.

My voice gets lost on the wind created by Jess's wings. He knocks me off my feet, flying forward. His blazing sword lights through the dark room, and panic threatens to send me to the floor. If I stop Jess, Dad will send Ezekiel to Hell. If I don't stop my watcher, Dad will end up in Hell.

My heart is torn in half, beating and bleeding for the two demons I love. Two demons who I know are capable of more than just drowning in the Hell pouring through their veins. But the firelight shines too brightly to see clearly. They need more.

Summoning all the power I can manage into my hands, I do the only thing I can think of to stop someone from dying. I cover my eye with my hand, concentrating on the fading mist of the Veiled Realm, and I blast it open. The world shudders around me. An ear-piercing noise forces me to cover my ears with my hands. Mist fogs the room, the hole in the veil bigger than ever before. My skin steams against the cool world blending with the Earth plane.

Everyone freezes, staring at the gaping hole. More power glows from my trembling hands, and I take an automatic step forward. Jess jerks his attention to me, his whole beautiful face morphing into the angel I first saw when he prophesied I'd ruin the world. He glowers at me like he wishes he finished his job the last time we were on the Earth plane together, in a world he can easily send his flaming sword through my heart to save the world.

And maybe he was right about me from the start.

I can't help myself. I can't stop my inner demon from winning.

"Faith," Kristin whispers from behind me. "What have you done?"

LOVING A DEMON

"FAITH, RUN THROUGH!" Ezekiel yells, punching Dad in the jaw.

Dad flies onto his back next to Jess. The angel's flaming sword disappears as he gathers Heaven's light to reseal the veil as the sun steals both Dad and Ezekiel away to the place neither can kill each other. The place they'll be safe from Jess.

I stare at Dad attack Ezekiel on the other side of the veil, ramming him into a tree. He manages to evade him, rushing toward me on his side of the veil. But the hole is sealed shut, keeping us apart.

"Faith, come to me. Hurry! I thought you'd be safe, but Jesaiah will kill you for that." Ezekiel tries to grab me, but all he does is shock my skin as he presses against the veil. "Please, Faith. Break the veil again if you have to."

In a world where Ezekiel is cut off from my humanity, he seems more human than ever. Desperation puckers his brows, and he uses his own power to blast at the veil between us. It sparkles around me without damaging the veil. But he continues to try.

"I can't, Ezekiel," I whisper. "You know why."

He summons more power, tossing it anyway. "Faith, please. Don't say another word. Don't mention anything to anyone."

He's referring to the deal we made on the beach, the one attached to the mark I gave him over his heart. A deal that if it came to fruition in this moment would mean I might still be okay. If I die at the hands of Jess, I can still find peace, and Ezekiel can still manage in a world that wronged him. He can fight the dark for me.

"Faith, promise me," Ezekiel says.

I nod my head. His fear for me is warranted. Nothing would stop Jess from ending my life to revert my soul back to me if he knew of the deal. And even if he doesn't and still rams that flaming blade into my heart, at least I still have a small chance at forgiveness.

Jess swivels in my direction, his flaming sword glowing in his hand once more. "Faith, drop your hand." His cold voice crawls under my skin to extinguish the fire burning in my veins.

I swallow, licking my lips. "I—"

"If you break the veil again, I..." His voice trails off. He can't even find the courage to finish what we both know might happen. "Please, I'm trying to help you."

I can't move. I can't catch my breath. I can't portal through to Ezekiel. If I do, it'll break our contract. The agreement was for me to go with my watcher. But I catch sight of Dad behind Ezekiel, gathering power. He can't kill him in the daylight realm, but he can try to overpower him until sunset when he can attempt to rip his heart out again.

Ezekiel reaches for me, his hand only grazing the barrier. "Faith, please. Try one more time. We'll work it—" Ruby red power explodes through the air. Dad drags Ezekiel away from me and deeper into the gnarled forest of the light prison world.

I scream out. "No!"

Cool fingers lock around my wrist, prying my hand from my eye and the view of the light prison world and Ezekiel. I yank away from Jess and his flaming sword. The world falls silent, Jess stopping the hellhound pack and Kristin, the whole world from seeing me through his shield. My local pack can't protect me if they can't see me. The flaw in the contract wasn't something Dad anticipated. He never expected Kristin to turn against him. And I'm sure she'll see his fury when he returns. The whole world will.

I stumble away from Jess and outside, trying to run from my avenging angel as he turns his frustration on me. I trip over the stairs, landing on my back. I can't get away fast enough. Now being free to see me because of Kristin's broken spell, he can fulfill whatever purpose he believes he has, even if he made a promise to me. Angels don't create contracts, and trusting Jess was an act of faith, but my faith has always let me down.

I brace myself, shielding my chest with my hands. "Please, Jess, forgive me. I know I shouldn't have broken the veil, but I—" I groan, squeezing my eyes shut. "Forgive me."

Jess tenses at my words, gripping the hilt of his sword. He expands his brilliant wings out and blocks the early morning light from my eyes. "That might've been my only opportunity to get to Raphael, Faith. He will have a shield protecting him the moment night falls. Was he really worth it to you? Look what he was trying to do."

I rub my hands over my eyes, the daylight realm flashing in and out of view. "You don't think I know that, Jess? I'm not stupid. I see him as the demon Heaven made him. I know what he's capable of. And he's going to use Ezekiel against me."

"Then you should've let me do the right thing and save the world from him," he says.

He makes sending my dad to Hell sound so easy. He makes his life and existence sound so horrible that there's no coming back for him. But he doesn't know him like I do. He acts on behalf of humanity and can't see what I see.

"Like you were trying to save the world from me?" I ask, my voice barely audible. "People can change. Demons can change. You have to give him a chance."

His sword disappears, and he runs his fingers through his light brown hair. "I've given him far too many. I know you don't want to hear this, Faith, but even if Raphael can change, he'll always carry a darkness within him. I know you feel it."

"Of course I do. It's in my veins. It burns through me, trying to surface every chance it gets. But he still has something in him I'm willing to fight for. Your light blinds you, Jess. It's so intense you can't see anything around you. But your light makes me see everything. And I just need to figure out how to remind him."

He growls in frustration, flashing Heaven's light to the sky to blend in with the early sun. "You know if you showed this kind of devotion to something or someone worth your energy, you could make the universe a beautiful place. Yet, here you are, fighting and making excuses for someone who inflicts so much pain and heartache on you I can even feel it through Ezekiel's hold on your soul. It causes me so much agony to bear witness to your precious, beautiful life bending and breaking at the hands of a demon you exist for."

I drop my arms to my sides, opening myself up to Jess instead of trying to block my heart. "He's my dad."

"He created you to serve a purpose for him, but your purpose changed. And you chose your demon, Faith. You can't tame them all," he says. "Maybe if you would have taken your soul back from Ezekiel—"

I push up on my elbows. I refuse to let Jess make me feel small or worthless or like my whole life revolves around demons. "You just don't get it."

He folds his wings, dropping to his knees by my side. "Then make me understand. I'm trying to get you to see that you can have a new purpose away from the chains Raphael wrapped you so tightly in."

I sit up straighter and pull my knees to my chest. "My mom sacrificed her soul to save my dad. She thought he was worth saving, and Dad did the best he could raising me, even through all the Hell. He never once pressured me into falling by his side until you came along and damned Ezekiel, who lost his wings because of me. So, if you think that just because Ezekiel has my soul I didn't choose my Dad, you're wrong. You're wrong to assume I have to make a choice and pick a demon. I deserve a chance to save them both, Jess. You owe me that at least."

"Faith," he says, releasing a small groan. "What you're asking—"

"Please, Jess. You claim to know your purpose, and you claim you want to help me change my purpose, but can't you see that maybe it has already changed? That maybe this is my purpose and what I'm supposed to do? Because my dad has his faults, but he's served Heaven well even as a demon. He doesn't deserve to be forsaken and damned."

He rubs his hand over his face. "And neither do you. You know Ezekiel and Raphael will never stop fighting. And if Raphael sends Ezekiel to Hell, you'll..." He can't finish his thought. The idea of sending me to Hell morphs his beautiful features into an expression of pure agony.

His eyes shine in the sunlight, darkening the honey brown color without dimming his light. A glittering tear splashes his cheek, and I groan, feeling his torment in trying to do the right thing and trying to do right by me. It's not the first time an angel has cried on my behalf, and it doesn't get any easier to witness.

"Jess, I'm not going to let my dad kill Ezekiel," I say.

I consider telling Jess about the deal I made with Ezekiel, and how if I die, my soul will revert back to me, but Ezekiel made a good point. It'd be in Heaven's best interest to end my life and save my soul. It'd make it easier for Jess to fulfill my final request, and then there'd be no one to stand up and save my dad.

I should feel guilty. I should want to make Jess feel better and give him some kind of hope. But Heaven's never been open and angels manipulate the situation more so than demons. If I tell him, he has no reason to help me.

"Ezekiel's strong," I add. "Dad will come to his senses. He might not feel his love for me, but he'll remember it's there. He doesn't truly want to damn me."

"And you think I'm going to put your fate in Ezekiel's hands, Faith?" Jess asks. "Or trust Raphael will do the right thing?"

I shrug. "I did. I still do."

"But they've lost you, their Faith," he says.

I rub my hands across my cheeks. "Is it too late to change

my name?"

He doesn't laugh or smile. In this moment, I miss Ezekiel being my watcher. He'd smile and take a breath, gather his hope and lift me off my feet. Jess continues to stare at our shadows stretching out in front of us.

I bump my knuckles against his shoulder. His muscles flex as he reaches up and wraps his cool fingers around my hand. I let him hold it. The gesture isn't anything romantic. It doesn't send my heart racing. I don't yearn to corrupt Jess or push my boundaries. I don't know if it's because Ezekiel owns my soul or if it's because I'm in love with my beautiful demon, but the only feelings I have for Jess are pure and full of pity.

Taking a deep breath, I tug Jess to his feet and run my free hand across his shirt to straighten it. He doesn't meet my gaze, tipping his head back toward the sky like the azure depths hold the answers to his silent questions.

I squeeze his shoulder. "You know, Ezekiel was the one who always picked me up off the floor."

He doesn't react and continues to stare at the sky.

"He also let me have the final say in the decision making," I add. "So, here's what we're going to do. You're going to drop your shield so I can go let my pack of hellhounds know I've handled the angelic threat. Then, we're going to get Cadence and Kristin somewhere safe before you portal me through the veil to retrieve Ezekiel at sunset."

"Faith—"

I hold my hand up. "Wait, I'm not finished. After we get

Ezekiel, we're going to go over the damn contract he made with the pack to see if Kristin left any loopholes to work with, because if you try to send in the angelic army and Ezekiel doesn't hold up his end of the deal to protect the pack, they'll eat him alive."

Jess unfurls his wings. "And then what? It doesn't solve my problem with Raphael."

I curl and uncurl my fingers. "I don't know yet."

He unfurls his wings and holds out his arms to me. "Come on. We must seek guidance. I've been cut off from the world for weeks and need a moment to think things through."

I step back. "We don't have a moment, watcher. And you can't make me do anything against my freewill."

He tilts his head to the side. "You don't have freewill with your soul in the hands of Ezekiel, so I can scoop you off your feet and fly you out of here if I—"

I summon power in my hands. "Stop it! You say you want to help me then stop sounding like my dad."

His mouth drops open like I physically slapped him. I guess comparing him to Dad was as offensive as swearing to his poor pure ears.

Snuffing out my power, I say, "Now wait here. My plan is to make sure my pack is calm, grab Cadence and Kristin, then prepare to get Ezekiel. We'll figure out everything else later."

Jess spins away from me, putting his hands on his hips while he turns his attention back to the sky. I take it as him relenting to my plan and rush to the door of the mansion. To my surprise, I find the Sunrise Cove pack hanging around, some asleep on the floor in wolf forms, others out of sight.

Kristin and Cadence stand together, their heads close as they discuss something so lowly I can barely make out a few words, including my name. I carefully step through the broken glass, and a wolf howls, drawing attention to my arrival.

"Faith, you're still here," Cadence says, rushing from Kristin. "What's going on? I don't understand any of this. Kristin said—"

My hair gusts in a rose-scented breeze from behind me, and Cadence brings her hand to her mouth at the sight of Jess. Something changes in her confused expression, and her eyes light up. Without having to hear her thoughts, I know Jess reveals himself to her from behind me.

"Oh, Faith. Heaven must really love you," Cadence says.

I grimace. "Don't let Jess fool you. He tried to send me to Hell in the name of humanity. Heaven barely tolerates me."

Jess touches my shoulder. "If that were true, I'd leave you to your fate of being a demonic vessel."

"Heaven's Traitor's daughter was intended for more," Kristin says, turning herself into my prophetess. It wouldn't be the first time she's said something like this.

"Like ruining the world," I say, hugging myself.

"Now who told you that?" Cadence asks, speaking up.

I glance at Jess.

She reaches out and flicks his shoulder. "You angels. How dare you say something like that to Faith."

I step between Cadence and Jess. She's no stranger to how angels work or how they manipulate situations with their good grace.

Jess straightens his shoulders. "No good comes from loving a demon. They ruin everything they touch."

If Cadence had demonic power, she'd summon some right now to threaten Jess with. The angelic army has never been fond of her relationship with demons, and it probably doesn't help that she's dating my dad, but she knows better than anyone how untrue his words ring.

I spin to face Jess. "Angels aren't supposed to lie, Jess."

"I'm not lying."

"I'll prove it."

He tightens his jaw.

"I'll prove to you that loving a demon won't ruin the world," I say. "I'll prove to you that it can save it."

"I hope you're right, Faith," Jess says.

I am.

It's the only thing I'm certain of.

BETRAYAL

"**B**LOOD TO BLOOD, a demon's kin, take the light and let it in. With Heaven's grace you'll be strong. Take your power and move on. A father's protection is no longer due, I give you the power to see yourself through. From dark to light and light to dark, you'll withstand the fight and bear the mark."

I squeeze my eyes shut, bracing myself for yet another brand to mar my skin. But this one isn't a witch's kiss or an angel branding. It isn't a lock to control my sight. The brand is Kristin's way of helping me when she can't.

A cool sensation flourishes over my skin instead of pain,

and I open my eyes. I peer in the mirror as a paw print glows red on my shoulder. Calvin, in his wolf form, presses his cool nose to my cheek once and then licks me before hopping from the chair.

"I figured this would be nicer looking than my handprint," Kristin says, running her fingers through one of her familiars' fur.

"Dad's going to fli—" I snap my mouth shut. Dad won't see the mark. He won't know that Kristin, while contracted to Dad, will always put me first. Ezekiel once mentioned that both Kristin and my mom left an impression on my soul. I'm sure I've left an impression on Kristin's, too.

"Ten minutes, Faith," Jess says from behind me.

Ten minutes until sundown.

Ten minutes to find Dad and Ezekiel.

Ten minutes until I have to say goodbye to Dad. Hopefully not forever.

I tug my shirt back over my head and stand. If I know Dad, I know he wouldn't have wandered far from where he can sense me. Jess's kept his shield down for now so Dad wouldn't assume the worst and think my watcher ended my life. Because the world would fare far worse if we leave him believing he needs to seek revenge.

He needs to see that I'm choosing my side.

He needs to remember whatever he chooses to do next will impact my perception of him.

Feeling the link through my humanity isn't easy for him

with Ezekiel's presence, but I refuse to believe he's cut off from me completely. It is his blood running through my veins. His fire burning my heart. But the emotions he could easily access before, the love, the devotion, those are faint memories. I have to get him to tap into something darker, more prominent.

And tonight, he'll feel my betrayal.

A knock sounds on the door to what was supposed to be my bedroom. It was easy enough to make my new supposedly loyal hellhound pack believe all is good. Dad will now regret that Ezekiel signed the contract, because he won't have the same control as Ezekiel, even if we aren't around. And for now, Jess promised the angelic army will stay out of it. We'll let Dad continue to play his game.

Cadence peeks her head in. "My ride's here to pick me up. Are you sure I shouldn't stay? I can handle Raphael."

Jess moves to the window and peers out. It takes everything in me not to throw myself through the glass to fall at Dylan's feet as he shades his eyes in the blazing setting sun.

Kristin shakes her head. "I'm going to tell him I sent you home this morning to alert the angelic army of the success of the deal he was supposedly making with the hellhounds."

She nods. "Got it."

"What about you, Kristin?" I ask.

She shrugs. "I'll be fine. He needs me."

I frown. "He'll put you through Hell."

"Wouldn't be the first time. It'd be worse if I break my contract."

I hate thinking that even after everything Kristin's done for Dad, she's still obligated to serve him for who knows how long. Neither has ever mentioned the deal they made after my conception, but what I do know is she made the deal to help me and possibly her own life. I can't imagine how things were back then, in a time where the alliance would murder one of their own as some sort of act of salvation. But then again, time seems to be rewinding on me as I try to push forward.

"Eight minutes, Faith. Time to go." I throw my arms around Kristin, wishing I could take her with me, and then I hug Cadence next. Who knows when I'll see her again? Jess's obviously not going to parade me around as the poster child of Heaven's army since I'm technically by his side to help myself in the end. We both know it, but neither of us will say it.

I turn to Jess and take his outstretched hand. His wings wrap me in their cool softness. Covering my eye with my hand, I peer through the veil and around the forest of twisted trees, silently screaming toward the sky. Jess blocks the view of the world completely, pressing his forehead to mine, so all I can do is stare at his blurry form.

"Close your eyes," he says.

As much as I want to resist, I do as he asks. My stomach drops out from under me, and I snap my eyes back open, staring at the dream beach around me. Something's wrong. I should have crossed over with Jess through the veil. I shouldn't be inside my own mind.

"Jess!" I yell. "I swear—"

"Faith," Ezekiel whispers from behind me.

I spin around to face my beautiful demon. A dark look haunts his eyes, and he wobbles, his image flashing in and out of existence. Rushing to him, I fling my arms around him to only grab air. He appears just out of my reach, sending panic through me.

"Ezekiel, what's wrong?" I ask.

"You should leave. I don't want you to see me like this," he says.

I frown, reaching out to try to grab him again. "I'm not—"

The world around me explodes in blinding light, stealing Ezekiel away from me. A chill runs through my blood, washing away the heat of being so close to Ezekiel as our beings touched together.

A hand covers my mouth, silencing the scream ripping from my throat. Jess hugs me against him, petting my hair, hushing me with the soft hum of his voice. The world distorts for a moment, and dizziness washes over me and then disappears.

"I'm sorry I had to do that," Jess whispers so softly in my ear. "I can't have you throwing up all over the place minutes before you need to rescue your demon boyfriend."

I blink a few times, letting out a small breath. "I thought you knocked me out to let the universe take care of me."

His lips twist downward, his eyebrows puckering. "You have so little faith in me."

"I wonder why," I say, motioning to the flaming sword

clutched in his hand.

"It's just in case."

"And you have so little trust in me."

"I—"

A familiar yell sounds through the quiet, warm world of the daylight prison realm, cutting Jess off. The sun sinks into the horizon with only seconds to go before the veil thins and releases the demons for the night.

"Give me her soul or I'll send you to Hell and you can spend the rest of eternity with the reminder that you damned her with you!"

Summoning power in my hands, I race through the trees, faster than Jess, and in the direction I hear Dad's voice.

"Do it!" Dad yells.

Bones crunch, sending my heart into my stomach. Anger rushes through me, my head pounding to the same rhythm of Ezekiel's heart, which sounds strange, louder than ever. My hands smolder with my power, burning away my flesh as my inner demon grabs hold of me, pushing away everything good left in me, reacting to the place it feels most at home. My ruby fire turns vibrant orange—as orange as the fading sunset.

I dodge past a tree and come to a small valley, catching sight of Dad pinning Ezekiel to the ground, his hand submerged in his chest, gripping his heart in his hand. The edges of my vision darken, the sight of my dad trying to rip Ezekiel's heart out unleashes my inner demon completely. It jets from my body, screaming and flailing its arms, nearly galloping on all fours to reach my demons before me.

We throw power together. My inner demon jumps on Dad's back at the same time I hit his arms with my demonic orb. A screech echoes through the air, and the world shifts. Dad lets go of Ezekiel's heart without pulling it free and suddenly he's on top of me, shoving me into the ground.

I flip him off me with my burning hands. My inner demon never left my body. I was seeing myself through the visions that plague me in this realm. Though I imagine it to be separate from me, the monster that roams from me is still me.

I summon more power in my hands, pressing it against Dad's stomach. The veil thins, releasing us back into the Earth plane. He yells out as pain from my intense power now unlike his eats away his flesh to reveal his true body.

He stops fighting, realizing who I am. "Faith, you're here. I thought the watcher—"

"Stole me? Killed me?" I ask, getting to my feet. I drag Dad from the ground by his tattered suit jacket so he can't spin around.

He cranes his neck to try to see me. "I knew better than to doubt your power, but I—"

I embrace him, pressing my cheek to his back. "Dad, you nearly ripped Ezekiel's heart out. What you did—"

"He'd have given me your soul before I could," he says.

"And then what, Dad?" I ask.

He doesn't respond. "Faith, I'm only trying to protect you. That demon doesn't have your best interest in mind. And now that your watcher is free…" He sighs. "That witch is going to pay."

I squeeze my eyes shut. "Don't hurt her. I swear, Dad."

He releases a breath. "You're right. It doesn't matter now. You're as powerful as ever. I know that now. Now we can continue on with—"

"Nothing."

He tries to spin around again, but I don't let him. "Faith, what's this about? Why won't you let me see you?"

"Because." I sniffle, trying to keep myself together. "You've changed. You've left me no choice."

He stiffens. "What do you mean?"

"I'm sorry, Dad."

He roars, trying to pull away, but I hug him from behind, feeling his heartbeat against my fingers. "You can't do this, Faith. I'm your dad. Please, we've been through so much to have it come down to this. You're my daughter. You love me. You don't want to see me burn."

I squeeze him tighter. "And that's why this is goodbye. Because if I stay, I will."

"What?" The heat in his voice flickers out.

"You knew the path I wanted to follow," I whisper.

He reaches up and touches his fingers to my arm. "They'll use you for all they can and then destroy you."

I swallow. "It's a chance I'm willing to take."

"It's us against the world, Faith."

"But I'm choosing the world."

"You're making a mistake," he says, his voice deepening. "I won't be here when you lose everything."

"I'm doing this to save you, Dad," I whisper. "Remember that. I love you."

"Faith, please." Dad's voice sounds just above a whisper. "Please."

"Goodbye, Dad."

I release him and take a step back. He spins, power engulfing his hands and fire in his eyes. I raise my hand to him, and cool fingers touch my shoulder. Jess releases a beam of light, causing Dad to cover his face and duck.

"Faith!" he screams, falling to his knees. "How could you?"

Dad glances toward the sky, searching for the angels who took me away, though I still remain hidden before him. A hot hand slides into mine, and Ezekiel watches me stare at my dad reacting to my betrayal of choosing Heaven over him.

He yells out again, shooting power toward the clouds blocking the glittering stars, and then he bows his head.

I have lost so much over my short life—my mom and grandma, my best friend and my new friends. I lost my home, my soul, and my beautiful angel—but Dad? I haven't lost him yet. I can see the man I love, the man with his own personal demon to battle, still fighting to hold on. Still fighting for me even if his world is now dark.

Dad composes himself, getting up from the ground to dust off his pants. Straightening his tie, he peers around the night and strolls past us, all signs of his humanity now gone. But it isn't lost forever. Because all it takes is one small flash of light to break through his darkness.

I will be his light.

I will be his hope.

And I am his faith.

He will remember.

So will the world.

Epilogue

DEVOTED DEMON'S DAUGHTER

"COME ON, JESS. This is torture," I say, staring at Ezekiel through the veil. "What's an hour?"

"Exactly. What's an hour?" He unfurls his wings, trying to stand between me and Ezekiel to get us to stop peering at each other through the veil. "And your hand's going to get stuck like that one of these days."

I glare at him, though he can only see one of my eyes. I wouldn't care if my hand did get stuck like this, it'd be easier than having to deal with the ache in my shoulder from holding it to my face all day. But I can't help myself. I've turned into Ezekiel's self-appointed Demon Watcher, because I'm afraid to take my eyes off him even for a second while I'm on the Earth plane and he isn't.

"Like I said, it's torture. Come on, just today, and I won't ask again—"

"You said that last time."

I swat his arm. "I won't ask again for two weeks this time."

He groans. "Even five seconds in that place with you two is miserable. If I wanted to be in Hell, I'd lose the wings."

Reaching out, I run my hand along the tops of his white wings. "I can arrange that."

He rolls his eyes. "Get your own pair."

"Don't think I won't try," I say, pressing against the veil.

A hot hand grabs onto my wrist, startling me, and I yelp as I fall through the veil and into Ezekiel's arms without Jess's help. Ezekiel grins at me with the most amazing smile I've seen in a long time. His smile is enough to weaken my knees so he has to lift me into his arms.

"You're getting better at this," Ezekiel whispers into my hair. "I bet it's driving Je—"

My stomach heaves at the sudden shift between realms, and Ezekiel flips me around before I puke all over him. My eyes shadow and blur with tears. My stomach twists and turns a few more times, making my entire body convulse. This is why I wanted Jess to portal me here. Crossing through wreaks havoc on my mortal body without his angelic guidance.

Ezekiel sets me down, combing my hair out of the way while rubbing my back. "I think the more you cross on your own the easier it'll be."

Sweat drips on my forehead, the heat of the daylight prison world making it increasingly hard for my mortal lungs to breathe. Another reason Jess argues about bringing me here. While the world won't kill me, it's damn unpleasant for the minutes it takes to get used to it.

I groan, lying back on Ezekiel's lap. "Maybe I'll break the veil and pull you to me next time."

Huge wings block the sun, casting a heavenly shadow across us. "If you even think—"

Ezekiel ignites power in his hands. "You don't really think I'm going to let you threaten Faith, do you? She was joking. You know, you'd get it if you'd use your good grace to lighten up."

Jess glares, flapping his wings hard enough to make Ezekiel brace himself on the ground. "Forgive me for taking my job seriously."

Ezekiel grumbles against my shoulder. "If that were true, then you would've sucked it up and transported Faith so she didn't have to suffer."

"Suffer? You—" Jess inhales a deep breath. "Faith must learn the repercussions of her powers. It's not suffering. It's a learning experience."

My stomach heaves again, and I groan.

"I hope your impatience was worth it," Jess says.

Ezekiel kisses my head.

I compose myself and smile at Ezekiel. "Totally worth it."

"Ugh, demons," Jess mutters.

Ezekiel tosses power at Jess's feet, making him fly a few feet in the air. Jess summons his heavenly light, lighting his features through the hazy brown air. He'd probably attempt to use it if we were in the Earth realm, and I wasn't cradled on Ezekiel's lap, bracing myself.

"Maybe you should've considered what I'd become before you stole my—"

"Enough!" I press my hand to Ezekiel's chest while holding my hand up to Jess. "While it tickles my demon blood to have you two fighting over me, knock it the Hell off. You guys want to help protect the balance of the universe, but you keep yanking me between you."

"Forgive me, Faith," they both say at the same time and then glower at each other.

I laugh. "How could I not?"

Ezekiel scoops me off the ground, meeting me for a sweet kiss, making Jess turn his back on us. Ezekiel strolls us deeper into the gnarled forest of trees and away from Jess. My watcher's still learning his boundaries, but at least he doesn't turn into a creeper and disappear from sight to follow us undetected. I thought Dad was bad about me and Ezekiel before but Jess never gives us a moment alone.

A drop of sadness sneaks into my heart as the veil thins and releases us back into the Earth realm to watch twilight fade into night. Voices sound through the air, drawing my attention away from Ezekiel and the vibrant glow of Jess's wings.

We're at least a mile from the apartment we've been living

in, despite Jess's desire to move into the sanctity of a church even if Ezekiel couldn't ever go in. We've had to make a lot of compromises as we learn to coexist. Jess blessed his room to have what he called the Hell-Free zone. Ezekiel claimed my bedroom at night as the Watcher-Free zone, always tempting me to ignore the outside world despite Jess making sure we're always busy trying to interrupt Dad's Hell raising. And for me, my special space is the living room, which I've deemed neutral territory for everyone.

"The angelic army will learn they can't take what is mine." Dad's voice cuts through the air, sending a shiver through me. "Whoever brings my daughter to me will be heavily rewarded."

A few demons cheer. Others release power toward the sky. Dozens of hellhounds howl.

I groan.

"No one will get you, Faith," Ezekiel says.

"Make the angelic army regret trying to light her in Heaven's grace. Prove to my daughter the only place she belongs is by my side. Show her she means nothing to Heaven when it comes to the world. Show no mercy. They've never showed it to us."

Jess reveals his flaming sword. "Faith, do you hear him?"

I nod. "Drop your shield. I can put a stop to this now."

Jess looks at me in his peripheral vision. "So, can I."

A flash of red light explodes through the air, knocking all three of us back before we have a chance to argue. The demon gathering disappears before our eyes, the whole world shifting. I sit up on my elbows, peering around the dark night.

"Blood to blood from a demon's heart, bend the night, pull it apart. Thicken the veil to wrap around you, hide the sight, block him from view. As long as Heaven's light shines, you will never see, what's in store for you as Hell's revenge sets your body free."

A strange sensation crawls over my skin, and I jerk my hand to my eye. Kristin's spell hums in my ears so quietly, but whatever magic she casts still reaches me.

Ezekiel swears. "Did you feel that?"

Jess hops to his feet and looks around. "Ten souls sacrificed at least."

Ezekiel stands and offers his hand out to me. "We knew it was coming. Raphael's too smart to test his luck against Heaven without Faith."

I remain on the ground, ignoring Ezekiel's hand, still watching the demonic gathering unfold before me. Dozens of demons bow before Dad, showing their loyalty to the new purpose he's set out before them.

"Faith?" Jess asks. "Do you still see them?"

I nod. "They're bowing."

"This is only a small set back," Ezekiel says.

I drop my hand and turn to my beautiful demon and my watcher. A mixture of emotions runs hot through me, threatening to send me curling my knees to my chest. I hadn't expected saving Dad would prove to be so difficult. Or that I'd have to decide what's more important.

Because Dad's never giving up on me.

He's as loyal to me as I am to him, except he wants to take it into his own hands to see to it I make it through.

And I'm afraid.

He'll ruin the world for me, and if I want to find my good grace, I might have to let him. If I don't, I will be ruined for the world.

I'll always be known as the devoted demon's daughter.

TO BE CONTINUED...

Other Young Adult Series by Ginna Moran

PARANORMAL

Destined for Dreams Series
Demon Within Series
Finding Nate Series
Going Ghostly Series
Spark of Life Series
When Souls Collide Series
Demon Watcher Series
Call of the Ocean Series

CONTEMPORARY

Falling into Fame Series

STANDALONES

Life After Lila

Acknowledgements

THANK YOU TO the women who always help to perfect my novels, from plotting to critique and editing to proofreading—Sarah, Katie, and Jan, I'd be lost without you.

Thank you to my reader group and those who send me emails, your excitement and enthusiasm makes me love what I do even more. You are all amazing!

Lastly, thanks to my family and friends, whose love and support help make this possible. Thank you for allowing me "five more minutes." XOXO!

About Ginna Moran

GINNA MORAN IS a writer from sunny Southern California. She started writing poetry as a teenager in a spiral notebook that she still has tucked away on her desk today. Her love of writing grew after she graduated high school, and she completed her first unpublished manuscript at age eighteen.

When she realized her love of writing was her life's passion, she studied literature at Mira Costa College in Northern San Diego. Besides writing novels, she was senior editor, content manager, and image coordinator for Crescent House Publishing Inc. for four years.

Aside from Ginna's professional life, she enjoys binge watching television shows, playing pretend with her daughter, and cuddling with her dogs. Some of her favorite things include chocolate, anything that glitters, cheesy jokes, and organizing her bookshelf.

Ginna Moran loves to hear from her readers so visit her

online at www.GinnaMoran.com. You can also find her on Facebook, Twitter, Instagram, and Snapchat. To stay up-to-date on new releases, sign up to her newsletter. You'll not only get exclusive access to the VIP Exclusive Access page on my website to view special content, but you'll be able to participate in monthly giveaways!

Ginna Moran is currently hard at work on her next novel.